"IT WAS A CRAP-SHOOT every morning when I woke up, anticipating my mother's mood, wondering what time she'd slithered through the door. Sometimes she wasn't home from the previous night's show and she'd disappoint me for the millionth time. But she had no idea, since she never involved herself with anything I did, thus adding another checkmark on the list of things she simply didn't know about me. I guess I'd feel worse calling her a completely selfish, irritating, and inconsiderate nut-case, but I have less guilt if I don't say those things out loud. Maybe it's the difference between yelling at someone you love and hearing somebody else yell at the person you love. The perspective changes and you risk hurting worse."

DON'T JUDGE

A

Girl

BY HER

Mother

This novel is entirely a work of fiction. The names, characters and incidents portrayed in it are the work of the author's imagination. Any resemblance to actual persons, living or dead, events or localities is entirely coincidental.

Cover Art by Sarah Carson
Book Design by Nutz & Boltz Productions, LLC
Author Hair and Makeup by Michelle Halleck
Author Photo by S. Raasheedah

For every single person immersed
in the writing chasm, keep climbing.

DON'T JUDGE

A Girl

BY HER

Mother

K.H. FINDER

RUBY RED INK, LLC
CHANDLER, AZ

PROLOGUE

"No one can tell what goes on in between the person you were and the person you become .... There are no maps of the change. You just come out the other side. Or you don't."

—Stephen King

IRIS

KNEW EVERY SINGLE WORD, my voice beneath each of theirs, whispered in unison from my position in the left wing. It was the play's final show and Mack gave the best performance of his career, though I knew he struggled to continue. His face wore a glistening sheen of perspiration and no makeup could disguise his hollow-set eyes; God knows what he took to control his pain. He finished his part admirably and headed to dressing room, allowing the rest of the cast to end the play.

I was thankful for the hiatus between productions; that he promised to take it easy and seek proper treatment for his migraines and fatigue. After the final bows, I waited for the small cast at the wardrobe racks, anticipating their joy and celebration for a successful run. The curtain fell softly, facing passionate applause. But Mack didn't show, no one did. Instead, Curtis appeared in the doorway, his headset dangling around his neck.

"Iris, come quickly!" he signaled.

"Why? Where is everyone?"

He rushed us to the cramped corridor near the backstage door where a team of EMTs hovered over Mack's body. He was on the ground, skin exposed, limp and lethargic. They lifted him to a transport board, still wearing the shirt I designed, intended for his last scene. I begged him to wake up, watching in shock. Though his eyes remained closed, I pleaded for his ears to hear my words.

PART 1

"Words are, of course, the most powerful drug used by mankind."

—Rudyard Kipling

CHAPTER 1

MARLEY

SOMETIMES THERE'S A DIFFERENCE BETWEEN what I say and what I mean. In my line of work, I report stories with carefully crafted sentences and crisp threads of words, but sometimes, the story I intended is not the story that is heard. Words give meaning to my work, an opportunity to communicate with clarity and unbiased perspective. They're selected with pride and purpose, expressed with an intentional voice and relatable demeanor. Even so, I'm occasionally misunderstood.

With that said, I feel inclined to admit that I tend to be on the defensive when it comes to my life outside the office. At work, I feel smart and capable, certain of my position and unwavering in principle. Yet, once I walk outside the doors of the television station, the cracks of my shell become deep crevices and I'm vulnerable to the weaknesses that take over my mind.

In my adolescent years, I kept a journal of thoughts and feelings; mostly things that made me mad, occasionally a story of happiness—far less of those to choose from, but still worth mentioning. I didn't write every day, but I'd write to burn off steam, the likely explanation for the pages of frustrations opposed to fewer colored-pencil doodles.

In my later teen years, similar tensions persisted when I longed for a simple response from someone, but instead received silence, feeling ignored or rejected. If I'm speaking honestly, guilty emotions had already begun infiltrating my adolescent life, and I don't think anyone noticed, not even my mother.

Fast forward a couple of decades, and now my daughter, Alex, has the potential to become like me; the girl I was at her age. I don't think I could allow her to morph into that state of unhappiness. Some days, I look at her and see a bit of me, and I'm unwilling to take pride in our similarities or acknowledge the likeness beyond our chestnut colored hair. Most of the time, I shrug those glimpses away and focus on our differences; thankful that she's courageous and willing to take risks, disconnected from the superficial things that once harnessed me from dreaming big and taking action.

And some days, I feel like I'm losing her. Her outstanding character makes her appealing to the masses. She's pulled in every direction with invitations from friends, school demands, and time away from our home spent with her dad. Now my mother, Iris, is in the mix, altering my role in Alex's life and even taking over in areas that should be mine.

The truth is, when I was fifteen, I calculated my exit date to the precise hour I'd back my car into the driveway, stuff it to the ceiling with my most treasured belongings, and wave goodbye with no plan for visitation. Not a single drop of emotion in my soul led me to wonder, or even consider, what my mother may have been feeling about my longing for independence. I spent more time daydreaming about my new digs, decorating my roommate-shared space, and intentional time away from the only person in the world who made me feel alone. So, when I compare those feelings with what I presume to be Alex's state of mind, I don't see any similarities in the circumstances. She hasn't said anything about moving out. We have plenty of time.

VIVID DETAILS FROM MY CHILDHOOD are scarce. Not really milestone events as much as pivotal decision-making markers. When my dream job in media became a reality after years of juggling insignificant college courses with the interesting few in order to earn a degree, I met Rachel. Though one of many on staff at the news station who openly welcomed me on my first day, she stood out differently than the rest. We clicked. Only three years older than me, she became my mentor, confidante, and eventually, my best friend.

She'd been working at the station long enough to give me a crash-course in getting to know the ins and outs, big deals and small ones, pointing out those I could trust and the ones I should work with at a distance. Mostly, she encouraged me to draw a very visible line between work life and life outside of work—something, I realize now that I hadn't considered, but should've by then.

Rachel found a way to help me understand the juxtaposition between my self-perception—feeling accomplished and confident, versus the opinions of my older and more experienced colleagues who considered me green, unskilled, and presumptuous. She was able to coach me without making me hate her. And though our pairing may seem strange to an outsider, given her propensity for brutal balls-to-the-wall honesty and my gentler, more empathetic approach with others, her frequent laughter reminded me to relax and try to enjoy life each day.

Early on, we got into the habit of walking out together. But one night, she caught me off guard with an invitation to a party at her house the next day. So much for the bold separation between professional and personal life. As it turned out, it wasn't the last time I'd cross the line.

I WALKED ON PINS AND needles my entire life, until I got a place of my own. I'm speaking literally, and believe me, I tried to get out earlier. When incarceration sounded like a better option than living at home, I knew my mother and I had a very serious problem.

For as long as I can remember, she worked intermittently as a costumer for a couple of local theater companies when she felt like working. When she didn't, you'd never know the difference by looking at our house. Since theaters were typically small, her workspace was our living room. I've never described Iris using words like tidy or careful or precise. She's always been a free spirit, sort of traipsing through life, or tramping, if you will, to the beat of her own drum. Her schedule accommodates her life, her interests and her needs.

I can't remember a single day that our house wasn't a complete disaster. Iris rarely cooked, but when she did, she didn't clean. I learned to leave everything on the counter until she rediscovered the mess a few days later and tried desperately to keep my friends out of our house. When Iris was working on a show, the conditions worsened. I spent a good portion of my time alone, reading books and keeping a watchful eye on the neighborhood happenings through my bedroom window.

She'd lay patterns and cut fabric on the carpet, with pins in the costumes and on the floor. Getting to my room was always a task because she'd absolutely freak if I stepped on anything she had laying on the ground. I tried tiptoeing through her mazes, still often catching a pin underfoot.

You see, Iris isolated herself in her own little universe, with no regard for the world around her. She still does this, I've learned, even though she rarely sews anymore. I could've come home as a teenager doing any number of inappropriate things and she wouldn't have noticed. I began conversations with her and she didn't hear me. The phone would ring repeatedly and she wouldn't budge. I told myself that it was only because she was so focused in her work that she didn't remember her own child in the same room. How does a kid learn to justify a parent's misbehaviors?

Iris was consumed with emotions and situations that she compared to colors. In true form, she'd say: *Why don't you get rid of that dreadful indigo scarf and wear something with more personality. You look like a misfit.*

As a costume designer, she was *up to her eyeballs* in colors, textures, and patterns. She's always loved fabric and anything that *might work* for a costume. Even today, she hoards things that most people would toss into the trash or kick to the curb—feathers, lone buttons, raggedy jeans, purses and anything that might be found in vintage junk shop or second-hand store. Back then, she hardly made the time to wash our clothes or launder our linens, because God forbid, she'd take the time to worry about anything but work in her extremely busy life. I don't know how she did it, but she could stay awake all night to make an impressive custom three-piece suit and fall asleep the second I came home from school.

It was a crap-shoot every morning when I woke up, anticipating my mother's mood, wondering what time she'd slithered through the door. Sometimes she wasn't home from the previous night's show and she'd disappoint me for the millionth time. But she had no idea, since she never involved herself with anything I did, thus adding another checkmark on the list of things she simply didn't know about me. I'd feel worse calling her a completely selfish, irritating, and inconsiderate nut-case, but I have less guilt if I don't say those things out loud. Maybe it's the difference between yelling at someone you love and hearing somebody else yell at the person you love. The perspective changes and you risk hurting worse.

So why are we living together now and how did this happen? According to Rachel, I've made *progress* on the issues that I'd suppressed. Apparently, I've begun to recognize that Iris and I are two different people with different life goals. I finally see that it's fine that we aren't best friends, we don't see things eye to eye, and we don't have to. I was doing great, until she drifted back into my life wreaking unwelcome havoc on my mental health. Does she love me? I think so, but I only remember her saying it one time. Do I love her? Yes, but—let's leave it at that.

IRIS

DINNER PREPARATIONS BEGAN IMMEDIATELY after my morning yoga class. Reusable grocery bags were folded under my purse in the upper section of the shopping cart, and for the third day in a row, I modified my personal schedule to accommodate my grand-daughter's needs. Marley prepared for her network obligations in New York where she would promote the T.A.D.A. campaign, along with representatives from each of the fifty states, a movement created to *Talk About Drug Abuse*.

I promised Alex's favorite meals during the days that her mother would be gone, just as long as she understood that I'd still be attending my evening dance classes. Alex agreed immediately and said she'd plan time with her dad. In my opinion, Andrew's habitually random entries and exits in Alex's life have left an irreplaceable void. But on the other hand, if he was constantly present, his immaturity would only display poor examples and instigate irritation for both Alex and Marley.

There was a time when I approved of Marley's relationship with Andrew. When I truly believed that no funny and whimsical man on earth could ever get my straight-and-narrow daughter to accept his easy-going ways, Andrew showed up and eventually changed my mind. He'd swept Marley off her feet from girlhood teens into twenties adulthood. The spark they shared glistened, radiating immeasurably—recognizable even to strangers. From my perspective, it was astonishing. I wondered how my own flesh and blood could actually commit her life to a man; so differently than any relationship I'd ever experienced. Marley and Andrew's shared passion for love and life stared me straight in the face, forcing me to question my longstanding views on exclusive companionship; whether maybe I'd given up on the integrity of indefinite companionship too soon.

Standing in the kitchen cleaning vegetables at the sink, I heard the clicking sounds of the garage door rising. Unconsciously checking the time, I knew the school day was far from over. Something was off.

I shook my head and smiled wildly when my unexpected suitor entered mischievously through the hall. It was Marco, my handsome Latino salsa partner of six weeks. "Tell me you didn't just let yourself into this house using the keypad on my daughter's garage!"

"I can't stand being away from you for all these days, my darling." Marco cradled me in his arms and gazed into my eyes, feeling entirely comfortable with our decade-plus difference in ages.

"I can't stand being away from you, either, my love. But you simply cannot sashay in here without warning or a simple phone call. How about knocking on the front door? I live here with other people, you remember?"

"Darling, you should have protected that secret code if you didn't want me using it."

Marco released his embrace, strolling into the kitchen with an array of wildflowers wrapped in tissue and a bottle of red wine to enjoy midday. Puckering his lips, he placed his gifts on the counter and scooped me into his arms again. He twirled me into a playful dip and kissed me slowly on the mouth.

"I'm begging you, my dear. Please give us one afternoon together before you dedicate all of your precious time to your over-indulged granddaughter."

"Ah, my love. I can't give you the rest of the afternoon, but I can certainly spare a few minutes." I placed the flowers in a glazed ceramic vase and pulled two wine glasses from the cabinet. "But please, you mustn't stroll in here casually, without giving me a few moments of warning and time to prepare."

"I promise, my love. Never again," he smiled, slowly pulling his belt through the loops of his pants and dropping it on the kitchen floor. I smiled, pouring the wine. He unbuttoned his sleeves and the front of his shirt, exposing his full chest. I leaned in and kissed him on the lips, then handed him his half-filled glass. I tugged gently on each sleeve as he wriggled out, scooting down the hallway, dropping his shirt to the floor before entering the bedroom.

I turned on some music and pulled the sheer curtains across the window. Marco positioned himself directly behind me as I turned around, ready to undress me and massage my exposed skin. "You're one of a kind, sweet Iris," he spoke softly, caressing my shoulder blades with his lips.

I wasn't one for small talk, but I smiled and led Marco to the bed. He was completely undressed when the hallway door to the garage slammed shut. It felt like two seconds before I heard his voice.

"You're kidding me, right, Iris?" Andrew announced, catching more than a glimpse.

"Damn it," I grumbled, popping out of bed to close the bedroom door, disgruntled and unwilling to engage with Andrew. "I didn't even think of closing it."

First I thought, I am a grown woman permitted to behave in whatever manner I choose. However, I am technically a guest in my daughter's home, and should probably manage my activities according to a reasonable code of conduct. Although, Andrew doesn't live here. What gives him the right to talk to me like that or walk in here unannounced like he owns the place?

Marco redressed himself slowly and finished buttoning his shirt before speaking. He caressed my hair and held my sullen face in his hands. "Don't let this upset you, my love. Next time we'll be more discreet. Please . . . " But I put my hand to his mouth, stopping his speech.

"I'm sorry, darling. This is my fault," I said, forcing a weak smile. The door from the house to the garage slammed again and we heard the garage door descending. "Just a minute."

I returned to my room after watching Andrew drive away from the house, wondering why he'd come over in the first place.

"Are we free?" Marco asked, reaching for my hand.

"Yes, we're free. But I'm afraid I'm not in the best frame of mind right now."

"Why don't I stay with you for awhile."

I contemplated Marco's offer as I sat at the dressing table, seeing him in the mirror's reflection. He laid on the bed, smiling simply, with his gaze focused on me in peaceful silence.

"Why do you enjoy being with me?" I asked without turning to face him.

He sat up and stood behind me, placing his hands on my shoulders.

"There are many reasons, my darling." He stroked my arms and watched me in the mirror, noticing that my expression had changed. "Why would you ask such a thing?"

I sat quietly. I didn't respond when Marco gently kissed my cheek. Or when he said goodbye. Or when he walked out of my bedroom. Or when the garage door opened and closed again.

I moved from the dressing chair to the bed after hearing Marco's car leave the driveway. Overwhelmed with many thoughts, yet capable of checking the time, I knew I had one hour to gain composure and prepare for the rest of the day.

ANDREW

I PARKED ACROSS THE STREET and three houses over from Toby's. He and Alex had become quite the high school couple. The sun lowered behind the mountain peaks, yet it wouldn't set for at least another hour. If the kid really paid attention, he'd have no trouble spotting me. I had a clear view of his bedroom window on the street side of the family's ranch style home. And if I really wanted to hide, I'd be more discreet.

It wasn't long before Toby sauntered out the front door with a basketball, headed for the stationary hoop adjacent to the driveway, and faced away from my car. He set a gallon jug of water on the gravel and covered his eyes with sunglasses. I noticed my body ducking to just below the rim of my dashboard, squashed in my seat, feeling awkward and inexperienced at surveillance.

My Toyota Prius hugged the curb, common and unsuspecting, while the air conditioning kept the interior at a comfortable seventy-two degrees. I checked my phone for any new emails or voice messages, played around with the radio, and ended up turning it off. I felt a bit antsy and I'd only been there a few minutes.

Within fifteen minutes, Alex parked her car in front of Toby's house. Her unpredictable arrival made me strangely nervous. I dove for the floor on the passenger's side, hoping she wouldn't see me. My car looked similar to many cars on the road, and wouldn't generally stand out, as long as she didn't spot her dad's face in the driver's seat. How was I going to get out of this if she did see me? Panic set in, surprisingly. Why would I be afraid of having this conversation with my own daughter?

Seconds later, though it seemed much longer, I peeked over the gear shift and watched Alex pick up Toby's water jug and follow him through the front door into his house. Great, I was safe, and my heart rate slowed.

Just as I regained composure, a loud series of knocks rattled on the passenger side window of the car. I'd like to say that I didn't jump or make a sound, but I did a little of both. Since the car was on, I rolled down the window automatically. An attractive woman was standing on the other side of the window, smiling.

"I'm sorry. I didn't mean to scare you," she laughed.

I laughed uncomfortably. "You startled me, that's all."

"Mind if I sit down?" she asked, though she'd already opened the door.

"Have we met?" I asked, as I scrolled my brain for anything that could have seemed familiar about her.

"That all depends. Does me seeing you on television and

recognizing your voice from the radio count as us meeting before?" She sat sideways on the seat with one of her legs crossed under her thigh and the other one resting with her foot on the floor. Her pink heels matched the polish on her toes.

"No, I don't think it does," I grimaced.

"I've been watching you from my living room window for the past thirty minutes."

I raised my eyebrows.

"Now tell me, what on earth are you doing here?"

I didn't know what to say. I wasn't prepared for a nosy neighbor to question my motives for sitting across the street from my daughter's boyfriend's house.

"Actually, I'm not sure. This is where my GPS lead me," I said, trying to think on my feet. I tapped the navigation screen with my index finger. "These damn things can be more trouble than they're worth."

"C'mon. You can come up with a better story than that. You haven't taken your eyes off that kid across the street for the last half hour. You think he's up to something, don't you?"

I've never met this woman in my life and in five minutes, she's cornered me. Do I look guilty?

"You know, I've had a leery feeling about him for a few weeks now," she offered. "Whenever I've come in contact with him, he's been very polite and has a nice smile. But even the nicest kids do the darnedest things. Something about him just seems off, doesn't it?"

I sat in silence looking out the front windshield, wondering what was going on inside Toby's house. My daughter was in there with him, doing who-knows-what.

"I'm Cypress," she said, detaching me from the wandering thoughts in my mind and reminding me that a stranger was sitting right next to me.

I put my hand out to shake hers. "Hi," I replied hesitantly, without repeating my name. She'd made it perfectly clear that I was no mystery.

It was dusk and the light went out in Toby's bedroom window. Moments later, he and Alex came out the front door together.

"I've got to head out," I said.

"No problem, I have a few extra minutes," she pulled the passenger door shut. "I'll go with you."

Was she nuts? Who says that to a complete stranger?

"I don't think so." I glanced at Toby and Alex. They were both in Alex's car and the headlights illuminated.

"I have no problem with it," she insisted. Cypress fastened her seat belt, showing no visible plans for getting out of my car. Alex turned her car around on the street, lights beaming toward mine, and headed east out of the neighborhood.

"I guess you've left me no choice," I said, pulling into the street with Cypress as co-pilot. I followed a few car lengths behind my daughter and her boyfriend, hoping nothing else would botch my surveillance.

"THAT'S STRANGE," I MUMBLED AFTER trailing Alex's car from quite a distance. They'd pulled into a drive-through and I couldn't very well pull in behind them. I hung back near the supermarket, camouflaging my car between a beat-up Ford Ranger and a slick silver Mercedes C-class.

"What's strange about two kids stopping at a fast-food joint?" Cypress asked brazenly. I'd almost forgotten that she was part of this charade until I heard her voice and grumbled.

"Oh, no . . . ." I popped the gear shift into place making my way to the nearest parking lot exit.

"What're you doing?" she yelled.

I've gotta hand it to my daughter. Her driving skills show real talent. But if I wanted to continue tailing her, I had to weave between cars in three lanes to make a left-hand turn at the intersection before the light turned red, or I'd definitely lose her. Once around the corner, I slowed as much as I could without totally pissing off the driver behind me. I made my way to the right lane and finally looked at my passenger.

"You realize that I don't owe you any explanations, right?"

"Lighten up, would you? I thought you'd be much easier going!" she snapped.

With both hands on the wheel, I squeezed tightly and just shook my head. "Well, that worked out well, didn't it?" Alex and Toby had pulled into a neighborhood and in the midst of keeping my distance while remaining unseen and arguing with the stranger sharing my car, I lost them.

"So what now?" Cypress asked, sporting a huge smile.

I shook my head again. I could feel the tightening of skin between my brows. "I don't think I get you. You're so—"

"Seriously, what's your plan now?" she pushed.

I pulled up to a curb where a mailbox might stand in a neighborhood that didn't have a community bank of post office boxes. Leaning to my left, I pulled my phone from my back pocket to text Alex, then stood it up in a pull-out cup holder. "She should get back to me pretty quickly," I said confidently.

"Your daughter?" she laughed. "And if she doesn't?"

I checked behind and next to me before pulling out to make a U-turn. "Then I guess she doesn't," I sneered. By the time I got to the main road, I heard the triple chime of an incoming text. I felt one brow peak and a slightly satisfactory smirk appeared on my face.

Cypress reached out for my phone and reactively, I lurched with a bear-sized claw to snatch it back from her. Unfortunately, in order to keep adequate control of a nearly two-ton moving vehicle, my reach could only extend so far. Guess who still had my phone in her hand?

"Dammit, woman! Give that back to me!"

She cackled uncontrollably, slapping her knee. Was she laughing at my inability to grab the phone or at what she was seeing on the screen?

I pulled to the curb as quickly as I could, slammed the car into park, and threw my car door open. Why I chose going around the front as opposed to the rear of the car to get to her side, I have no idea. But when I got there, she was still giggling, and her thumb was swiping through my photo files. I yanked the handle to open the passenger door and she'd locked the damn thing from inside. "Son of a bitch!" I turned away from the car to take a quick breather, hearing a car door slam in mere seconds. As I turned around toward my car, I watched that crazy woman take off with it. She literally left me in the freaking dust, so much so, that I momentarily shielded my eyes and waved off the flying dirt.

No phone.

No car.

No options. Well, that's not exactly true. There are always options. I just didn't like any of them. I wasn't too far from home, but obviously, my keys were in the car along with my wallet, a new (still in the box) pair of high-end sunglasses, and any loose change I could've used was rattling around in the lower panel of my door.

I had a momentary out-of-body vision of myself, turning in slow circles as I assessed the reality of my situation. The streets were bustling with vehicles; it was the time of day that most people were heading home from work. As I considered my less-than-desirable options, I noticed a news van parked about a quarter of a mile from where I was standing, which also happened to be in the direction of my home. I wondered what was going on after seeing two more news vans pull into the same area. I was slightly more curious because I couldn't see any police or emergency vehicles hovering in the vicinity. Instinctively, I picked up my pace and arrived on the scene in minutes.

It was a relief to see a van from Marley's station, but I made my way around all three cameras filming live from their satellite vans, and I didn't recognize a single reporter. I noticed two police cars parked nose to nose through the parking spaces that lined three store fronts in the strip mall.

"Hey, you know what happened?" I asked a guy who was looking pretty comfortable leaning up against a block wall that faced the crews.

He cocked his head up and smirked, "It must be a slow news day or somethin' if they're all out here covering this."

I looked in their direction and then back to him. "I don't see it. What are you talking about?" An officer and his K-9 came around the exterior of the corner unit. "A drug dog?" I asked the guy.

"Sounds like the dry cleaners kept the real dirty stuff in the back room."

He looked pretty proud of himself, chuckling at his attempt at a quick-witted joke.

"Gotcha," I said, bidding him farewell with a two-finger salute and heading toward the one familiar face I finally spotted in the sparse crowd. "Flick! Dude, what's goin' on?"

"Hey Andrew," he said, stabilizing his camera on his left shoulder and jutting his right hand out to shake mine. "What brings you over here? Thought you might get a pinch before the head-honchos store it up for safe keeping?" he snickered.

I just laughed with him. Everyone seems to think they're a comedian, I guess. "No, actually, funny story, but I won't go into it. I just saw the vans and decided to check it out like the rest of these yahoos."

"Yeah," Flick said, putting his gear into the truck. "Good to see you, bud. You take care, and stop into the station when you're in the neighborhood."

"Hey Flick, any chance you can give me a quick ride?"

——————

I WAS ON MY OWN in the front seat of the news van with Flick while the young frat-bro turned street reporter swiped his phone screen in the back seat; his ears enveloped in a large head-set.

"Really appreciate the lift," I said. "The craziest thing just happened to me and the more I think about it, I feel like a complete idiot."

"Can't be all that bad," Flick said, taking a quick glance at his passenger. "I'm happy to help. After all, Marley'd have my head if she found out I'd turned you down."

I smiled, leaning back on the headrest. I cracked my knuckles.

"But I'd 'a said yes anyway," Flick declared, "being that you're pretty well known around here, you know?"

"Most of the time," I paused, "I wonder if it's a good or bad thing, Flick. But today, I guess it worked out in my favor. On the other hand, I wouldn't have needed your help in the first place if that nut job hadn't recognized me."

"I'm not following," Flick said, slowing up to a red light intersection.

I shook my head. Telling Flick meant giving up full control of my side of the story, as Flick was known for embellished re-tells in the name of entertainment. But actually, this story seemed entertaining enough, no matter what Flick would do to hype it up. I left out the Toby-surveillance part and moved right on to Cypress.

"Dude, I was sitting in my car, working on a project and this woman started banging on my window; scared the shit 'outta me."

"Ha!" Flick bellowed. "I would've loved to see that."

I laughed with him. "She actually opened up the passenger door, got inside my car, and wouldn't get out."

"What'd she want?" Flick asked. He pulled the van onto Coconut Trail. "Remind me which one."

"Right there," I pointed. "Good memory, man!"

"I really have no idea, but I was so frustrated, I had to get out of my car to just think about how I should handle it. Next thing I knew, she'd moved into the driver's seat and took off with my car!"

"Ah . . . " Flick shook his head. "You're kidding? That's unbelievable!"

"I know, right?" I agreed. "My wallet, my phone, my keys are all in the car!"

"Maybe we should get GQ back there to run a segment right here in your driveway. See if the producers would give it a go. Hopefully, you'd get your stuff back and the station could benefit from your pretty-boy face. Maybe even get that crazy lady in a bit of a pickle."

I shrugged, looking back at the young kid. "Could get him some kudos, maybe. Newbie with not much to his name gets recognition for breaking news. Let's see if he's more interested in his ego than following protocol; this isn't an assigned segment, you know?"

"Listen, the station doesn't have to run it. If they don't, you move on to plan B—whatever that is. You just have to get your car back with everything you own still intact."

"Hang on, lemme think this through a minute," I hesitated. If the station actually ran the story, it would be much more than Flick shooting the breeze with a few co-workers. It would mean statewide attention.

"Mr. Dead Poet's Society would have to spin it in the right direction."

"Let's see if he'll do it," Flick said, getting his attention.

Turns out the kid's name is Sawyer Finn, Syracuse grad with East Coast roots and a family tree that somehow links with one of the nation's founding fathers. Flick wasn't sure which one, exactly, but he was pretty sure he got everything else right.

"Yeah, I'll do it," he said, hanging the headset on the window hook and making his way out of the van. "Anything to beat this miserable heat," he complained, patting his powdered face with a handkerchief. "Sawyer Finn," he announced, darting a strong hand toward me.

Mid-shake, Flick cut in. "Here's a first," he joked. "Someone who doesn't know who the hell you are." His laugh was contagious and we were all suddenly laughing for different reasons. "Sawyer," Flick said, "it's my pleasure to introduce you to the one, the only, Andrew Donovan."

"Pleasure to meet you, man, but—fill me in. What are you known for around here?"

I tipped my head and decided to keep it simple. "Actually, I do a bit of everything, but most recently I've been doing a radio show in sync with the morning news program, so my face gets flashed on the screen for a few minutes a day and some people know my voice pretty well."

"He also has a kid with *the* Marley Christopher," Flick announced.

"Ah," Sawyer nodded, more impressed with the recent disclosure. "So bullet point the details for me and let's get this taped," he said, looking at his watch.

"You sure you have time to do this one?" I asked, feeling slightly insulted.

"I think a shot of Andrew in his driveway—this is his house, you know? Then a quick interview, just the basics, then we're done," Flick interjected. "It's enough to get the word out without making it more than it is."

"Hey, it's a big deal!" I spouted.

"Sounds good," Sawyer cut it, confidently. "Flick, you get the camera and I'll get a statement."

"Yes, sir!" Flick laughed. "Kids," he mumbled, shaking his head. "Hey Andrew, what about Alex?"

"Shit!" I grimaced.

"Who's Alex?" Sawyer inquired.

"My daughter. Yeah, I've gotta call her before this airs, even if it doesn't air."

"I'm ready whenever you are," Flick said, tripod secured and camera in place. "I won't get your house number in the shot, okay?"

"What the hell is going on?" a female voice shouted abruptly, making her way to the driveway from the curb.

I jolted at the sight of my vehicle. "You're seriously asking me what the hell is going on? You're the lunatic who took off with my car!"

"I didn't take off with your car, I was finishing what you started."

"What does that mean?"

"Someone had to keep an eye on those kids," she said.

I looked at Flick. "Does this make better sense now? I can hardly believe she's actually serious!" I looked back at Cypress. "Give me the keys!"

She dangled them in front of my face. "Lighten up, cowboy," she smiled. "Who's this hot tamale with the camera?" she asked, approaching Flick in the driveway.

Sawyer pulled out his earpiece and took off his blazer. "I guess we're done," motioning a circular wrap-up hand motion toward Flick.

Within seconds, the camera was down and into the back of the van. Flick smiled at Cypress, "I've met a lot of beautiful women in my time, and believe me, you are beautiful—but definitely out of my league. G'day ma'am."

"Thanks, guys," I saluted.

Flick leaned out his window, "Lemme' know if she doesn't work out. I know a few guys who love the wild ones," he howled.

ALEX

I'VE BEEN WAITING FOR THIS email for a week, though it felt much longer. I sent an opinion article to the editor of our school newspaper, requesting an opportunity for publication in the next issue. The only contact information I submitted was a generic email address with an anonymous signature. I didn't tell anyone about my article or my intentions, though I've checked my email inbox at least three times a day, deleted tons of spam, and kept my fingers crossed that I'd get some type of response. I decided that even a rejection would trump no response at all.

I was stoked. The journalism department would support a trial column, open to the entire student body and staff. They would allow me to write, submit to them for proofreading, and then they would upload to the newspaper link. They would allow comments from students, although stringent rules and a code of conduct would be enforced. The trial period would begin with ten school days.

It did, however, require proof that I was a student at the high school. My dilemma: Am I willing to submit my name and blow my cover? Who could I trust? My original opinion article focused on the subject of teens and cell phones. It was more of a *let's take a poll* of opinions than the intention of swaying anyone.

Here's what got me to thinking: I caught a glance of an afternoon talk show where a girl my age was bawling on screen, horrified and ashamed of a mistake she'd made. My first reaction was that she was overreacting. But I turned up the volume and decided to watch for a few minutes.

Unfortunately, someone took an inappropriate cell-phone picture of her and then had the pea-brained idea to share it. Once the picture was passed around through texts and other postings, it obviously reflected badly on her. The talk show host gave her some time to plead her case but nothing she could say would ever change the outcome. Her explanation might have swayed some people to believe that it was an isolated incident where she made a really bad choice. But mostly, it was an example of something that wouldn't soon be forgotten.

Not only had the picture been taken, but it had been sent to many other phones with her name attached to an inappropriate hashtag. Many kids who received the picture, forwarded the photo and tag-line to their friends. And so, the cycle continued. Unfortunately, the picture is still being circulated and will forever be floating through the internet waves.

Personally, I can't think of one person in my circle of friends that doesn't have a cell phone capable of texting, emailing, surfing the web, and sending photographs. Everyone knows that high school is a very common age to make impulsive mistakes, whether they're meant to be malicious or not. So, I wonder if my fellow classmates understand how their lives could be forever changed by the click of a button. A picture that their friends think is hilarious and send out imme-diately to their whole address book, might in fact, embarrass the hell out of the person in the picture. It was one little thing that caught my eye and unearthed this idea of current event commentary. Honestly, I'm still a little surprised that the journalism department agreed to give this a go.

MARLEY

IT'S HARD TO PINPOINT WHEN all of this started. I say *all of this* because in my emotionally fragile state of mind, I lump everything together into one label; it's just easier that way. When I have the energy to think about things in my logical state of mind, it's very clear that *all of this* can be sorted into pieces, layers, function versus dysfunction, if you will. There was a time when I wondered why no one ever told me that certain things in life were destined to happen, or that every decision forces an equitable response that begins a new pattern of behavior. Now I wonder if anyone did, and I just didn't hear it that way.

I've always felt smart, like I had a good handle on my education and future goals; never clueless like a particular person who comes to mind. I feel lucky that I've had a handful of really good friends over the years to spend most of my time with, hanging out, eating, playing sports, loving life. But now, referring to nearly twenty years' time, my life is consumed by a daughter who means the world to me, her life-of-the-party father, a demanding job that I love, my exceedingly difficult mother, and my best friend whose therapeutic counsel keeps me sane. It feels like a juggling act, but without them, I'd be different and life might be simpler. Sometimes I wish it was.

I made it through college on a basketball scholarship that guided me to the person I am today. I could talk for hours about the support I received from my coaches and teammates, the family unity I felt with them that I never experienced at home, and the identity I developed as being part of a team.

They focused on my strengths and abilities, rather than pointing out my weaknesses. And differently than earlier in my life, I formed relationships based on trust and loyalty, instead of biology and necessity.

If my mother weighed in, she'd share a different angle of insight. She *brought me into this world*, she'd say, and *raised me until I was nearly eighteen. That would count for more than a little something in your upbringing, you know. Your coach came in on the tail end of your childhood*, I've heard her say too many times.

So as a former athlete, I sometimes think about my life and the people in it as my teammates. We're not all friends all of the time, but when it counts, when it matters, we can do our jobs for the good of the team. Sometimes we can't—or don't. And sometimes I feel like I'm the only one in the game.

The way I see it, I'm the *Center*, the key player in all decision making regarding myself, my daughter, and my work. I'm responsible for being up front, *in the paint*, and playing to score as a leader. I'm a pivotal player—in ready position —during any aggressive play.

I see my daughter, Alex, as the *Small Forward*. She's the most versatile, both physically and emotionally strong, and she's got skills! I'm amazed by her creativity and drive at school and in sports. At her age, I was interested and willing, but whoa, at a completely different level of maturity.

Then there's Alex's father, Andrew. We've been together, lived together, parented together, broken up, got back together, lived separately, hooked up again and again and again, but the bottom line is, we've never been married. Which means, we've never divorced. And for quite sometime, we've lived in close proximity, but not together. Alex loves her dad very much. He's our *Power Forward* as the most adaptable player with a huge scorecard, if you will.

My mother, Iris, is the *Shooting Guard*. She drives every

play to the net with gusto, but she can skillfully defend the strongest threats, as if she predicted their presence before they arrived. As a kid, I remember her playing for her own team ninety percent of the time, all for one and one for Iris, until she swooped in when I wasn't expecting her. It was always a good feeling for me when she actually showed up, but I spent most of the time on my own, wishing she was nearby.

Rachel is the *Point Guard*. She's quirky and a true friend who can handle the junk of my life. Her raw honesty helps me reason through things and see others for who they are. I'm far more work for her than she is for me, but as the ball handler, she trusts me with a pass when she knows I'm up to it and passes to someone else when she knows I need a break.

These are the players who keep me focused and busy as I navigate through the daily grind. There are days when *all of this* seems too much; an unbelievable mountain that I must traverse without any training to get me to the other side. And there are days when *all of this* seems exactly how it should be.

———

TODAY, I GAVE MYSELF PERMISSION to stay buried in the comfort of my blankets and the curses of my own debilitating thoughts. I know for certain, simply by the absence of sunshine and the date on the calendar, that today will not be good for my mental health.

Living in a climate where sunshine and clear skies are predictable more than three hundred days each year proves suitable for my attitude and perspective. And though I've never tried it, I have pretty strong feelings that moving to a colder and wetter climate would be a detriment for me, both physically and mentally. As it is, my joints ache and mild headaches ensue on the occasional rainy day, and I bundle up in layers at the first hint of temperatures below seventy degrees.

The clock on my nightstand reads six forty nine, and I only have eleven minutes to get my act together.

Today is Alex's birthday. Each year on this day and the days leading up to it, I become irritatingly nostalgic, followed by pathetic lamentation. It's a fine line between pride and rationality, when my mind is flooded with memories from the past.

The day my sweet Alex was born, my life changed forever. I say that knowing that I was not the first person on the face of this earth to give birth to a child and experience *the change*. But, from my point of view, it was a change that altered the vision I had in place for my future. It's like that for the mother, I think, especially for mothers who raise their children without the presence of a permanent father. And for that fact alone, I could go on incessantly about the reasons why I'd rather stay all bundled up, protected by the gray skies, wrapped in the cocoon of my bedroom, drowning in the safety of my delusional suppositions.

Six fifty-four. It's earlier than I'd planned, but if I wait any longer, I'll never be able to fake my way through the excitement of the morning. I rip the covers away from my body and rise to the land of the living. Without passing a mirror, I feel what my face must look like, and I will it to relax. I grab my chenille robe, bringing a smidgen of happiness to me, as the softness warms my cool skin. The moment I reach Alex's door, I can feel a smile tugging at the corners of my mouth, excited to sneak into bed and snuggle with my daughter before she wakes up for school.

Hoping I won't startle her, I gently turn the handle and ease open the door. I do this most mornings, but not until seven fifteen. I want to spend a little extra time with Alex today. My eyes adjust to the darkness of her room, but it takes only a moment for me to realize she's not in her bed.

Atypically, she's an extremely responsible teenager, but I'm amazed by the immediate panic I feel in that instant. I call her name throughout the upstairs before dashing down to the kitchen. There's no sign of Alex, except for a note written on a fluorescent orange paper, taped to the coffeepot handle.

Dad picked me up early for a birthday breakfast.
I'll be home around seven. Love, Alex

"Dammit," I whispered, slumping over the counter. He did it again. I know he loves Alex as much as I do and he has every right to take her out for her birthday. But he stole my thunder. Again! And he doesn't have the right to keep on taking it away from me. I'm her mom; the one who's here for her every day; the parent she counts on. Why couldn't he have invited me to join them? He could've told me about it last night and we could have all gone together. Damn you, Andrew.

"Mom?" Alex called out, when the door closed. Her mood was noticeably elevated.

I stammered to my feet and wiped under my moist eyes. She rounded the corner as I met her in the hallway, thankful that she never saw me crunched in a ball on the floor below the coffeepot.

"Did you get my note?" she asked.

"Yeah, yeah. I just saw it. Happy Birthday!" I said, giving her a big hug. And there was Andrew, standing behind her, catching the sight of my pathetic face buried in our daughter's beautiful chestnut hair. I lifted myself away from her, holding her shoulders and looking into her eyes. "What a nice surprise! Where did you go for breakfast?"

Andrew alternated his gaze back and forth from Alex to me. "We just went up to that bakery on Fourth for those chocolate chip pancakes she likes."

I smiled at Alex, squealing giddily, then bit my bottom lip. "Can you believe you're sixteen?" Andrew looked proud. I'd say he even looked happy. He has no idea how emotionally weak he makes me feel sometimes. I don't know if it's him or if it's just me making a big deal out of something small.

I've got to figure out a way to shake this recurring day of depression. It's been sixteen years and I'm still hurt and wondering what if—(insert any number of a million or so options). There's one thing that's certain. Without him, I wouldn't have Alex. She's the one person I know I don't want to live without.

CHAPTER 2

MARLEY

"**D**ON'T MIND ME," IRIS called from the couch when the doorbell rang.

"Mother, please don't start tonight."

"What on earth are you talking about? I'm one of the only friends you've got right now. Real ones, anyway."

I sighed, contemplating. Making friends and keeping them had gotten more difficult since becoming a local celebrity. It wasn't easy differentiating between those who wanted to get to know me because of my title and those who were sincere. However, I knew I could depend on Rachel, and had been counting down the minutes until she arrived.

"Thank God," I said, as I opened the door.

Rachel stared at me with a look that did the talking: what just happened?

I yelled, "Bye," and closed the door. "It has been one thing after another this week and my mother's cynicism is not what I need right now."

"Don't go getting all upset with Iris. She's helping you out a lot lately, even if you don't want to see it."

"I know, but right now I need you. Not her. I need someone who can hear me out and be on my side, and agree with everything I say. Not someone who is logical."

"Thanks, a lot!" Rachel laughed.

"That's not what I mean, and you know it. I'm just so angry at Andrew right now and I have a million things that need to get done before I go to New York."

Rachel pulled into the restaurant parking lot. It was one of our favorites, with dimmed lighting and cozy booths. We'd been there dozens of times and no one had ever cornered me with the, *We've met before, haven't we?* line.

Sliding into the booth across from me, Rachel smiled.

"What?" my patience was dwindling.

"You'll never believe who's going to be at the launch party in New York!"

"Is it someone I'm going to be excited about or someone who will make the trip extremely difficult? And why do you still have that ridiculous smirk on your face?" I asked as the waitress poured our wine.

Rachel leaned in closer and began whispering. "Dax Townsend."

"No way," I mouthed, dropping my forehead into my hands.

"I know! I couldn't believe it either."

Dax Townsend was known to most of the American public as a former NFL player turned sports commentator, but we met as fellow athletes before his true glory days when he was a just lowly college football hero and I held my own as a Lady Sun Devil on the women's basketball team at Arizona State.

"Does he know that I'm representing the Phoenix affiliate?"

"I don't know. I was just notified this afternoon, so I'm

assuming it only recently became official. You seem surprised, so that means he hasn't contacted you?"

"No!" I gasped. "Why would he?"

"I don't know. I thought he might, since you're involved in T.A.D.A. on this end."

"I cannot believe my week! How am I supposed to handle this? Do I call him or just see how things play out? Maybe we won't ever run into one another."

"Come on, Marley. Be real. You can't get on an airplane, fly all the way over there, and not have a conversation with him before you get back on a plane and come home. Why is it so weird, anyway?"

I gulped half of my glass of wine. "I feel like I've gotten in over my head, not that I ever planned on things getting this crazy. There's so much going on right now, not to mention Iris butting into anything and everything."

"What do you think she'll say about Dax?"

I swallowed my last sip of wine. "She'll say something snarky and inappropriate for her age."

"I'll help you. We'll come up with a plan, but for now, let's talk about Andrew."

"Really?" I winced. "Don't we have anything else to talk about?"

"We don't even have to talk, you know that. We can just sit here and eat and drink in silence. Or, I can talk to you about random petty things. But, that's not why I picked you up tonight. You wanted to talk this stuff out. It's just a lot and it can be draining."

"Right again," I agreed. "I thought forty was supposed to be the new thirty. Forty sucks right now," I grinned. "I'd give anything to be the happy girl I was ten years ago."

"You weren't particularly happy ten years ago," Rachel smirked.

I shook my head. "Dax is really going to be in New York?"

Rachel nodded. "Don't get freaked out yet."

"Right," I replied hesitantly. "And everything just got a little more interesting."

IRIS

IT COULD BE SAID THAT I didn't intend to stay at Marley's this long but that would imply considerable forethought and a defined plan, both of which would be misleading. The truth is, I'm comfortable here. I enjoy time with Alex quite differently than Marley's teenage years. And when I'm ready for a change of scenery, I'll pack a bag and walk away from certainty and predictability. When I've had my fill of something new, I know someone will be here when I return. It's strange, really, but I'm becoming very fond of our shared space. The solitude I once insisted upon now concerns me with fears inconsistent with my younger self.

Have you ever traveled outside the country, beyond the borders of the mighty United States of America? The experiences are not only mind-bending and hectic, occasionally heartbreaking and sometimes glorious, but true and unaltered snapshots of real living by real people in circumstances and accommodations often unreflective of America's modern conveniences. To trade big-box warehouse shopping for a walk-up outdoor market or biking to replace an un-fueled vehicle would propel the average American into a fit of frustration, wouldn't it? The urgency for immediate gratification is far less observable in other places of the world. It's refreshing in some ways; a time for renewal and pause, to reflect and regroup, but don't most Americans say, *it's good to be home* and go back to their usual habits?

I know Marley has complaints, maybe even some regrets about how I raised her into adulthood. I would imagine that most parents judge themselves and for the most part, I think I did pretty well. Take me out of the equation for a minute and use Marley as the barometer. If the kid evolves into a strong confident career woman, isn't that a good gauge for how she was raised? I'd be dishonest if I were to say it was just me raising Marley, because I always relied on friends to help me. I think she benefitted a lot from her early interactions with others, forcing her to learn flexibility and acceptance of others. In some ways, I wonder if that's why she tends to sway too leniently with some people in her life instead of taking a firm stance when she feels vulnerable. It's strange though, she treats me differently.

Marco has asked me to travel with him to South America for a couple of weeks. It would be new terrain for me, visiting a geographical area with so much to explore and meeting a culture of people who might teach me a few new things about living well. It'll give Marley and Alex some alone time together again. It's easy to see that Marley, especially, misses their one-on-one dinners and weekends without dear-old-mother tagging along. I think I'll go with Marco, but the mere pondering that I'm doing is nearly driving me crazy. In the days of old, I'd never take this long to *consider* how or whether my absence would affect anyone else. I just did what suited me. I'm not sure how I like the revolutionized Iris, but I feel like the changes are involuntary within me.

Take Alex's teen romance with Toby, for example. Don't get me wrong, I'm all for high school dating, but when Marley was Alex's age, I had no worries or concerns. She didn't have a set curfew (although she never took advantage of her freedom), we didn't talk about safe sex or God-forbid, abstinence. I wanted her to date more often, play the field, not get tied down with just one boy but live freely and without commitment. I let her make her own decisions and I rarely asked questions, though I voiced my opinion far more often than she asked for advice.

Now my very bright, tech-savvy granddaughter, bursting with confidence and driven by eccentricity, has for the first time in my life, positioned herself at the forefront of my thoughts. Even above and in front of my own interests. That, my friends, speaks volumes.

My darling Alex, I have dreams for you. I think about so many things that were once foreign yet now seem so important in life. Maybe my experiences have guided me here unknow- ingly; a place where there's a family unit rather than a single portion. There's been a shift in my universe and my internal compass is beginning to point outward toward others rather than stuck on myself. It may be too late for me to fulfill Marley's expectations, but I truly believe there's still time for Alex and me.

At my age, I wonder how long I have left. I don't worry unnecessarily, but questions certainly cross my mind more often in this season of my life. In the meantime, I'm not too old to enjoy it! I'm not going there, I just won't do it. So what if Marco is younger than me? Or that I enjoy certain pleasures? I've always done things my way and that isn't going to change.

ANDREW

I ROUSED MARLEY WITH A gentle massaging of her left thigh. She was sleeping in her favorite place; a position I know well. Her legs curled peacefully as she rested on her right side, very close the edge of the bed. Her neck was embraced by her small satin blanket, loosely bundled under her chin. I caressed her ear with the slightest brushing of my lips; watching the rustling of her eyelashes as she came out of her deep sleep; a picture I'd studied a million times. I slipped off my clothes before sliding into the familiar place, nuzzling my face beneath hers. She jolted up and away from me.

"Dammit, Andrew! What the hell?" Marley spouted, rubbing her eyes and waking agitated.

I was pretty sure that she'd take few Ibuprofen later in the day. "Shhhh," I motioned, placing my index finger in front of her lips.

Marley swatted my arm away, rising naked from her bed. She stood facing me and I repositioned myself to sit on the edge. "Is this what we've come to? Sex whenever you want it and especially after a long night at the bar?

"No!" I smiled. I shouldn't have, but I did.

"Usually when you feel like it, letting yourself into my house and taking me at your convenience. It's a sick and convoluted habit that we've both allowed for way too long. You get drunk, bored, or wired, and have no other offers, so you let yourself in for a quick lay?"

"C'mon—you know it's not like that," I said, taking her hand and nudging her closer. "It's more than that. We love each other."

"Oh my God," Marley spun around, walking into her bathroom and flicking on the light. "Yeah, we love each other." She covered herself with the robe that was draped over the vanity chair. "You're drunk. You know I hate that! You being here right now isn't about love, Andrew."

"What? What does that mean?" I said, offended, following her and sitting on the edge of the tub.

"The whole thing is messed up." Marley laid on the floor next to me, covering her eyes with her forearm. "At this very minute, love has nothing to do with it."

"Of course it does. Who's been telling you we're messed up, Marley? You didn't think so the last time I came over to see you. Where'd this come from? You've never said that before."

Marley clenched her fists as I rambled. She looked so angry at me. "You know what? We'll talk after you sleep," she said.

"I'm fine."

She may have sensed my hostility, generally surfacing after several drinks, despising the reality of my dual-self. She shook her head. There was a time that she never wanted to leave my side. She always said that the sober version of me was fun and handsome, hysterical sometimes, and extremely sensual at others, but we've spent more than a decade trying to figure things out.

"You're not fine. You reek, you need a shower, and enough time to clear your head."

"There's somebody else," I blurted. "You met someone. I'm right, huh?"

Marley cocked her head. "Excuse me?"

"You would never do this to us unless someone else was in the picture." I paced the small room, stepping over Marley at each pass.

"Do you hear yourself? You're just talking crazy. You see other women all the time, even sleep with them, and it doesn't stop you from coming back to me. There's something very wrong about that from both of us! Me seeing someone else shouldn't even factor into this conversation. I'm just done. That's it. No more."

"You can't do that, Marley. I love you. You can't cut me off."

Marley sat up, leaning on the wall, consciously lowering the volume of her voice. "Yes I can, Andrew. And I will. This has gone on way too long."

I felt my head fall into my hands.

Marley sighed. "Just come sit with me for a minute," waving toward her on the bathroom floor.

I laid down and she guided my head to her lap. She ran her fingers through my hair and no one spoke for awhile. It was comfortable. Natural. Easy. It was awful.

"What's wrong with this?" I finally asked.

"There's a lot wrong with this, Andrew," she whispered. There's a difference between the love we share and the fact that we're not in love. It's a love that we haven't been able to commit to for the last sixteen years. If we were meant to be together for the long haul, we would've dedicated our lives to one another a long time ago. But, we didn't. And the truth is, we both know that we never will."

"I need you," I said seriously, but barely expressed a sound.

"I need you, too. Just not like this."

I nodded and knew she was right, but losing her intimately would be difficult. I knew she'd put a stop to all of this one day, but I never thought much about when that day would come. I know every inch of her body, can recognize the patterns of her breathing while she sleeps and I know exactly what actions induce her pleasured responses. Among the long list of women in my past, not one has matched the perfection I see in Marley.

"You have to stop coming into my house whenever you feel like it, and I don't just mean in the middle of the night." The mood began to lighten. Her breathing was more peaceful. "And you should probably leave the key before you go."

"Garage door opener, too?" I half-joked, but I knew she wasn't kidding.

Marley lifted my head from her legs, placing it lovingly on the floor. She laid next to me and we held one another, shedding trickling tears. Who would be the first to let go?

I rolled enough to touch my forehead to hers, speaking directly into her eyes. "I'm sorry."

Marley nodded. It was painful.

Making an official physical break in our bond was hard; we'd tried before. More than once. More than twice. Maybe we should've insisted. After this long, it seemed worse. It was an admission that our love wasn't enough, no matter how much we wanted it to or how resistant we were to accepting the truth.

"I don't know if I'm sorry," Marley said.

I scrunched my eyes.

"It's just time. For both of us."

"There's still Alex."

"I know. She'll understand. She's a big girl and she's got both of us. She'll be fine."

We were way past the point of staying together for Alex.

The unsettling reality transformed awkwardly. "Is this what's going to make the difference?" I asked.

Marley opened the palm of her hand and placed it at arm's reach. "It's a start."

I delicately gave her the key, cupping her hand with both of mine. Immediately, Marley jerked her hand away and frowned.

"You're still mad?" I asked, surprised.

Marley stomped her foot. Short of having a temper tantrum, she was on the verge of a full-blown pity party, desperate to be alone. She marched to her bedroom door, pulling it wide-open, making it perfectly clear that she was prepared to physically escort me away from the room that had comforted us for so many years.

We've never been together at my house since she moved from Coconut Trail. Not once. When she found out that other women had been there . . . it became a big *hell no*! But what difference did it make, really? Being in Marley's *clean* space didn't erase the accused uncleanliness of my ways. It was just another way Marley justified the ongoing agreement, and it's worked out fine for me. Until now. I stood in the archway that separated Marley's bedroom from her bathroom, looking at her in question.

"C'mon. Get your stuff and go home."

I didn't budge.

"I don't want to be angry, Andrew. We're done," she sighed. "We talked it out again. You gave me your key. Just get dressed and get out." She looked tired and emotionally drained.

I shook my head, deflated. My leisurely pace didn't match her desire for speed, as she continued coaxing me to the door. With mild resistance, our voices escalated as we made our way down stairs. Wearing jeans and holding my t-shirt, I met Iris at the front door, greeting me with a mocking smile.

"Good morning, darling," she smiled at Marley, nearing the bottom of the staircase.

Marley chucked my flip-flops out the door before it nearly knocked my heels, slammed by Iris' hand.

MARLEY

IRIS RAISED HER BROWS, SUSPICIOUS but pleasantly amused.

"I don't want to talk," I barked, heading upstairs to my room. Spending the rest of the day in bed fit my fancy but not my schedule. Ibuprofen would be a Godsend if it could cure my aching head and simultaneously uplift my spirits. I reached the landing and heard my mother call my name. Without turning around, I stopped mid-step. Iris was a loose cannon, a meddler, an instigator, a provocateur (probably her fondest title), yet sometimes her unpredictable nature evoked generous and nurturing wisdom. I clenched the banister, unsure of her intentions.

"You don't have to look at me but I want you to hear me," she paused, making no attempt to ascend the staircase or shelter my emotions. "Getting him the hell out of here was the smartest thing you've done in a long time." I cocked my head downward and caught her eyes. "I would've done it a hell-of-a-lot sooner, but we both know, you're not me."

She just couldn't do it, I thought. My own mother couldn't make it through one stressful moment for me without reverting the conversation back to herself. I shook my head.

"He's changing you, Marley. He's been breaking you down. You deserve more than he can give you and I think you're getting closer and closer to seeing yourself the way I see you."

I looked away, cringing, and knelt down on the stairs. What did that mean? Was that her back-door way of saying something in my favor? Or was it in my favor?

"Who knows if this'll be the end for you and Andrew, but there will be an end, believe me. It'll end for good and hopefully soon. You'll be better after the end, Marley, no matter how hard it is to get there."

ALEX

I FELT A SUDDEN PANIC in my stomach as I crouched to Mom's side. Was she hurt? Was she breathing? With the master bedroom only a few paces away, surely she didn't choose to sleep hunched-over the steps of the staircase, did she? I lowered my head very close to her face, desperate to observe a proof-of-life exhale from her crumpled body. A strand of my hair must've grazed Mom's face, jolting her upright and colliding with my forehead. Both of us screeched with surprise, embracing our heads from the sudden discomfort.

"I was just checking on you," I admitted, beginning to tear.

"Oh, honey . . . come here," Mom said, reaching for me. "Why are you crying?"

I sniffled twice, using the inside of my shirt's neckline to wipe under my nose. "I don't really know. It just scared me to see you on the steps like that and then you startled me when you woke up. What happened?"

She hugged me a little tighter. "Ugh, a lot happened, babe. There's a lot to tell you, but I don't think I can sit here any longer."

"What's wrong?"

"I'm getting too old to sleep on steps, that's what's wrong," she laughed. "Can you help me up?"

I smirked watching Mom steady herself with a hand on the railing. "You're not that old."

"O-kay. You just wait to see how long it takes for your body to start acting older than your mind thinks it is."

I bounced down the stairs, taking two at a time, maybe showing off just a bit.

"I'll be there in a sec. I need to stretch a little. Want to get the coffee pot going?" Mom called down from the landing.

I arrived in the kitchen only to find Grandma sipping tea from an antique chawan tea bowl, which she claims was designed especially for a Buddhist prince in India more than a century ago. I'm not sure how she acquired it, but oddly, no one seems to question the authenticity of her worldly treasures. And believe me, she has many stories.

"Good morning, darling," she said, greeting me while her eyes focused intensely on her daily Sudoku puzzle.

I kissed her cheek, catching a trace of yesterday's perfume. "How long have you been up?"

Grandma knew exactly what I was up to—attempting to solicit information that could render my mother *off the hook*. "Ah, you know me," she said vaguely. "I'm in and out all night."

I filled the coffee basin with bottled water from the pantry and scooped four heaping spoonfuls of coffee into the cone-shaped filter. I closed the lid and turned it on as Mom rounded the corner, taking a seat on a barstool next to Gram.

"Coffee is going to hit the spot," Mom grumbled, wiping her eyes with the back of her palms.

I gracefully jumped up and back to sit on the kitchen island. My shoulders came forward while the pressure of my palms rested on the counter top. The room was quiet and peaceful, but something felt off.

Mom popped every knuckle on both hands; maybe in an effort to delay conversation.

Grandma must've sensed Mom's stewing and took the liberty of jumping right in. She lowered her thin bedazzled readers and looked over her nose, speaking in a controlled, yet clearly audible voice. "If you're second-guessing yourself for one minute, you'd better do yourself a favor and slap the thought right out of your mind."

Mom responded with a piercing look.

"I knew it," Grandma proclaimed, and tossed her prized mechanical pencil on top of the newspaper. "Just when I thought you'd been pushed to your limit, you cower and start to back-peddle."

"What does that mean?" I asked Mom, diving into the one-sided lashing.

Mom glared at Grandma and took a deep breath before addressing my question. "I asked your dad to give me his key to our house. And his garage door opener, too."

"Why?" The impulsive response reflected my surprise.

Mom pondered before answering. "Your dad was over-using his privilege to be in our house whenever he felt like it—even when we aren't home," she said.

"What does that mean?"

Grandma rolled her eyes, swallowed hard, and got back to

her puzzle. "Just give it to her straight," she mumbled under her breath.

"I mean—we never stop-by or drop-in at his house just because it's closer than going home or just to use the bathroom," Mom explained. "He acts like this house is as much his as it is ours—like he doesn't respect our privacy."

"So he can't come over anymore?"

"No," she blurted. "I'm not saying that at all. I'd just like to know when he's coming over, why he wants to be here, and how long he's planning to stay. I don't want to look over my shoulder anymore and see that he's just let himself in."

"You don't trust him being here without us?" I asked. "Did he do something wrong?" I pushed.

Grandma elbow-nudged Mom. "Good question," followed by applause for me with the tip-up of her chin and a left-eye wink.

"Getting some privacy back into our lives," she gestured toward me, "has everything to do with us. We have to consider that Grandma is living with us now, and she deserves her privacy, too. I should've made that clearer to your dad a long time ago."

I could see Grandma roll her eyes and look down at her puzzle again. "Then why are you still re-thinking what you said to him?" she asked, not lifting her head or her pencil.

Mom downed half her coffee before answering. "Andrew has been present in some way or another for Alex's whole life, which by the way, is a significant portion of my life, too," she told her. "It's a strange feeling making a change like this—no matter how strongly I believe in the decision."

"I get it, Mom, I think," seeming to take her by surprise. "It's just going to take some getting used to." I sat quietly on the counter stool with my cereal bowl, not sure what to say. Mom came over and hugged me from the side.

"Let's just see how it goes."

"Yeah," Grandma sighed. "Let's see how it goes."

MARLEY

RACHEL PLACED TWO COFFEE CUPS on my desk and peered over my shoulder. "How long have you been here?" she whispered.

I surprised her with a sudden jerk. "What are you doing?" I shouted.

She took a seat in the chair across the aisle and I swiveled around.

"What am I doing?" she asked, placing heavy emphasis on the *I*. You're the one sprawled across the desk."

"Forget it," I said under my breath, shuffling and redirecting toward the piles I'd never accomplish that day.

Rachel noticed me eying the coffee. "Go ahead, one is yours. Just like every day. You look like it would do you some good about now."

"Thanks." I was glad she didn't stick around. I powered up the computer and heard my phone ringing inside my purse, having no interest in it—the caller, the possible message, the sound of the person's voice on the other end of the phone.

Someone raised the volume on one of the televisions lining the newsroom walls. I lifted my head enough to notice that several people were gathering in front of a particular screen, while the other five televisions were suddenly muted. A split screen displayed text commentary, *Former professional football player, Dax Townsend,* on the left side, while the other screen ran live video footage of emergency vehicles on the scene of what appeared to be a serious multi-vehicle accident.

"Marley, grab your things and meet me in the truck. We

need to get to the hospital," Rachel said.

"What's going on?" I asked.

After nearly reaching the door to the back parking lot, Rachel came back to my desk in a huff. She leaned very close to me, forcing eye contact. "Make a decision. Are you here to work or do you need to take yourself off the schedule for the rest of the day?"

I grabbed my purse and the last-minute travel bag I kept fully stocked in the bottom drawer. I realized I forgot the coffee cup still sitting on the corner of my desk and retraced my steps.

Aside from the camera guy, Flick, Rachel and I were driving alone in the truck—which meant we were absolutely not alone. Talking about anything in front of Flick is like broadcasting to the entire networking area, without the benefit of electronic or wireless media. Flick does a fine job of spreading news with a viral effect on his own. He's extremely funny, crass, and easy to get along with, yet, to compound his reputation for being comical, he makes no attempts to conceal his penchant for gossip. He's well received by most people at the station, however, very few make a conscious decision to confide in him. In a way, it removes any workplace drama when he's around and you can always count on Flick for a good belly-laugh.

I reached into my purse for the phone that kept chiming. I glared at Rachel for sending the repeated text messages from her seat.

WHAT HAPPENED TO YOU?

I replied.

TALK LATER

Rachel spent the next ten minutes briefing us on the details of the accident, what we would be covering on location, and the constant updates from the station and police scanners. Flick secured a prime location for coverage, making sure the hospital emergency doors would fit inside the upper corner of the frame with room for me in the shot. Positioned among a string of media correspondents in front of the hospital, I was still in the truck, slathering on a decent make-up face before airing the first segment.

"Ever done a story on someone from your college days, Marley?" Flick inquired. I shook my head, taking one more deep breath before putting on a serious expression for the camera. He counted backwards with three fingers, cuing me with a pointed index to begin reading the teleprompter report.

"We've recently confirmed that Colton Townsend, son of former Arizona Cardinals Wide-Receiver, Dax Townsend, has been rushed into emergency surgery following internal bleeding and injuries caused by a three-car automobile accident on the Loop-101 at Broadway this morning, around eight forty-five. Townsend's son is a nineteen year old sophomore at Arizona State University and follows in his father's footsteps as a football superstar in the PAC-12. Townsend was the driver of the metallic gray Ford F-150, visible in the footage, and is believed to have been the middle car in the collision. He was carrying one adult male passenger, also an ASU student, who has sustained injuries and is being treated at this hospital, as well. Additionally, the other two drivers were alone in their vehicles and are receiving medical treatment at two different Valley hospitals. At this time, we are awaiting a medical report from a spokesperson for the Townsend family. We'll keep you updated throughout the day as this story unfolds."

I removed my ear-piece and handed the microphone to Flick.

"You okay?" he asked, as I walked past him.

"It's not my best day," I shrugged. "I'll be back." I pulled off my press badge and tucked it into the pocket of my blazer, walking impulsively toward the building. After entering the emergency room through automatic sliding doors, I slid past the front desk into a side corridor that lead to a pair of elevators. A couple of years ago, my mother had a hernia repair in an operating room upstairs and I waited in a family waiting area on the fifth floor. I wondered if Dax was waiting impatiently in that same space?

The elevator ascended and stopped at the fifth floor. The doors opened and I stepped timidly into the hallway. I spotted him, a man I'd seen in the studio dozens of times since attending college on the same campus, but typically only acknowledged with a cordial smile or quick word. During and since our undergraduate days, we'd spoken informally, a bit professionally, but never about our children. Soon, we'd be working together on the drug abuse awareness campaign. I paused, leaning on a corner pillar, attempting to survey the area. Is he really up here alone? I turned in each direction and took a few steps toward him, but he caught sight of me immediately, even from a distance.

Dax approached sternly. He stood eighteen inches away and looked directly into my eyes. His silence was unexpected.

"Hi," I whispered, drawing out the word.

"No press was to be allowed in the building," he said.

I brought both hands up as a sign of peace. "Right—that's right. I'm not here as press." I was unsure if he'd accept my expression of concern. "I'm here as a parent, maybe even as a friend. My daughter just celebrated her sixteenth birthday and hearing about your son just hit me in the gut. I came to offer support because I can't imagine being in your shoes right now."

He extended a hand and led me to a secluded waiting area

around the corner, away from windows and people and noise. It was strange but natural when we embraced for a moment, then sat quietly, with an understanding of the crazy mix of emotions we shared in that small moment of time.

———

THE SUN BLASTED THROUGH THE fifth floor windows with a brightness that revealed the calming southwestern beauty; a sharp contrast to the sterile and clammy hospital interior. Dax and I stood beside a straightened row of waiting room chairs in the silent corridor. Current editions of family and parenting magazines held vigil in tidy end table stacks, prepared to occupy the minds of anxious guardians awaiting reports from physicians.

I straightened my posture, wiping away a few falling tears. "I'm so sorry. I never should've bothered you," I confessed.

Dax shook his head and took my hand. "No, it's good. I'm glad you found me. I was kind of in a trance up here."

"You know we're going to be working together on the T.A.D.A. campaign?" I winced.

He nodded. "I do, and I'm really looking forward to it. I was actually planning to touch base with you before the New York launch, but here you are."

I peered out the window at the news van and tried to calculate how long I'd been gone. "I should probably go," I smiled.

Dax looked outside. "I knew they'd come." Looking at me, he asked, "Do me a favor and just report the facts. I know you have a job to do, but imagine dragging your own family into the news. I'm just thinking about my son."

I nodded, my eyes were glassy.

"And tell Rachel thanks for calling, but I'm not up for talking."

I must've looked confused.

"She's been calling me every fifteen minutes since the story broke this morning. I haven't answered a single call from anyone, but I appreciate her concern."

"I'll tell her." Rachel hadn't said a word about trying to contact Dax. Feeling the need to justify my actions, I let up a little on my own guilt for barging into the hospital. He probably wouldn't have answered my call anyway.

On my way downstairs, I touched my pants and patted my chest. No phone in my pockets or tucked into my bra. I snuck out of the hospital unnoticed, I thought, when Rachel called my name abruptly. A bit of attention garnered curiosity from the valet desk and onlookers enjoying the perfect spring weather from chairs and benches in the meditation garden.

"Where have you been?" Rachel scowled in a parental tone.

"Relax," I said, trying to hush her. "I'm fine."

"You've been out of sight and unreachable for twenty minutes!"

I picked up my pace, forcing Rachel to follow me into the covered parking garage.

"Please stop yelling at me and take a breath, would you?"

Rachel raised her eyebrows, waiting for a valid explanation.

"Obviously, I've had a rough night, you could see that when you came into the station this morning."

"That much, I already know. Why did you disappear? You couldn't just say, 'Hey Rachel, I'll be back in a few,' instead of leaving your cell phone in the van and vanishing into thin air?"

"I don't know! I wish I had a better answer for you, but I guess I needed some air. My head wasn't on straight."

"And now it is?"

I shrugged, "I feel a little better, clearer, more aware of what's going on. I just started walking."

"Please bring me up to speed because I'm having a very

hard time understanding you today," Rachel said.

"You're barking at me," I glared, but Rachel waited for an answer. "When I realized what happened to Colton Townsend, I felt something in my body that has never happened before. Like it was more real because we know Dax. And maybe more difficult to handle because Alex is nearly his son's age."

"I've been calling him all morning, but he hasn't answered any of my calls."

"I know. He told me."

Rachel positioned her face right in front of mine. "What? When did you talk to Dax?"

"That's where I went," I said, leading Rachel further into the garage. "It was like an out-of-body experience. I walked into the hospital, got on the elevator, and took a chance that he'd be upstairs in the waiting area where I sat waiting for my mom to come out of surgery. It turns out, he was."

"I can't believe you went in there, Marley! Do you realize the harm you could have brought to yourself or the station? Specific instructions were expressed for all media to remain outside of the hospital!"

"I didn't go in as media. I went as a friend."

"A friend? You're not a friend!" Rachel blurted in a loud whisper.

I deflated. "I might not be a friend, but I'm not a stranger either. We're acquaintances enough and it seemed like he trusted that I was there to offer support and not overstep my boundaries as a reporter. And soon, we're going to be spending a lot of time together."

"He told you that?" Rachel questioned suspiciously.

"Come on, Rachel. The poor guy was alone. The kid's mother wasn't even there. I hate that feeling when I'm forced to handle something for Alex without the support of her dad."

"Andrew's usually there."

"He might be there, physically, but it's me making the decisions. His self-centered approach to everything makes it very difficult to accept his opinions sometimes. Convenience is very important to him, and maybe even more important than what's best for Alex. Anyway, I just had a horrible feeling that Dax was alone."

Rachel slightly readjusted her tone. "How was he when you saw him?"

"After I told him my reasons for being there, he let his guard down. He was kind of business-like when he first saw me, thinking I was there as a reporter, of course. Then, he let me give him a hug, as a friend," I emphasized.

"How's Colton, besides what we've been hearing on the scanner?"

"From what I understand, he's still in surgery. I didn't see any doctors while I was up there, so I'm not sure if Dax heard anything yet, either. We didn't really talk. I was literally there only a couple of minutes."

"He's gonna pull through this, I just know it," Rachel announced.

"Dax or Colton?" I asked. "It sounds pretty serious."

"Both of them, and the other people involved, too."

"He asked me to pray for his son."

"You won't be the only one prayin', Mar, but he can surely use yours, too. A lot of people are saying a lot of prayers right now, for all these people. You can count on that. A public figure like Dax brings out empathy in a lot of people, especially fans—as if they were legitimate blood-relatives in the same family."

I closed my eyes and took a deep breath.

"You ready?" Rachel asked, already a few steps in front of me.

"In a minute. There's one more thing. He said he appreciates you calling."

"I know," Rachel said, taking my hand. "He's a good guy. I'm sure it means a lot to him that you took the time to see him as a dad and not just a celebrity football star."

"I hope so. At the very least, it brought me out of my funk and made me feel better," I smiled. "Can I borrow your phone for a minute? I just want to touch base with Alex and then I'll be ready. How much time do I have?"

Rachel looked at her watch. "You're already late."

CHAPTER 3

MARLEY

BEING ON LOCAL TELEVISION SEEMS to have changed how I'm perceived by people. I don't know this for sure, but I feel like it's true. Mostly, I'm referring to online commentary. *People* seem to give themselves permission to freely—and frequently, voice their assumptions and criticisms of me, and that happened far less often before I took position in an evening anchor's chair. Now there's that generalization of *people*. Why do I do that? I even use my index and middle fingers on each hand, air-quoting when I speak about *people*. Well, who are they . . . those *people*? I use the term loosely, as if they should bear any weight on my own perception of self. In actuality, it has taken me quite some time to become less affected by their comments. If I can be honest, it frustrates me that I even have the slightest bit of interest in what *people* say about me. Yet, here I am, thinking about those very public online comments again.

I felt the plane lurch subtly at the jet-way. The flight attendant opened the forward door after welcoming the whole cabin of passengers to New York's JFK International Airport. I flew alone, with plans of meeting a camera crew from the local affiliate, at the national headquarters for the T.A.D.A. campaign. That wouldn't be until this evening though, and my head was full of potential daytime plans.

I wheeled my over-sized luggage behind me as I passed through the double-wide sliding doors that lead to the curb. I inhaled deeply as my mind travelled back to a previous visit to New York. The scents and sounds of the city brought imme- diate reminiscence, even though I was a good forty-minute drive outside the perimeter of Times Square. A smile appeared on my face with day-old make-up and teeth that needed a good brushing. For the time being, I was just a regular person. No one who should be recognized or even worth a double take. I was relieved to be out of my home-zone and on my own before the T.A.D.A. events began.

"Marley Christopher, is that you?"

I'll admit that I heard someone speak. It was the voice of a man. At that particular moment, I didn't recognize his voice. I either assumed or hoped that the question wasn't asked of me, but for someone else with a similar sounding name. I willed myself not to look in the direction of his voice. I turned to my purse as an intentional distraction and began fiddling for some- thing. Anything that would take a few seconds to locate.

"Marley Christopher?"

Dammit. I felt my teeth clench, but forced a disgruntled smile as I turned my head in the direction of his voice.

My mouth opened, but I didn't say anything. Not at first. My heart started beating with an intensity that I couldn't control. Thank God I was wearing sunglasses, because I closed my eyes in sheer panic. I had to take my eyes off of him and concentrate on a couple of deep, controlled breaths. It seemed preposterous that moments after arriving in New York, I could be staring into the face of Dax Townsend. But, I was. And I knew I'd have to eventually. I just wasn't ready to deal with him yet.

"I thought that was you." He came closer into my space and cautiously hugged me. Then, he put a hand on each of my shoulders and looked me directly in the eyes. "I knew you'd be in New York, but never thought we'd arrive at the same time."

"I know. What are the chances, right?" laughing uncomfortably. I noticed a bench just a few feet away, and I inched toward it. My suitcase turned on it's side, no longer able to glide on it's wheels, but I dragged it anyway. I felt like my legs were going to buckle under my body. "Do you mind if I sit?" I winced.

"No, no. Not at all. Where are you staying?"

He's serious, I think. I hadn't seen or spoken to him since the few minutes in the hospital. Now we're sharing a casual conversation on a cement block bench at an airport located nearly twenty-five hundred miles from the television station where we occasionally pass one another with a quick wave and smile. I knew I'd have to talk to him, but that was supposed to be tonight. Not now. I'm not prepared.

"Marley, you look like you don't feel so well."

"You know, all of a sudden, I'm not sure I do. But it might have something to do with the fact that I haven't washed my face or had a decent meal in about eight hours." I raked my tongue over my teeth. They didn't feel right.

"Let's get you something to eat. Where did you say you were staying?"

"I'm not sure I did. Did I?" I wrinkled my nose. "Some-where near 42nd and Broadway."

"Me, too. Why don't we share a cab?"

I smiled, sort of, rubbing my eyes and wondering how I was going to get my day back. It sounded like Dax was taking me to breakfast, whether I was comfortable with it or not. Had I picked up on that correctly? I'd planned on a few hours of quiet—except for the sounds of the city. Alone. But of course, those were not the words that came out of my mouth.

"That sounds great!" What? How can I speak something different than what my mind was thinking? Before I have a chance to re-apply lipstick to the face that frightened me when I opened my compact, Dax was standing at the curb, hailing *our* cab. And how close were our hotels?

"Dammit," I managed to mumble out loud. I didn't mean to do that, either.

"Ready?" he asked, smiling, chipper, and awake.

All of a sudden, my luggage had been placed in the trunk of the cab, and off we went to eat breakfast in the city. I was so not okay with everything that had just happened.

"Yes! Absolutely," I say, smiling in the backseat we shared.

———————

THE AIR FELT THICK. EVERY window of the car was rolled up tight and snug in its casing, while the rain poured down over Queens. I looked around for backseat air conditioning vents, locating only two very small ones on the back of the driver's console. An overwhelming feeling of too much warmth or claustrophobia came over me; the side windows fogging with other people's finger-written names reappearing more clearly with each passing second.

I dropped my head back to the headrest, closing my eyes and praying to God that I could trick my mind into believing that my body felt fine. I felt clammy as the clusters of sweat began to form around the base of my neck and across the bridge of my nose. Dax was talking non-stop and pointing to various points of interest outside his window. He was so charismatic and jovial. I hated it. Quiet would've been so much better.

"If it was a clear day today, you'd be able to . . . " Dax said, halting his speech and putting his hand on the side of my face. "Marley."

My eyes were still closed as I put my hand over my mouth.

"Sir, please stop the car immediately," he said to the driver.

"Stop the car?"

"Yes, she's sick."

Before Dax was done explaining my immediate need to the driver, I had my door cracked open. The car was still in motion, but out of necessity, I leaned out toward the passing traffic with my seat belt fastened tightly across my lap and emptied the contents of my stomach onto the blacktop.

"Marley!" Dax called.

I felt his grasp around my waist, guiding my upper body to a seated position. I felt the driver gun the gas pedal. "He must be in a real hurry," I tried to smile. So irritated by his horrific lack of concern, I didn't feel too embarrassed in front of Dax. Yet. I closed the door, feeling somewhat relieved. A moment passed, maybe two, and I held up one finger.

"Stop the car!" Dax yelled to the driver.

"She's sick again?" the driver asked with his heavy foreign accent, laughing.

If I had all my faculties, I would've had something to say to that man. But at the moment, I could only focus on the passing asphalt, as the car slowed. I don't think the driver ever really stopped the car. Whatever. We warned him.

"Should we get out of the car, Marley? Maybe take in a few minutes of outside air?"

"No. I'm fine," I said, attempting to crack a very pathetic

smile. "Really. I feel so much better."

Dax reached across the backseat and placed his hand over mine. The truth is, I've been day-dreaming a long time for that to actually happen; for Dax Townsend to take me by the hand and share an emotional minute with me. But this scenario was nothing like the picture I'd painted in my mind. To be completely honest, I didn't want to be touched by anyone, anywhere, at that moment. Even if it was Dax Townsend.

Overall, I was feeling better as each minute passed. Along with regaining composure, came the reality of the situation, as well. I'd spent years reading about Dax in the media, following his career and occasionally wondering what it would be like to really know him. Whether we'd travel across the globe, share glasses of wine, watch movies, or just toss a football in the park, I never imagined that I'd vomit out the side door of our shared cab.

Thank God the weather cleared. The skies were still grayish, but the rain had stopped. He dropped me off at my hotel in Times Square, the campaign kick-off venue where I'd stay for the next three nights. Obviously, breakfast was cancelled. He mentioned meeting up with some friends during the day, but he'd return to the hotel before the cocktail event started at seven.

"Thanks for sharing your car with me," I winced, after he stopped me from paying for our ride.

"I'm just glad you weren't alone back here."

I agreed with him, though I felt mortified for putting him through such an unpleasant moment. I waved as the car drove Dax Townsend down Broadway, away from the hotel. I checked in with the front desk and headed to the elevator, arriving at my room impatiently. "Thank you," I whispered when the door unlocked on the first try.

The view from the twenty-first floor was exquisite. It had been quite some time since I'd visited the city, and this was right in the heart of all the action. I reached into my luggage and retrieved the binoculars I'd stashed in the small interior pocket. I didn't even need them to read the huge billboards marketing Broadway plays, musicals, upcoming television shows, and the big brand names and ads for the latest technologies. But I was intrigued by the windows above each of those giant store fronts. People actually live here in Times Square, and it's not just a place for them to visit. I gazed with amazement and wonder. Thoughts of my quiet suburban home outside of Phoenix, Arizona contrasted greatly with life in the heart of New York City.

"Oh my God!" I gasped. As I panned the windows with my binoculars, I caught a glimpse of a very handsome man. It was tough to actually see the details of his face, but I knew for certain that he hadn't quite finished dressing for the day. I pulled the binoculars away from my face and backed away from my window. Did he see me?

So many of the windows offered birds-eyed views into the apartments; very few covered with draperies. I still wasn't feeling great and decided that a shower would make a world of difference. I began undressing and remembered the guy in the window across the way. I left the curtains open, but headed to the bathroom before undressing completely.

My phone rang. "Where did I put it?" I peeked around the bathroom wall, seeing my purse on the desk. It wasn't all the way over by the window, so I tip-toe-ran quickly to retrieve it. Caller ID said it was Andrew and I answered right away.

"Good, you're there."

"The hotel is great," I said, sprinting back to the bathroom.

"Listen. I have to head out of town for a couple of days."

"Why?"

"A conference came up in Austin, and I'm the chosen one, I guess."

"When are you leaving?"

"I'm actually at the airport right now. That's why I'm calling. Your mom swears she'll keep her eyes on Alex."

"We'll see about that," I said, disappointed that my work kept me from being around when Alex really needed me.

"Hey, can you see the TKTS booth from your room?"

"I don't know. Let me see." I headed for my window, undoubtedly still groggy from my motion sickness. I don't know how it happened, but with all those windows in front of me, I locked eyes with the naked guy, as he waved from his window across Broadway at the stupid naked girl.

———————

I'D BEEN IN NEW YORK exactly long enough for my stomach to settle and I was suddenly starving, though it still felt loosely knotted after talking to my mother on the phone. She couldn't even keep track of Alex for twenty-four hours and I was going to be across the country for four days. It was very hard for me to resist micromanaging from more than two thousand miles from home.

Dax sat casually in an acorn colored club chair near a window in the lobby, paging through the New York Times. Not a fraction of the news pages were left without print, covered with black and white articles, advertisements, and press from around the world. While many loyal readers traded in the hard copy for digital news, I wondered if Dax preferred the overloaded print pages over other news outlets.

"Hey!" he stood and smiled. "That didn't take long." He'd called my room a little after noon to see how I was feeling.

I gestured toward the pair of empty chairs. "Can we sit for a minute?"

Like a perfect gentleman, Dax waited for me to take my seat. Not sure what to make of my hesitation, his puzzled, yet content face, nudged me to break the silence.

"I have to apologize," I began.

Dax tilted his head, perplexed.

I shrugged. "This morning, I was so caught up in the unexpectedness of seeing you at the airport, then not feeling well after the flight, I just wasn't thinking clearly."

"You don't have to apologize for any of that."

My flustered thoughts presented in a gentle bit of waving hands to clear the air. "I didn't say that correctly. Let me start over," I paused. Our eyes met and we shared a comfortable smile.

"It's only been a couple of weeks since your son's accident, and now we're here in New York, and I didn't have my thoughts prepared well enough earlier to ask you how he's recovering."

Dax sat up a little taller, the pride of fatherhood plus a sign of relief showing in his face. "I'm so pleased to report that Colton is recovering remarkably well."

I responded with an audible exhale. Why had I been holding my breath?

"He spent three nights in the hospital following surgery to reset a bone in his upper arm. He took it easy for another week at my house, and fortunately, he's getting back to his old self. But, he's back at school and he's got quite a few people who can help him out if he needs anything. He also has trainers monitoring his therapy and pain."

"I'm so relieved to hear that," I whispered. "I didn't want to bother you, and, well, Rachel thought I was a little intrusive, seeking you out at the hospital on the day of the accident."

"May I?" Dax asked, reaching for my folded hands. He wrapped both hands around mine. "You have no idea how comforting it was when you came to find me in the waiting room that day. So many people reached out to me in one way or another, but you—you were the only person who sought me out as a regular guy, the dad of a college kid who was in a terrible car accident, not a celebrity athlete or media attraction."

I felt my heart beating faster than normal. My teeth bit my bottom lip.

"Obviously, you had to report the facts later in the day. But during those quiet minutes that we talked together on the fifth floor of the hospital, you came to me as a friend, a concerned parent, someone who had genuine interest in the well-being of my son. I will never forget the strength you gave me during that short visit, Marley."

I nodded bashfully but couldn't think of anything to say that seemed an appropriate response to fill the quiet air.

Dax released my hands and straightened his posture. "Okay, now that you've gotten that off your chest, are you ready to head out into this beautiful city of lights?"

"Absolutely," I stood. "Can we start with a little something to eat? I'm hungry all of a sudden."

Dax grinned. "If a sandwich sounds good to you, do you think your growling stomach can hold out through a fifteen minute cab ride so I can take you to a deli I think every New York visitor should experience?"

"You're already making jokes about my stomach!" I smiled.

"No, sorry," he laughed. "That's not what I meant."

"How can I pass up that offer?" I joked. "I'm glad you're here, Dax Townsend. I lucked out with an experienced New York traveller as a partner in this campaign. I guess my itinerary lies in your capable hands."

As the cab pulled in front of Katz's Delicatessen, Houston Street was bustling with people, a couple of street musicians, and a line out the door.

"This is unbelievable!" I blurted. "I never expected to see

this many people standing in line for a sandwich. They're out the door and around the side of the building."

"Is it too much? Do you want to find something quieter?" Dax offered.

"No way. Tell me about this place."

Moments after Dax began his history lesson about Katz's, the group of people in front of us chimed in with their own knowledge of the legendary restaurant. Only about ten minutes outside before making our way into the iconic building, Dax and I witnessed the excitement on the inside. It certainly wasn't quiet. In fact, I quickly became schooled in pastrami, pickles, and Matzo balls.

The employees behind the counter were welcoming from the get-go with a boisterous "How ya' doin'?" and naturally outspoken conversations with anyone who'd chime in. As I watched the gigantic sandwich masterpieces being handed over the counter, I knew without a doubt, that I'd never be able to scarf down an entire pastrami on rye.

"I'm guessing they don't make half sandwiches?" I cringed.

"I doubt it," Dax agreed. "But, I'm willing to split whatever you order, if you're comfortable with that."

We missed our turn to order by approximately two seconds, and the guy behind the counter was spewing something funny, yet sarcastic, to get our attention. I stammered and laughed, Dax quickly took the lead. I caught a glimpse of one of the butchers leaving his post and getting the attention of the others. He came back with a framed picture in hand, aligning it with Dax's face.

"It *is* you, I knew it!" he spouted.

High-fives and jumping excitement stopped time for a few seconds. Cell phones came out of pockets and pictures were taken, hands were shaken, and pats on backs were shared among the employees and their realization that Dax Townsend was in the house. Their house.

"Dude, where have you been?" someone shouted. "This picture is dated nineteen ninety-nine."

———

THE TIME CHANGE WASN'T IDEAL, but I hoped Iris's phone was as close as her predictable Cabernet.

"Of course I'm still awake. You know I don't sleep well without a goodnight kiss from Jimmy Fallon. What's keeping you up this late?"

"I just walked in, but I've been trying Alex's phone all night. Would you get her for me, please?" I asked.

"Alex isn't here, Marley. At least I don't think she is."

"You don't think she is? What does that mean? If she's not there, then where is she?"

"Just a minute. Don't get yourself into a panic. You always overreact. I'll just check her room."

The pause with no information felt infuriating. I walked the length of the hotel room, flinging open the curtains in frustration and watching the movement in Times Square. I hate it when she tells me what to think and feel about my own child!

"Marley?"

"I'm right here," I scowled.

"She must've forgotten to take her cell phone with her, because I found it on her dresser. She's not in her room, but she called me earlier."

"What did she say?"

"She said she was with Toby and she'd be home later." Alex didn't flaunt it, but Toby had been her exclusive boyfriend going on five months.

"When was that?"

Iris looked at the clock. "Hmmm . . . .about three hours

ago, I'd say."

"I don't care what time it is when she gets home, I want you to have her call me."

"Dear, she's fine. You need your sleep for the work you have tomorrow. Don't exhaust yourself over nothing. I'm here for her. I told you that before you left. How about this? If she's not home at a reasonable time in my book, I'll call you myself."

"I'm calling Toby," I announced. Iris' tone felt so condescending.

"Don't do that," Iris suggested. "I know you think that life is a lot different now, parenting a teenager, but believe it or not, I've been in your shoes, Marley. I remember the things that drove stakes through our relationship when you were her age."

I was stunned, irritated by Iris's comparison.

"I know you think I'm completely oblivious to our differences, but the truth is, our differences lie only in our reactions."

"Mother, this is not the time for a psychology lesson."

"Get some sleep. Trust Alex. And call her tomorrow."

I didn't say anything but I didn't hang up, either. I knew Iris wasn't done.

"Figure out how you're going to talk to her without ripping her a new one and then spend the rest of the time working on what you need to take care of in New York. And take a nap. God knows you overwork yourself. Alex isn't alone, Marley. I'm here and Andrew is just a phone call away. Somewhere along the line, you developed an illusion of control. And no matter how hard you try, you can't control everything."

Iris had a point, but it didn't ease my concern. I hung up the phone wondering what I thought I'd actually be able to accomplish through the phone lines from a couple thousand miles away. At forty, I still didn't want my mother to be right. Ever.

The knock on the hotel room door was soft but startling. I opened it with the chain-latch still fastened.

Dax stood in the hallway wearing shorts, a t-shirt, flip-flops and an Arizona State Sun Devils baseball cap. I was still wearing the suit and heels I arrived in before calling Iris.

"I thought it might be too late—that you'd already gone to bed or something. But you look like you're heading out again," he smiled.

"No. No," I started, closing the door to unhook the latch, then opening it fully. "What are you doing? Would you like to come in?"

"Actually, I came to see if you wanted to hit the streets of New York for awhile. I thought you might like to join me."

I smiled. Moments before, I stood in front of the window feeling defeated by my mother.

"You know, I just took a look out there and considered taking a walk myself."

"Great! Should I change my clothes?" he asked.

I looked down at myself and laughed. "No, please. I think you have the right idea. Why don't I meet you downstairs in five minutes wearing something similar to what you've got on."

"Deal," he said, letting himself out the door.

My cell phone rang, caller ID revealed our home number.

"Hi, Mom," Alex said calmly.

Relief came over me as I sank onto the bed and listened to Alex's voice.

"Grandma said you were worried sick and wanted to talk to me. I'm sorry I didn't have my phone."

"Thank you for calling me, honey. Where have you been?"

"Toby went with me and some friends to watch a soccer game. I called Grandma earlier."

"Especially while I'm away, will you do a really good job of keeping her informed of what you're doing?"

"Yeah, sure. How's New York?"

"It's going well. What do you think about this? I'm going out to see the city as soon as I hang up with you."

"Wow, I'm impressed!" Alex said, seemingly aware of the time. "You're not going alone, are you?"

"Look who's concerned now," I laughed. "As a matter of fact, I'm going with someone from the campaign. I'll text you some pictures, but don't stay up too late."

I hung up the phone feeling content and reassured. Alex was a wonderful girl with good judgment and a grandmother who promised to watch over her.

ALEX

I WAS TWO MILES FROM home when I answered my cell phone and shifted gears on the manual transmission. Every single time he called, his goofy facial expression commanded my phone screen and forced me to smile—no matter what kind of mood I was in. This time though, it was a new picture; one I hadn't seen before. He must've replaced his contact photo when he was messing with my phone. It was parked in a charging dock on the dashboard, requiring just one touch to answer. I down shifted into third and coasted toward the stoplight, simultaneously sipping from a bottled water, answering the phone, and lowering the stereo volume, multi-tasking like a pro.

"Hey!" I said, accepting the video call through Skype.

"Hey!" he yelled back, freakishly close to the webcam.

I could only see one of his eyes and part of his nose. "Where are you?"

"I'm almost home. What are you doing? I can't tell where you are. Back away from the camera a little."

"Just a minute. You can't be driving when I tell you." He

made a stupid face.

"Tell me," I insisted. "You're so weird," I smiled.

"Seriously, Alex. You're gonna flip."

"Oh, my god," I mumbled. I had a million things to do and I was already late getting started. "Thank God for green lights the entire time. I'm home now."

"Is the car off?" he badgered.

I flung my seatbelt around my left shoulder, grumbling because the latch slammed the window of the door. I pulled my messenger bag over my shoulder, slid the phone off the dock, and pointed the camera toward the front door.

"See?" I barked. "I'm home. The car's parked and I'm sitting down on the front porch steps."

"You can't sit there. You should go inside."

"What? What's wrong with sitting out here?"

"You'll thank me in a minute. Just go upstairs into your room and close the door."

"Toby, seriously—quit the mysterious act." I played along and skipped every other stair up to my room. "Okay, I'm in my room. What is it?" I shut the door; my bag dropped from my shoulder to the floor and then I screamed louder than I'd ever screamed before. I turned away from my closet, jumping and running in place where Toby was standing. "You jerk!" I covered my eyes for a few seconds before turning around again and wailing on him. In between swats, I yelled. "What the hell? What are you doing?"

He was much taller and stronger than me, enough to restrain my wrists, although his laughter and obvious amusement didn't ease my frustration.

"What are you doing?" I growled, checking outside the window and my mind raced. Did I see my grandmother's car when I pulled into the driveway? Were we alone? I opened the bedroom door and peered down the staircase. It appeared that we were alone, but how?

"Calm down," Toby pleaded, still wavering between pride in his accomplishment and his attempt to regain composure. "You're freaking out for no reason."

"No reason? You just scared the living daylights out of me!" I looked him straight in the eyes. "We were on the telephone. Why didn't you just say you'd be waiting for me? And why are you waiting in my room and not outside? Where is your car, anyway?"

"That's what I'm about to tell you."

I threw out both arms and open-wide palms in front, waiting for his untimely explanation.

"I got a ride and came in through the garage."

"Toby. There are so many levels of wrong with this. Where should I start?"

He looked more devastated that I wasn't over the moon about his surprise than he was about me being upset with him.

"What's the big deal?"

"Don't you see anything strange about it?" I shook my head.

"Come on, Alex."

"Why don't you just go. I already told you I have a ton of work to do."

Seconds of silence filled the room.

"I don't have my car," he reminded. "Alex, I'm sorry. I wanted to surprise you; have a little fun before your mom came home."

Toby took my hands in his.

"I'm really sorry. I never thought you'd react this way. I didn't mean to scare you. It seemed like a good idea."

I heard the garage door. "Get your stuff," I whispered. "I'll take you home, but just to keep the peace. Don't try explaining anything."

"Hi, Ms. Christopher. Bye, Ms. Christopher," Toby said as we passed her in the family room.

"I'll be back in a few minutes, Grandma."

She wrinkled her nose curiously. "Okay, darling. See you soon." She pulled back the sheer front window curtain, just enough to watch us get into the car and pull away from the house.

MARLEY

THE ELEVATOR DOORS OPENED AND my cell phone rang in unison with my first steps into the hotel lobby.

"It's Rachel," I whispered to Dax, holding up one finger and stepping a few feet away to take her call.

"Hey!" I answered enthusiastically.

"Good, you picked up!"

"What's goin' on? Everything okay?"

"Yeah, yeah. Everything's fine. Just wanted to hear about your first day in NYC."

"Well, after I got off the plane, everything was a whole lot better. Actually, about an hour after I got off the plane, I started to feel normal again."

"Oh no, you were sick?"

"Not only was I sick, but I had an audience." I rolled my eyes at myself, remembering that horrible hour of my life.

"Ugh, Marley, I'm sorry! What happened?"

"It's more like, *who* happened? Just when I spotted a nice quiet seat on a bench outside the airport, I'd no sooner inhaled a mouthful of New York air, and Dax caught sight of me. He called my name and made his way to my quiet place, interrupting the most needed break from airline cabin claustrophobia, and struck up a conversation that lasted until he dropped me off at my hotel."

"That must've been awful," Rachel joked.

"Under normal circumstances, Rach, he would've been a very welcome sight. But I'm pretty sure my complexion had an aura of green and gloom."

"Ah, honey, I'm sure you looked much better than you felt. No biggie. You two are going to get to know each other pretty well in these next days and months of the T.A.D.A. campaign anyway. He's bound to have his own day or two of feeling down."

"Maybe," I doubted. "But listen, I've gotta run. The lights are on in the city and I have to take advantage of the short time I'm here. There's no place in the world like it."

"Damn, I wish I would've gone with you!"

"Well, let's plan it. Really, let's make it happen. Just you, me, and the girls after the campaign slows down a bit. It'll be a blast, except for the plane ride getting here and going home."

"Okay, I'm in for that. You check out the lay of the land and figure out our schedule for next time."

I turned my body to see if I could get eyes on Dax. He was leaning against a mid-lobby pillar, legs crossed at the ankles, talking to a hotel employee. He caught my glance and we shared a comfortable smile before I turned away to finish up with Rachel.

"Will do. Tomorrow is a huge day, so my plan is to stroll for an hour or so before heading back here to prepare a little more before the morning meetings."

"You're in a group tonight, right? You better not be trolling those dark New York alleys alone, Marley Christopher. Don't go and lose your mind on me, now."

"C'mon, Rachel. You know I wouldn't chance being iden-tified by a CSI. Everything is fine, but I really have to go. I'm the last one."

"Keep me posted and let me know if you need me to send anything from here."

"God, I hope not. I've put so many hours into planning for this week, I really don't want any roadblocks. But thanks, though."

"Have fun, Marley!"

I tucked my phone into my purse and couldn't hide the smile on my face as I approached a very patient looking Dax. He skillfully concluded his conversation with Vincent, the Night Manager, by holding out his arm at my shoulder height and leading me toward the exit. He dropped his arm and guided me into the slow spinning turn-style which acted like a stage curtain rising on the magnificent 7th Avenue.

"And how is Rachel?" he asked, positioning himself next to me on the street side of the sidewalk.

I grinned. "She's good, curious, just checking in with me."

The lights and sounds didn't lend a hint of reality to the actual time of day. There were so many people still on foot and inside storefront windows as we made our way to Broadway and 47th Street. The red hue from the bleacher seats in the middle of the intersection offered an invitation to *be one* with the city. People of all ages took refuge on the bleachers or the lawn furniture positioned in the center of Times Square. We opted for curb seats facing the Renaissance Hotel.

"My daughter would love this," I told Dax.

"Tell me about her."

I paused, taking in the moment.

"Ah, a smile. Is that all you're willing to share?" Dax tipped his head slightly to the side.

"I don't know. Not necessarily. But how about you? Your boy isn't much older than she is. What about him?"

Dax put both hands out in front of him with a proposal. "If we're actually going to get into a real conversation, why don't we walk to a place with comfortable chairs, a menu, and a table with a view?"

I checked the time on my phone. I could feel my teeth biting my lip as I looked at him and hesitantly agreed. He seemed like a nice-enough guy and aside from re-reading pages of statistics and outreach goals back at the room, it wouldn't hurt to stay out longer than planned.

"You're probably right," I agreed. "Which way?"

"Do you have any favorites?" he asked me.

"No, actually, I'm pretty new here. I've only had a couple of short visits."

"I've got a place in mind, if that's okay?"

"Sure!" Before I knew it, Dax was flagging down a taxi and we were riding instead of walking. I could feel the excitement inside my body, unsure if I felt safe or frivolous, nervous or ready for an adventure. I quickly convinced myself that living in the moment might actually be fun.

———

I TOSSED AND TURNED IN my bed for what felt like all night. I looked at the clock on my bedside table and realized I'd only been lying there for two hours. Just two hours?

Each minute dragged into the next and finally I got up and walked directly to my computer. Of course, my computer. The only place where I can be completely honest, and no one knows who I am.

I thought of Andrew. How long would things go on like this? I'm sure I still love him somewhere down deep in the pit of what we've created, but I don't have the energy to think about the other night. I don't have the energy to think about anyone except Alex, on top of managing my own life. But in the past, I've wavered. I've told him I was done and then my actions were different. I can't do that again.

I started journaling on my laptop three months ago, originally out of anger and frustration. Oh, and—don't forget guilt. But, over the last twelve weeks, the rambling notes have transformed into a respite of therapy and occasional flickers of hope. I keep everything in a pass-coded user screen and secret desktop folder. The writer in me loved the idea of daily journaling into the universe, but the pessimist in me harbored a fear that someone might actually find it. It didn't take long for me to pacify my hesitation and I've been hooked on detox writing nearly every day.

I dated the entry and began writing: After I finally sleep and wake up at a reasonable hour, the _Talk About Drug Abuse_ campaign will launch in New York. This is the day my team and I have been planning for months. I'm excited because of the awareness it will spark, but I'm hesitant because of the added obligations to my schedule. It requires a commitment with the national NBC affiliate, watching our every move under a microscope.

As for Alex, she's my superstar daughter, member of her high school debate team and National Honor Society student. But underneath her confident exterior, I'm sensing a change in her. I know things have been difficult since Andrew and I have become more distant with one another. As much as we told ourselves that we'd figure out what to do so her life would be the least affected, it's clear that our entire family dynamic is changing. Not to mention my cavalier mother joining our family, wreaking havoc on our lives with her antics alone. She came to visit the first week of summer break and decided to stay. Indefinitely.

What to do about Alex? I haven't spent a whole lot of time fretting about my sixteen-year-old girl. She appears so young and innocent still, but if I was being honest with myself, she too, is growing up and navigating through her own problems.

She uses her cell phone, of course, for more than just calls. I don't know of any teens who don't carry one. Is it unreasonable for me to be reading her text messages after she goes to bed at night? Am I being over-protective? I work in an industry that reports dozens of crimes each day, not including the devastating transgressions that result in life-changing punishments or worse, life-ending ones.

Before signing off, I viewed Alex's social media page, updating myself on her latest entry and those of her friends. She knows that I have access, since that was part of the deal when she set up her account, but I trust her judgement—I just like to be sure.

It was late at home and Andrew was sound asleep, I presumed. I wondered if he'd left a last sip of bourbon in the glass on his nightstand. I rolled my eyes, disgusted again. What happened to us? How did eighteen years of non-marriage turn out this way?

I'm exhausted from thinking about it. I hated the smell of booze seeping from his body in the bed next to me. Who am I kidding? He hasn't changed from the day we met. Why did I think he would change? Maybe I'm the one who changed. I felt sick to my stomach, but didn't have the energy to do anything else but close my eyes and wait for morning. Hopefully, he wouldn't be in my dreams. Sadly, I managed to bring him with me to New York and I probably haven't even crossed his mind.

IRIS

I CLOSED THE FRONT DOOR, turned the deadbolt, flipped the front light switch off and peered through the window at the sun rising in the distance.

"Coming or going?" Alex smirked.

"Oh," I gasped. "You startled me, dear." I tightened the sash around my robe.

Alex descended the remainder of the staircase in her tank top and favorite cotton pants. "So I missed him by just a few seconds?"

I made my way to the kitchen, filling the silence with a smirk. I filled the teapot and lit the back burner. "Missed him? What do you mean?" My favorite Japanese teacup was poised and ready, next to the stove with a homemade herbal blend.

Alex gathered her cereal bowl, spoon, milk, and placed everything in a heap on the counter before kissing me on the cheek. "Grandma, what's the big deal? Of all my family members, I'd pick you, every single time, to be straight with me."

Placing both hands on Alex's shoulders, I smiled. "Your mother has given me the pleasure of watching over you these few days while she's away. That's a big leap of faith for her, you know what I mean?"

"I guess," Alex said, getting the cereal from the pantry. "But what does that have to do with you letting someone out the front door?"

I paused and scrunched my face. "You've discarded the possibility that I may have been coming in?" I joked.

"Based on what you're wearing right now and how you like to look before leaving the house, yes—I've let go of that possibility."

I snickered. "Your mother still holds a lifetime of strikes against me, and the answer to this front door question could very well trigger what she's been looking for to declare my last strike in your home."

"Grandma!" Alex shrieked. "Mom doesn't want you to move out!"

The situation was beginning to present a fine line between what I felt comfortable discussing with Alex and what I knew Marley would deem acceptable with her. "How about this, darling? Why don't we let this one go? I don't want you in a situation with your mother that you feel like you have to choose between telling her the truth or trying to protect me."

Alex squinted her eyes and looked dubiously at me.

Just like every first sip, I closed my eyes to savor the flavors. Alex pointed out this habit of mine, but as silly as it seemed, I gleaned great pleasure from my morning tea. "I know it might sound absurd to you, dear, but it's better simply not knowing."

Alex rolled her eyes, nearly finished with breakfast.

"I don't want to tell you something that isn't true."

"Whatever," Alex shrugged, giving up on the issue. "Can we talk about tonight?"

"Yes, absolutely! I'm excited about it."

"I was hoping we could switch it to tomorrow instead," she cringed. "I need to stay at school 'til about four, but then I have so much to do tonight."

I positioned my cup on the counter, ready to steep a few more ounces. "Sweetheart, that's fine. Don't worry about a thing."

Marley's signature ring tone sounded on Alex's phone. "It's Mom," she smiled at me. "Hi!"

Marley must have asked what we were doing.

"Well, Gram just finished her first cup of tea, I'm done with breakfast, and we're talking about our week before I leave in . . . " Alex spotted the time on the microwave clock, " . . . oh shoot, it's late! I have to get ready in like twenty minutes! Wanna talk to Gram?" She took the stairs two at a time and I heard the shower turn on upstairs.

Cordial was good. Pleasant was better. I knew it would take time to heal wounds that Marley was still nursing from her childhood, but some of them, I hoped, would be enough to begin mending a bond that fractured long ago.

How much time would it take? With all of my being, I hoped I'd have enough time to make a difference before it was too late. For my sake, for Marley's, and God love her, for Alex. I never expected to be on someone else's timetable, I was beginning to question my own vitality. At this point, I'd be damned if I told Marley or Alex about what I'd learned in the last twenty-four hours. If I could manage it, I'd handle the treatment during the work and school days, be home in time for dinner, and no one would notice anything out of the ordinary.

Maybe it would amount to nothing. Just a few tweaks here and there, an adjustment to the daily medications, and maybe a slightly different diet. My head was flooded with maybes and optimistic what-ifs, looking forward to the alone time I'd spend with Alex throughout the week. I'd always lived *in the moment* but I felt like I was transitioning very quickly into living *for the moment*.

My health would define *time* differently, but I'd do everything in my power to work with what I have left.

MARLEY

IN THE MIDST OF A very meticulously planned schedule, I was thankful for a few moments outside of the conference room. I left my briefcase and binders on the table inside the room and stepped into the atrium for fresh air. Large ceramic pots bordered each pillar, overflowing with a floral variety rarely displayed so abundantly in Arizona's dry climate. I needed a break, some time to walk and stretch my shoulders, to clear my head. A perfectly timed, welcome distraction brought a smile to my face when I recognized Alex's ringtone.

"Hi, honey. I'm so glad you called! What are you doing?"

"Well," she hesitated, "Actually, I really didn't expect you to answer since I know you're super busy."

I slowed my pace and found an empty club chair next to a small fountain. Certain that Alex didn't intend to hurt my feelings, her comment stung. Was she hoping to just leave a message?

"Oh, babe. My work is never more important than you. You know that, right? If I miss your call, you know I always try to call you back as quickly as possible."

Alex mumbled a reassurance, but hesitated in getting to the real reason for her phone call.

"Alex. I'm right here. I'm alone and you've got my full attention." I knew something was bothering her, but I didn't have a clue what it could be. In the past two years, I'd come to realize that typical teen living could fluctuate dramatically from calm to hysteria and anywhere in between; emotions that I experienced so differently at that age. When I left for New York two days ago, Alex seemed stable, but really, I'd been so preoccupied with work, the launch, and preparing to travel, I could've easily missed that something was bothering her.

"It's just Toby. He's been different," Alex finally conceded.

Not the announcement I was expecting, but I could accept her concern. I felt a bit of relief when Alex mentioned Toby and not my mother, Andrew, or me. "Like what?" I asked, wondering if my assumption would align with Alex's response. I didn't dislike him, but of all Alex's *boy* friends known to me he certainly wasn't at the top of the list.

"He's fine, I think," Alex replied. "He's not really doing anything that I can put my finger on, but he seems off. It's just a feeling I have and we still hang out all the time, but I don't know. Maybe he's a little more quiet than usual."

Alex rambled a little longer, but I knew from personal experience that when something seems different, even when you can't pinpoint what *it* is, the hunch is usually right. "Have any of your friends noticed him acting differently?" My fear that Alex had alienated herself from her friends to spend more time with Toby came to the forefront of my thoughts. Was Alex capable of making good decisions in the midst someone else's bad ones? What if something much worse was really bothering her?

"Mom, I know he's not your favorite person and I almost didn't call you." Alex skipped the question entirely and went straight into defensive mode.

I didn't want to compromise Alex's willingness to talk. "Hang on, I never said that I didn't like him. I love you, obviously, and I want people to treat you right. Have you asked him if he's okay? Sometimes people just need to be asked."

"He says he's fine and then he changes the subject," Alex said.

My heart hurt when I heard her trying to conceal tears. I'd met Andrew in high school. It wasn't until college that we started dating, but even then, my emotions were still raw, immature, and vulnerable. I guessed that Alex was feeling a similar level of pain.

"Alex," I said, wanting her full attention. I spoke her name two more times before she responded. "How long would you say that he's been acting differently?"

"I don't know," she admitted.

I knew she was frustrated. "Honey, I'm sorry."

"You're never going to like Toby."

I felt unsettled about how the conversation ended. I didn't want to argue. How did I get through teenage life with my disengaged mother and absent father? Who was there for me? I tossed around memories of my playmates and others like salad ingredients, all complementing one another, but fine on their own. There were a few people I relied on during those years. Unfortunately, none of them were my own parents.

My internal dialog cranked ahead at full speed. As much as I thought I had everything under control, I realized that I had a huge mountain to climb.

When Alex was a baby, I remember thinking that life would be so much easier at each next stage. Maybe when she started walking. But walking brought tripping, running and falling, and I remember tricking myself into believing that once she could talk, we'd transition into an easier time. She'd be more grown up and independent. But her talking was constant. She asked questions and explained everything. For years, our home was only quiet after she fell asleep. I looked ahead thinking that once she started school, life would be much easier. But I was wrong again. As a school-aged kid, she seemed to have a fuller calendar, more social engagements, homework requirements, extra-curricular activities, a hungrier belly, and a long list of things that I never planned. Life wasn't easier as she got older.

I was irritated and felt like my hands were tied until T.A.D.A. *New York* concluded and I could return home to my first true love. My passion for work and service in the community was genuine, I was sure of that, but occasionally I questioned the impact that my time commitments were having on the family.

Dax sat down quietly in the chair across the coffee table. "You look intense. Everything okay?" he asked, as if we'd been friends forever.

I shook my head. "You know, just at the age when I thought I'd know a decent bit about life and circumstances, I'm humbled by what I still have to learn."

"I wish someone had said that to me once upon a time," Dax agreed. "I remember being eighteen, recruited by my first choice college, playing football for the team that I'd cheered on for most of my life. I truly thought I'd made it to the top back then. There was no going up for me, I thought, unless I could actually play professional football."

"You did play professionally, so I'm not sure I follow," I said somewhat sarcastically. I felt bad for the irritation in my tone but I was confused by his reference.

"Nah, it was great. Don't get me wrong," he said, batting his hand. "It's just that when I look back on it, I was pretty cocky. I didn't have any good reason to act so full of myself. But I tell you what—when a reporter approached me for an interview, I was all in. Every time. I loved the hype but I didn't quite understand the scope of who was watching and listening."

"What changed?"

Dax smiled and put his fist in the opposite hand. "Fortunately, someone took me under his wing and taught me a few lessons about life. And then another shift happened when I definitely wasn't ready for it," he paused, smiling with his lips together. "My whole world changed when I became a full-time dad. I've been wrapped around that boy's finger since the day he was born and even at his age, I don't see that changing any time soon."

ALEX

RACHEL'S DAUGHTER, MORGAN, SENT ME a text. We've been friends pretty much as long as our moms have been friends.

> WANNA GO TO THE MOVIES AND DINNER WITH ME AND MOM? WE CAN PICK YOU UP IN 20 MIN. WE REALLY WANT TO SEE YOU!

My phone was buried somewhere under the mound of blankets and sheets on my bed, but the faint sound got me squirming to find it quickly. It chimed a second time. I responded right away.

SURE, THX. I'LL BE READY.

I cracked my door and listened. It sounded quiet down-stairs, but I called out, "Grandma?"

"I'm here," she rattled, looking up from the bottom of the staircase. "You okay? I thought you'd be tucked away in your room until dinner."

"Rachel and Morgan invited me to go to a movie and dinner with them. So, I won't actually be here for dinner. Is that okay with you?" I asked hesitantly.

"You're the one who bargained with me to switch our outing because you had so much to do tonight."

I cringed. "I know, I'm sorry. I just haven't seen them in a really long time."

"I know, dear. Yes—go, have fun."

She appeared at my door. "Are you in your jams?"

"Yes, but I'm changing. They're going to be here soon. And thanks!" I squawked, pushing the door closed. I felt excited when they picked me up.

About ten minutes away from the theater, Rachel answered an incoming call before pulling into the parking lot of a conve-nience store.

"You kids want to pick out a few snacks for the theater?" she smiled, talking to us through the rear-view mirror.

We jumped out of the car as if we hadn't eaten for days.

"I figured you might." She handed Morgan some cash and continued her phone call in the car.

We made future plans to see a couple more movies

together during the pre-movie trailers. Finally, the feature began with a deeply emotional scene. I was immediately in full-blown tears, followed by a slightly less-weepy Morgan. We scrounged for scraps of coarse paper napkins in place of soft tissues that tore and shredded into damp crumbs on our laps. Rachel had tears, too. The heart-wrenching heaviness eased up until the last twenty minutes of the movie and all three of us were wet messes again. We exited the theater into the low-lit foyer and the puffiness under our eyes seemed to magnify in the dim light.

"That was *so* good," Morgan said.

Rachel and I agreed. The parking lot lights were beginning to illuminate as the sun was nearly set behind the mountains.

"Where to?" Rachel asked. "You two decide."

We threw out a few suggestions that no one immediately jumped on until I flippantly suggested a pizza place nearby. It was a surprisingly unanimous decision. The hostess seated us at a patio table perfectly positioned in the the front corner so we could people watch in both directions. Placing the food order was quick and easy, and drinks arrived in no time.

"Tell us what you've been up to since your mom has been in New York," Rachel prompted.

I gulped half of my cherry limeade. "I love that stuff," I huffed. "She's really only been gone a couple of days and I've had school, so, not that much, I guess."

"What's Toby doing tonight," Morgan asked.

I shrugged. "I'm not sure, exactly."

"According to the picture he was just tagged in, he's out playing basketball somewhere," Rachel reported, turning her phone screen toward us.

"What did you see?" Morgan and I were curious. "And how did you see that?"

His jump-shot was being blocked by a ridiculously tall guy

on the court. I recognized the username immediately.

"You girls know how easy it is to see things online when people don't keep their accounts private."

"Loaded pizza muffins and white chicken pizza!" the server announced, setting up a raised rack for the pie and individual plates in front of each person.

I savored my first bite and smiled, catching Rachel studying me. "Did my mom put you up to checking on me today?" I asked. Morgan's goofy facial expression answered the question.

"C'mon, Alex—can't we just invite you to dinner and a movie without being accused of a setup?" she asked.

I pulled apart a pizza muffin; steam rising in front of my face. "It's okay if she did. Either way, this is a lot more fun than what I had planned."

PART 2

"It's funny how day by day, nothing changes. But when you look back, everything is different."

—C.S. Lewis

CHAPTER 4

MARLEY

THE MEDIA WAS OUT OF control, roaming through the ballroom and the hotel with fervor and a hunger for moment-to-moment coverage of the event. Generally, I was included in the media category, but tonight, as a representative for the campaign, I felt stalked by those nasty overwhelming people, and I didn't like it one bit. I tried weaving through the crowd, but felt confined and way too far from calm. My head was up, smiling meekly at anyone who made eye contact and I kept a steady pace without overtly rushing. A large hand cupped my bicep from behind and stopped me in my tracks. I was immediately irritated and turned around, jerking my arm out of the grasp. I knew my face looked tousled with emotion.

"What're you—" I barked, then cowered, lowering my voice after seeing his face. "I'm so sorry."

Dax put his arm around my shoulder to physically guide me

away from the crowd and toward the bar. While I tried regaining composure for feeling so ridiculous in front of him, yet again, his comment lightened my mood.

"I never would have pegged you for a girl with a temper," he smiled.

"I don't know what it is," I said. "Usually, I'm the one behind the scenes doing the investigating, reporting on the topic, getting in everyone's personal space. Being on this side of the crowd doesn't feel natural to me. I guess I'm a little uptight tonight."

"I probably shouldn't've grabbed your arm like that. I startled you, didn't I? I apologize."

"What can I get for you?" the bartender asked from the other side of the apron-draped table.

"Marley?" Dax gestured.

"A glass of white wine," I said.

"Certainly. And for you, sir?"

"Bottled water, please."

I looked at Dax, surprised by his drink selection. Then again, not every man is like Andrew.

"I'm the first presenter tonight," he said, looking at his watch. "There's still about ten minutes till show-time."

I raised my brow. "I've read the program, cover to cover, and I don't remember seeing your name on the presenter list. I know I wouldn't have missed it."

The corner of Dax's mouth smirked. "I'm full of surprises."

I sneered, thinking I'd never heard him throw out such a cheesy cliché. "What do you mean? What kind of surprise?"

We walked to a window overlooking Midtown, partially secluded from the larger group of people hanging out near the bar.

"You know that friend I went to see this afternoon?"

"Yes."

"It was actually a meeting with the T.A.D.A. campaign director, Tim Maason. The keynote speaker for tonight . . . "

"Dr. Sofia Braunstein," I cut in.

"You're right. Unfortunately, to Dr. Braunstein's dismay, her emergency admission to Lenox Hill Hospital changed the plan. She's undergoing a series of tests on her temperamental and benevolent heart, leaving her unable to speak at the event tonight. So, I'm taking her place. Simple as that."

Shocked by his nonchalant explanation, I spewed questions. Within moments, he'd be speaking to a ballroom of five hundred guests, not including the dozens of media personnel and cameras hanging onto his every word. "Just like that? How can you—?"

"How can I . . . ?" he asked, wrinkling his face.

"What I mean is, how can you agree to a speaking engagement just hours before it starts? How do you know what to say? How do you prepare yourself for this kind of venue? And how do you fill a time-slot with a speech that you haven't written?" I jabbered.

"Marley, you seem really wound up. Or—is this the way you function every day and I've just never had the pleasure of witnessing your stress management?" he smiled.

I took a little offense to his question, but then pondered how much of it was the actual truth. If he was right, I was going to have an even tougher time getting over another embarrassing moment. I needed to loosen up—pronto, at least until I got through the miserable night that was intended to be memorable.

"I think I'm just anxious about all of the events this week."

"You're on camera all the time, Marley. Of all people, isn't this old-hat for a news anchor like yourself? You have so many opportunities to fill time gaps with unscripted commentary. What's different about what I'm doing tonight?"

"I'm a control freak. Let's just start there," I grinned. "I spent a lot of time planning for this event, making sure I was prepared from every angle, and I'm not even speaking. I had expectations, and so far, I've been way off base."

"Try to relax. Don't you want to look back on tonight with good memories? The launch is meant to be informative for the public and fun for everyone involved." He gently toasted my drink with his water bottle. "I have to make my way into the ballroom," he said. "Would you like to come with me or would you rather listen to my rambling from out here?"

It became very obvious that my options were limited, since he gave me only two and I hadn't thought of others. I stood undecided and wasn't feeling very creative in the moment.

"Why don't you sit with me?" he coaxed.

I nodded and smiled the best I could as we headed into the ballroom together. He explained that since his status had changed to keynote speaker, he'd be taking Dr. Braunstein's seat at table number three, with an available seat for his guest.

As soon as he entered through the double doors, Dax was approached by the media. Even after NFL retirement, he'd been generous with his time interacting with the public, so I folded quietly into the periphery until the band finished playing the last song in their set.

I met him at his table just before the emcee started his shtick, chock-full of New York-themed jokes and a brief welcome to the evening program. It began with enthusiasm for the support and awareness that the campaign was generating, but the audience was reminded very quickly of the serious nationwide need for the campaign. A slow series of photographs flashed on the screen in memory of teenagers lost to prescription drug abuse. Their names were spoken and memorialized, emphasizing their preventable cause of death; the main focus for the creation of the campaign.

Dax was announced in a sixty-second introduction including the highlights of his professional football accomplishments, community service and philanthropic endeavors, and statements regarding his personal experience with prescription drug use. My wide-eyed gaze felt paralyzing for a moment as I wondered how so much press had been collected on Dax in such a short amount of time.

He stood tall and proud, taking the steps to the stage with poise. He shook the emcee's hand, positioned himself behind the podium, and turned to his audience. By his presence alone, he had full command of the devoted crowd. His voice and the reactive whispers from attentive listeners were the only vibrations heard for fifteen solid minutes. His words were captivating and heartfelt, spoken from a dedicated, emotional, and inspirational man.

THE MASTER OF CEREMONIES CLOSED out the evening with a final note of gratitude and encouragement for sponsors and families in attendance at the gala. Dax was quickly surrounded by colleagues and fans alike, giving me the perfect opportunity to dissolve into the shadows. The head-table attention was pleasant, but I was ready to break away and decompress.

"Marley—hello! Phil Jennings from WNBC-New York," he announced, as I approached the center of the room.

I nodded and smiled, presenting him with my right hand. "Mr. Jennings, it's lovely to meet you."

Phil Jennings stood confidently, flashing a TV-style smile, perfected after years in front of a camera. I was very familiar with demonstrations like his.

"Actually, I should've introduced myself differently. And please, call me Phil. You remember, don't you? I'm originally from Phoenix; we met back in the day." He held onto my hand, gazing curiously into my eyes. "You've done very well for yourself in the last decade."

"That's very kind of you to say, Phil." My mind was stuck on *back in the day*, hoping he didn't use that phrase very often. "How long have you been in New York?"

"It's been about ten years or so, but let me give you a hint about the first time we met."

He started giggling, strangely. I caught Dax's eye across the crowded foyer. He returned a smile as I cast an S.O.S. and Phil Jennings continued talking.

"I got my undergrad at Arizona State, like you and Andrew."

My passive listening posture transformed suddenly into a slightly defensive one. First I smiled, tilting my head to the right. "I feel like I missed something between your introduction and where we are now."

Phil chuckled. "Oh, okay. I thought maybe you were just keeping me at bay, embarrassed maybe a little, because of the circumstances?"

I squinted.

"You really don't recall?" He paused, looking defeated, like I'd insulted him. He was uncomfortable, but certainly not ready to concede.

"What are you suggesting?" I inquired, still puzzled.

"C'mon—really? You don't remember me?"

I laughed, not knowing what else to say; clearly not invested in the bantering as much as Phil. "Believe me, I feel terrible for not remembering exactly, but . . . "

"Okay, how bout' this? Freshman year, Arizona State, a *huge* party at an off-campus frat house after the last football win of the season?"

My stomach clenched. He brought back memories of a

night I never wanted to remember; I hoped my face didn't reflect my thoughts. It was so many years ago, but the mention of it prompted an uncomfortable series of flashbacks. The morning after that night, I promised myself that I'd never party so carelessly again. The potpourri of pills were supposed to calm me down, ease my mind. Instead, they triggered the opposite—a frightening amplification of emotions. I looked away from Phil and brought my hand to my face; my head flooded with sickening recollections.

Phil touched my shoulder. "There you go, now you remember? I knew you would. There's no way you could forget that night. You know, you really lucked out with Andrew. He's such a great guy, he knows how to have a good time, and from what I understand, the guy's still a freakin' genius!"

With a pause, I took a deep, controlled breath. "You've got that right," I said, unsure if he picked up on my sarcasm.

Dax weaved gradually through the crowd with perfect timing. Arriving with a publicly practiced grin of his own, Dax introduced himself to Andrew's animated acquaintance.

"My God," Phil proclaimed, shaking his hand and patting Dax's shoulder twice. "Man—I've watched every single play of your career. You were an unbelievable athlete! It's great to meet you!"

"Thanks, that means a lot. It was good time," Dax said sincerely. "Now I get to take on other challenges," he smiled.

"Are you ready to go?" I asked Dax with anticipation. His facial response implied that he could go either way. If I wanted to stay, he'd hang out a bit. If I was ready, we could leave together.

"That's right!" Phil interjected when he made the connection. "You're both here to represent the Phoenix campaign. How did you two get so lucky to land the platform?"

We looked at each another and smirked, we'd never talked

about it.

"I can't speak for Marley, but for me, the timing worked out well with my retirement and the fact that my son is within a target age bracket for drug abuse education. I suppose the name recognition works well for outreach, too."

"And Mar," Phil added, "it just makes sense that they'd want you paired with Dax Townsend. A nationally recognized home-team legend with a very recognizable, and beautiful—I might add, evening news anchor? It's a win-win for the campaign. Anyone who knows the two of you knows that every-thing you touch turns to gold."

"I think that's a bit of a stretch," I said humbly.

"Be real, Mar!"

He did it again. I was becoming more agitated. Only two people in the world have ever called me Mar, and he wasn't going to become the third.

"Local viewers hear you every night, they watch you from their recliner chairs, take your reports as personal opinions, true or not, and they believe what you say. And sports fans around the world would fall all over themselves to be involved in something that could link them to an all-star like DownTown Dax."

Dax must've sensed my discomfort. "Hey, thanks for your encouragement. We'll do our best as a team and hope the local efforts go as well as you predict. We're just doing this to keep kids safe." He used two fingers at his forehead to sign off with Phil. "Nice meeting you, take care."

"Ready?" I asked.

"I was going to make my way to the door; check out the cab line."

"Perfect." I turned to Phil, expressed a kind goodbye, best wishes, and promise to deliver his message to Andrew. Dax invited me in front of him and we proceeded outside. At the curb, I turned to him, visibly relieved. "I can't thank you enough for choreographing that farewell!" I smiled. "I haven't seen or thought of that guy in more than twenty years, and by the way he carried on, it was as if we'd seen each other yesterday."

"He seemed nice enough," Dax shrugged.

"He's probably fine. I just felt like he was backing me into a corner, bringing up college and talking about people we once knew."

"We're just a cab ride away from anything you want to do." Dax checked the time on his phone. "Feel like taking in the city lights from the roof of a double decker tour bus?

I laughed. "In these clothes?"

"Why not? It's New York, the city that never sleeps. Or, if you prefer, I can drop you off at the hotel."

"And you'll go on your own? You'd actually do that?"

"I do a lot of things on my own," he smiled. "I'd miss a lot in life if I waited for someone to do everything with me."

I took off my heels and replaced them with thin flip flops from my purse. The straps of my heels dangled from my fingertips as we slid into the backseat of the cab. "Let's check out the city lights."

ON MY WAY HOME FROM the first day back to work, I called Andrew. He didn't answer and I didn't leave a message. I grumbled that he wasn't available when I wanted to talk. I knew he didn't owe me full access or immediate attention anymore but there are times when I just want to ask his opinion. And like breaking any bad habit, it's incredibly difficult.

My thoughts were scattered. It happens often when I'm driving, especially when the sky is dark and streets are desolate.

I've been looking forward to more time at home with Alex after work most days. I told her we'd talk tonight, but forgot to mention my plans with Rachel.

I have two more weeks of this late night schedule before making the switch to mornings. I'll have less air time but more involvement with research for special interest stories, including my work for the campaign. It's a change I'm really looking forward to, I think. But change isn't ever easy.

My cell phone chirped a text notification. Andrew came through for me.

Can it wait until morning? it said.

After all these years you'd think that he'd know how I read into things. Was he so busy that he couldn't answer my call? On the other hand, he didn't have to check in with me at all, but I'm having trouble deciphering his tone of voice via text. I hate that because I usually assume incorrectly.

Once I pulled into the garage and turned off the car, I carefully chose my words and returned the text.

No problem. Talk to you tomorrow, I typed.

I turned off my phone to prevent myself from putting it on my night stand and wondering if he'd text me back.

"You're up late," I said to Iris when I came into the house.

She was standing at the stove over a bubbling pot of herbal something-or-other that smelled wonderful.

"What's gotten you so cranky?"

"Why do you say that?" I asked, setting my briefcase near the door and tossing my blazer over the chair. "I'm not cranky."

"You always get this way when you're irritated with Andrew."

I was halfway down the hall when I stopped short of the bathroom door and cocked my head in the other direction.

"What did you say?" I asked, making my way back to the

kitchen and taking a seat in one of the chairs.

Iris placed a cup of tea in front of me and sat down delicately in the opposing chair.

"I said," she began, taking a sip from her cup, "you get grumbly with everyone when Andrew does something that you don't like. Did you see him tonight?"

"I haven't been in the door five minutes and you've come to this conclusion?"

"Am I wrong?"

She looked up at me and then down at her cup. She dipped her index finger in the tea and massaged it around the rim."

"No. Not exactly," I admitted. "But it's not really Andrew's fault."

"What happened?"

"I didn't see him or hear his actual voice. But I called."

"That's what's eating you?" she smiled. "He didn't answer your call?"

"I know. It's crazy. I've been doing this for years. He does something that I don't like and I get frustrated. Sometimes he's completely off my mind. In fact, when I was in New York, I didn't think much about him at all." Realizing that I just confided in my mother added fuel to my mood. And now she'd started counseling me on my destructive behaviors.

"I only see this side of you when it comes to Andrew. What is it about him, Marley?"

"I don't know. And why are you suddenly interested in my personal life?"

Iris caught my eye and reached her hand toward mine, disregarding my flippant question. "He frustrates you because he's not who you want him to be."

I sat quietly, mulling over her choice of words. Should I be upset with her too? I'm already agitated. And when she's right, it chafes me even more.

"I hate it when he does this," I snapped, leaving the table and heading upstairs.

Maybe it's me. Damn Andrew.

ANDREW

I'M NOT ENTIRELY SURE WHY I agreed to have dinner with Cypress. She tracked me down through a social networking site, which reminded me to put more security in place on my account. But I didn't respond to her message, and she sent another one two days later.

> I'm hardly someone that you can forget, especially since I took a mini road trip with you in your sexy Eco-friendly Prius last week.

After that message, I remembered the security issue. I logged on and made some changes. Physically, she was beautiful, but she was more of a one-night stand than a relationship type. I had no interest in seeing her again.

She made herself comfortable as a passenger that night, sliding her feet out of her heels and exchanging sarcastic banter. We followed Alex and Toby's car for less than ten minutes, only to discover that they were just doing what kids do. She continued to watch them when she took off with my car and reported more of the same. Since then, I took myself out of the chase, wondering if I was making more out of Toby than necessary.

The doorbell rang and I glanced at the clock, surprised by the time. I opened the door with a raised eyebrow.

"I'm not complaining, but never in my life, has a woman arrived on time for a meeting, a date, or any planned event, for that matter," I said. "Come on in."

Cypress walked through the entry, flashing a mysterious smile, carrying a cocktail shaker and a tall glass of ice. Although she'd never been inside my place before, she had no inhibitions about making her way to the kitchen and opening cupboards tenaciously.

"You look like you have a plan," I said. "Maybe if you tell me what you're looking for, I can help you find it," I joked.

"Sorry," she said, taking a seat on a bar stool. "Sometimes I get ahead of myself and forget that my conduct is surprising to some people."

"What are you looking for?"

"Cocktail glasses. I whipped up a round that I want to share with you."

I grabbed two highball glasses from the top rack of the clean dishwasher and set them on the counter. She placed a few ice cubes into the shaker, chilling the mixture of gin, schnapps, and a few other ingredients before pouring into the two glasses.

"What's the occasion?" I asked.

"Who needs an occasion to share a drink with a friend? To a great night," she said, toasting my glass with hers.

"To a great night," I nodded, gulping most of my drink and hoping I hadn't made a mistake by agreeing to another night with her.

"Well?" she said curiously. "What do you think?"

"Of the drink?"

"Yeah."

"It's fine," I smiled, holding up my empty glass.

"It's fine? You're kidding me. That's all you have to say?"

What does she want from me? It's a drink. I drank it. It's gone. It was fine. It was good. How long do we have to go on about it?

"It was great," I laughed.

She walked over to me and took my hand, leading me toward the door. Her cocktail shaker was stacked inside the empty ice glass and she held them in her other hand. What was she doing?

"Get your keys and let's go," she said. "I've got a whole night planned."

I felt my brows arch again. "Sounds good." I locked the door and followed her to the car.

She drove a sleek silver BMW loaded with gadgets and a hefty price tag. I opened the driver's door for her and headed around to the passenger's side.

"So tell me, why did you insist on picking me up?" I asked.

"Well, seeing how a person lives can tell a girl a lot about the man she's dating."

Dating? I wouldn't go that far. I'm not sure we'll be doing this a third time.

"Were you here long enough to learn anything insightful?"

"We'll have plenty of time to talk about that. And yes, I did. But I'll say that there's a lot you can learn about me tonight, too."

I felt oddly uncomfortable as I paid closer attention to where she drove. Not only had we turned onto Linden Avenue, but she slowed down as we approached Toby's house. I looked behind me, noting that she'd passed the house I thought was hers. She pulled into Toby's driveway and looked at me with the same mysterious smile I'd seen when she arrived at my place.

"What are you doing?" I asked.

She pushed a button in the ceiling of her car and the garage door opened.

"I want you to see where I live," she said, pleased with her surprise.

ALEX

A GREAT IDEA DOESN'T MAKE a difference until it's put into action, right? I knew my plan would work. I never questioned the how or why. And I really didn't want it to become someone else's idea if I didn't try it myself. This was my chance and I got the green light. The lingering question had everything to do with how well it would be received. Millions of bloggers around the world attempt to inspire readers and gain recognition with an online presence, but this column would give teens at my school a voice and the option to remain anonymous.

My goals are simple: present high school-interest topics and pose questions that encourage comments in a non-threatening environment. With a code of conduct imposed by the administration and no tolerance for slander or negativity, I hoped it would get a lot of traction. Over time, student opinions would only be the beginning in gaining perspective on other people's lives. If the weblink could present facts and opposing viewpoints, maybe having an open mind wouldn't be so difficult. Could people learn to coexist in peace?

As it turned out, creating visual appeal had become my biggest obstacle. If it didn't look good, people wouldn't be interested-bottom line, plain and simple, not even kidding for a minute. If the home page looked confusing, browsers wouldn't read it. I don't think that's being too presumptuous, because I'm a bit of a cover snob myself. When I browse the aisles of a bookstore or the library shelves for new fiction, I'm drawn to books with intriguing covers. Even though it's possible for a great story to be tucked between two drab bookends, the content will sit pouty-lipped and dejected when I pass by it for something else.

For the first month or so, I'm committed to writing a new

entry on the column three times a week. I want to flood the site with new material so that readers expect to see new information on a regular basis. At least one day per week, the topic will reflect a current event, taking place either in the United States or abroad, not isolated to the local news. Another day will address a typical high-school related issue, and the third entry will have a whimsical flare—something humorous or creative in an unpredictable sort of way; maybe a joke or a rough sketch.

I'll go live with *DogEar* very soon. The artwork is nearly done, intertwining layers of color, texture, bold block lettering with overlapping scripted font. I was surprised but more impressed, in my humble opinion, that with my limited experience using Photoshop, I could create such a masterpiece. What began as a simple idea of woven threads morphed into a multi-dimensional visual banner integrating theme and purpose.

What's killing me now is my internal struggle with telling, sharing, showing someone—not just anyone, versus maintaining absolute secrecy about the project. From the beginning of the daydreams that lead to the eventual conception of *DogEar*, I never wavered in my determination to launch it and remain in the shadows of its development. More accurately, I never questioned the anonymity, until recently. I know it sounds strange, protecting something that really doesn't need to be kept secret, but I feel pulled in that direction, at least for now, that the plan will be more successful without a face to my screen name. But, stay tuned. Everyone knows that secrets are nearly impossible to hide forever.

For now, I have to be me, doing what I'm supposed to do, acting the way I'm supposed to act. My extra job requires a constant awareness of relevant topics I can address online. Around three months ago, I created a folder on my computer dedicated entirely to entry ideas. At the estimated three entries per week gleaning from a folder of approximately fifty notes, I feel pretty good about my first harvest. But, I'd much rather be overly prepared than left in lurch for lack of good material.

I logged off my computer before heading to the kitchen for the rest of my belongings. According to the clock hanging next to my door, I had thirty minutes before the bell would ring in my first class. I was five minutes late getting out of the house. Five minutes makes a world of difference. Glancing at my feet, I accepted that my flip-flops would have to substitute for running shoes. If I had the sheer luck of finding a parking spot on my first pass inside the lot, I could be seated before the bell rang. I'm old enough to drive a car and daring enough to develop a world-wide website, but one more tardy would earn me a claim check for In-School-Suspension. I had to make some changes in my morning routine.

MARLEY

I ARRIVED AT THE LOUNGE about four minutes late. Pretty good for my record. After scanning the parking lot for Rachel's car, it appeared that her streak of punctual arrivals had come to an end. As much as I wanted to feel proud of my timeliness, the puzzling reason for Rachel's absence had gotten me a bit worried. She lived by the principle that *being early was to be on time, and being on time was to be late.* I really couldn't think of any occasion when Rachel made an exception to the rule, but I could think of many occasions when she'd given me a hard time about being late.

I checked my phone. No message. I gathered my things, a medley really, of random show-and-tell items from New York. I emptied my gym bag onto the passenger seat and used it as the carrying case for everything I wanted to show her. The large majority of items were collected in an oversized manilla envelope, but I had a couple of things scattered in my car.

I would've loved to meet Rachel at her house, wearing my pajamas and carrying a bottle of wine in each arm. If we'd planned to meet there, then I wouldn't have had the restrictions I was putting on myself by suggesting that we meet at *The Lounge*, like time restraints and less privacy, but that's what I needed tonight.

We meet there often, although the days and times always change. It's a public place, a bit of a hole in the wall, not where we'd go if we were inviting others to join us. It's somewhere that I don't worry about being recognized, because no one stops long enough to notice. Rachel and I can sit forever and talk, and no one makes us feel like we're taking up space or overstaying the acceptable sitting time at a restaurant table.

I saw her for the first time after being in New York when I returned to work on Monday, and we'd spoken on the phone briefly, but mostly exchanged emails with information about the campaign's national kick-off events. Reports were aired on our local news programs using video feed that the affiliate provided and I could tell by her enthusiasm that she was anxious to hear every detail from my three days in New York.

"Tomorrow night?" I asked her.

"Tomorrow night works. Where do you want to go?"

Her daughter, Morgan, the same age as Alex, was staying at her house this week instead of her dad's. I really didn't want extra ears weighing in on our conversation—whether she would blatantly join in or listen from the top of the stairs.

"Iris will be at my place with Alex, so how about *The Lounge*?"

"I'll be there. Eight o'clock ready for a drink," she agreed, looking back at me with a giddy smile as she headed to her editing room.

I still wasn't sure how much I wanted to share, but I felt like I had to tell her before losing more sleep.

Once the gym bag was zipped, I made my way into *The Lounge* to snatch up a table by the window. Rachel flagged me down as soon as I walked through the door.

"Hey, where's your car?" I asked, surprised to see her already tucked into a booth.

"My car? Oh, Morgan dropped me off. I told her you'd bring me home," she said, sitting in a chair across from mine. She seemed a little edgy. "What the hell, Marley? I know you're usually fashionably late, but you're more like fifteen minutes late."

"I didn't think you were here," I admitted. "I've been waiting for you in the parking lot for at least twenty minutes."

"Bullshit. I've had time to order drinks from Curtis at the bar and have them delivered to our table. I got here before eight and you definitely weren't here."

We could've gone on for awhile, but we both knew she was right.

"I don't mind taking you home," I said, pausing to take in Rachel's gnarly mood.

"Good, but that won't be for awhile. We have a lot to talk about," Rachel announced, slapping *Page Six* of the *New York Post* onto the table. "Can you explain why you haven't mentioned anything about this?" She had a very serious face and her eyes were locked on mine.

I had no idea what she was talking about, so I must've looked like a deer in headlights when, to my surprise, Dax Townsend was featured in a cover story. I felt the color flush from my face and my heartbeat raced when I realized that the woman pictured with him was not only easily identifiable in a crystal clear frontal photo, but it included my name in the caption!

"I've never seen this before. I didn't know about it," I stammered, picking up the paper in shock. It seemed unbelievable. The world is facing crises in small villages and whole countries, some struggling for peace and others without food.

"Marley, I don't think their Photoshop people are that good that they've artificially entwined your fingers with his and painted a genuinely natural happiness on your face that I haven't seen in a very long time."

"No. That's not what I mean. It's just that I never saw anyone take pictures of us that day, or even notice us, really."

"So you frolicked around the city with an amazingly handsome man known nationally, some would argue globally, and you didn't expect anyone to notice? They're called Paparazzi, Marley. They do this for a living and they don't ask your permission or let you know they'll be taking pictures of you."

I could see that I may have misread Rachel's excitement for seeing me in the newspaper with Dax.

"I know who they are, and, I'm sorry. I was just waiting to have this time with you, to explain everything from start to finish, instead of throwing out breadcrumbs each time we had a couple of minutes to talk. I had no idea that anything would end up in the news."

"The news? You report the news. This isn't the local crap that we run, Marley. It's not what we do on a daily basis, reporting to suburban folks who just want to hear the weather and sports updates. It's celebrity fucking news on *Page Six* of a publication that is read by tens of thousands, no millions, of people around the world."

I sat back in my seat slightly offended. "Are you seriously angry with me?" I asked, unsure. She didn't answer. "Rachel, look at this," I said, holding up my bag. "I brought ten pounds of random crap to share with you, plus whatever I want to tell you about spending time with Dax in New York. It's not that I wasn't going to tell you, we just haven't had time."

"I'm sorry," she said, backing off with her tone. "It's just that," she paused, "I couldn't believe my eyes when I saw you with Dax in a publication like this, and you've been home for days. You've kept your eye on him for years, kept me up to date on his status, and you didn't tell me anything about your relationship or what's going on with him."

"Just a sec. It's not a relationship. But it is a really long story. And it doesn't make much sense. I haven't even talked to him since we left New York," I admitted. "Nothing's going on."

"According to this, there's a lot going on," she said, holding up the paper.

"Let me see that," I said, scanning the article. I read the headline out loud.

TOWNSEND BACK ON THE PLAYING FIELD AGAIN

"That's what I've been trying to tell you, Marley!"

I felt my eyes open wide and shook my head from side to side.

"How did this happen? I don't even know what it means."

"Then we need to get to work and find out."

"Maybe I should call him?" I said.

It dawned on me that if Dax knew about the pictures, he hadn't been in touch. Maybe he didn't know yet. Maybe he did.

I HATE FEELING THIS WAY. I'm always in a rush going from place to place, task to task, and shuffling ideas in my head. The notebook I carry everywhere (a very cute one, I might add), is my saving grace, overflowing with sticky notes, paper clips, and bound together with a rubber band. I figured if I was going to carry this thing around for the better part of a year, then it should look appealing to me, rather than something that would extract frustrations from me like a sixteen-gauge needle.

The notebook has, in some respects, replaced my memory. I've gotten to the point where I must write things down or they float carelessly into the air. I wish I could finish that statement with, *never to be seen again.* However, I remember things at random times and immediately feel guilty for remembering too late or at the wrong time—which is not random at all. Was I born with a gene that lends itself more toward the probability of living a life filled with guilt? At least if the things floated into the air, never to be seen again, then I'd have nothing to feel guilty about.

And did I mention how displaced I feel? My mother, who has taken up residency in my home, has also taken up the space that once belonged only to me. It was my office. My place of solace. The room where old pictures in mismatched frames displayed the life I once lived. Where Alex's elementary school art pieces hung, stuck to the furniture with Disney stickers. The room with the tattered futon that matched nothing, but solemnly wrapped itself around me each time I snuggled into it with a blanket and a book under the watchful gaze of the antique floor lamp. All of those comforts and many more, were lost when Iris haphazardly dismantled the room and dumped everything that belonged to me, in the bay of the third-car garage so that she could move herself into that space.

I knew she was coming; moving into our home. I even gave her the invitation to join us for awhile. What I didn't give her was permission to bustle in here and take over without regard to the balance and rhythm of the life that Alex and I had finally woven together.

To simply use my computer to get on the web or type in my desktop journal, I've had to find a new quiet and comfortable space to sit in my own house. This is often a difficult task, depending on how many of Alex's friends are visiting, how loud Iris's music is playing, or what's going on in the family room. From there, I boot up my laptop, occasionally plug it in because the battery apparently drained, find a method for spreading out my paperwork, take a couple of trips to said area with a drink in one hand, my cell phone in the other, and of course, my notebook nestled under my arm (since I don't go anywhere without it). The convenience and comfort that *home* should provide is now null and void, since Iris has been with us.

At least for the sake of conversation, you should know that Alex was excited about her grandmother moving into the house. For Alex's whole life, she's only known Iris to be a free spirit, uninterested in gossip and trends; someone who lives in the moment and does what makes her happy. I don't think Alex thought for one minute that her grandmother would change much of anything in our routine, except for her presence at meals and scarcely being around, in general.

What neither of us predicted was the unspoken truth that Iris didn't have immediate plans of finding another place for herself. About a month after she moved in, it became quite clear that our house wasn't really being used as a transition residence anymore. It started to look more and more permanent every day. It's a hard topic to discuss, because unlike my mother, I do worry about offending her and being sensitive to her needs. I already carry a heavy load of guilt and I know I don't have the strength to add more weight because of something that might add strain to our present situation.

There are days and even stretches of time when I feel so burdened by guilt. It's as if my habitually hunched-over posture is a physical illustration of the weight it bears on me. There are times when I want to cover myself up. I mean really cover myself up with a sweater or blanket; something I can wrap around my physical body to hide the uncomfortable mess I feel like I am. I don't want to burden others with my instability, so maybe if they don't see it and I don't say anything to them about it, they'll be spared.

The biggest stress and guilt combination of all time shoots through me with the speed and heat of a cannonball, even bigger than the emotional distress caused by Iris and her antics. Fortunately, stress doesn't present itself three hundred and sixty five days a year, but when the storm hits, it's with the force of a category one hurricane called: The Andrew Factor.

I've loved him for so long and for so many reasons but there are times when love can't endure the aftermath. And for that reason, we cannot be together. Ever again. We've never been able to find a middle ground, except when it comes to Alex. He trusts her with me. I trust him with her. Yadda yadda . . . .

I'd have to really think about it in order to pinpoint the time frame, but for quite awhile, I've wondered what life would be like without Andrew in it. Really, the only reason we still have to keep beating ourselves up and continuing our natural cycle of whacked out crap is because of our daughter. But sometimes, I just wish he was completely out of our lives. For good.

I GLANCED AT THE TIME on my dashboard as I reached to grab my cellphone from the passenger seat. "Dammit," I mumbled. I've started procrastinating until the last possible moment, without any excuse for my tardiness, except that I'm suffocating in my own anxieties and trying to hide my struggles from everyone.

My internal dialogue started taking over my sense of reality and it's continuing to do a very good job. Overanalyzing and self-doubt were certainly not traits I inherited from Iris, but somehow, they're manifesting in me with a vengeance. Andrew rarely raises his voice. He never really blames or insults me, but on the other hand, he's difficult. He sees the world and consequences of actions differently than me, and we've absolutely stopped talking about the little things that weigh so heavily, because it's just so damn exhausting.

I don't even know how long it'd been happening before I paid attention to how bizarre we were behaving. Over the years, we randomly hooked up after living separately. Why did we do that? And how did I keep letting it happen?

I needed this night with Rachel. We hadn't hung out since she ambushed me with *Page Six* at *The Lounge*. My phone notified me of two voicemails, three text messages, and a low battery. I plugged into my phone charger, but left the messages for later. I'm trying to make a conscious effort to refrain from fiddling with my phone while driving. The last thing Alex needs is the stress of her mother injuring herself, or worse, her mother's actions leading to another person's danger, injury, or God forbid, death.

Stoplight. I checked caller ID. Wrong decision. I never should have done that. I tossed the phone back onto the passenger seat and continued driving to Rachel's house. Seven minutes later, I arrived in her driveway, shifted the car into park, and sat with the air-conditioning on while I called Iris.

"Yes, Mother."

"Do you know anyone by the name of Cypress?" she asked.

I thought for a moment, resting my head on my seat back. "No, I don't think so. Why?"

"Andrew left his phone on the counter while he was with Alex."

"Mother! You didn't touch his phone, did you?"

"Are you saying that you aren't interested in what I called to tell you?"

"I'm saying that you don't have permission to involve yourself in Andrew's business."

"Does Andrew's business include a meeting with someone named Cypress at a bar tonight?"

My heart sunk, although I knew it wasn't possible, since I felt it beating way too fast. "Mother, I don't know what his meeting is about, or who Cypress is, but I know that invading privacy in my home is not in your contract."

"I thought you'd want to know, Marley. You should be thanking me, not treating me like a child."

I thought that Alex would be out late with Toby, but I guess she's with her dad.

"So Andrew's at our house with Alex?"

"That's right," she said.

"Okay, I'd like to talk to her, but there's one more thing."

Iris sat idly on the other end of the line.

"Mother, please—don't say a word to Andrew about his phone. It isn't your business. He'll get me involved, and I don't need anymore unnecessary stress."

"Marley, your stress is enough for ten people."

"Goodnight, Mother. I'd like to speak with Alex."

I hate the way she makes me feel. On top of that, I hate knowing that Andrew is allegedly planning to meet with a woman tonight when I shouldn't have one care in the world about it.

"Hi, Mom."

"Hi, sweetheart. I'm spending some time with Rachel and I didn't get to see you before I left."

"Sorry. I should've let you know that I'd be a few minutes late."

"Are we still on for the morning?"

"Yeah. We have to leave by nine, since the orientation starts at ten."

"I'll be ready by nine. I promise."

———

AFTER A LONG NIGHT, I met Rachel in the editing room the next morning. With just enough time to regroup briefly off screen, I reviewed notes for the segment. Andrew's morning radio show would be joining the feed in thirty seconds and I heard his voice in my earpiece. Not only was it a slight distraction, but I was caught off guard when he addressed me directly. If I could hear him, that meant a multitude of others were privy to the conversation.

"Ye—es," I hesitated.

"Hey, call me later, would you? After my show, maybe ten-thirty or so."

A producer stepped forward, just close enough to the front of the camera that I knew we'd be on the air momentarily.

"Sure thing," I replied, sitting up taller and tugging down on the front of my blazer.

I announced nearly every headline, then directed the rest of each story to different local on-site reporters. Between the news and weather reports, Andrew's radio show took over the screen with entertainment and commentary between he and his co-host. They typically joked about national news bloopers or funny YouTube videos, but today Andrew directed the topic to focus on crazy dating experiences. Typically, the news component was a carry-over from his very early morning show, so this took me by surprise. He invited the viewers to answer a radio show tweet with the hashtag:

#crazycompanion

At the next break, I got Rachel's attention and asked her to listen in on Andrew's show, specifically the parts that didn't include the paired time with the news broadcast.

"You hate his show," she reminded me.

"I know, he usually talks about things that are a waste of time, in my opinion, but I have a feeling that today is personal. I can just hear it in his voice. He cares about this one more than usual. I'm not sure why. See if you can figure it out, at least while I'm stuck up here."

"And don't forget how irritated you get by his pompous on-air flippancy." Rachel eyed me with a look that spoke volumes.

"I know," I smiled. "Just this once?" I gave Rachel a taste of her own medicine, with a slight head tilt that pleaded for help.

Paired again with the radio show, I improvised a semi-scripted dialogue with the morning hosts.

Andrew bantered back and forth with me and my co-anchor. It happened to be Chris Dalton, the sports reporter who filled the seat during any anchor's vacation time. Unbeknownst to me though, during an off-air moment, Andrew convinced Chris to get his buddy, Dax Townsend, on the phone to chime in with any crazy dating experience during his years in the football spotlight. "*Dude, these morning listeners love to hear personal details about famous athletes, especially the hometown heroes! Dax is a good sport. I'm sure he'd play along.*"

Just in time for the last radio/news pairing before the end of the broadcast, Andrew introduced a *caller* with a crazy dating story to share; someone who's spent years in the spotlight for his athletic achievements, always willing to help out the local news and radio affiliates. In fact, he's our very own Arizona ambassador against the war on prescription drug abuse, alongside our morning news anchor, Marley Christopher. Let's all give a warm morning commute welcome to Dax Townsend.

I made eye contact with Rachel, wearing a headset as she

stood to the camera's right. With a slight cringe in her eyes, she mustered up a more than generous smile to remind me that I was still pictured in a split screen with the radio station. I could hear Rachel's voice in my earpiece, knowing that whatever she said would be heard by the others, as well. She counted down by three, announcing the screen change to radio only, getting the news anchors off the air and cued Chris Dalton to wrap the segment on his own.

I pulled my earpiece abruptly, rolling my chair away from the news desk to meet Rachel in her editing bay. She slid the glass door shut and leaned against the side wall, using only her hands to initiate a frustration that she couldn't put into words.

"It's going to be fine, just take some deep breaths," she encouraged.

"What was that?" I blurted.

"I'm not sure, but I'll find out before the end of the day."

"Did you hear Andrew on the mic this morning, asking me to call him at ten-thirty?"

"I did," she said. "I bet he had Dax planned all along."

I shook my head. "I don't know. Why would he pull a prank like that?"

"Mar, listen to what you just asked. This is Andrew we're talking about. You really have to ask? He never does things the easy way, and he's the first to joke instead of actually communicating like a normal human being."

Rachel pulled her phone from her back pocket to check the time. "It's about ten-thirty. Why don't you give him a call?"

———

"YOU REQUESTED A PHONE CALL," I spoke plainly when Andrew answered.

"Yeah. Why did I have to find out in the news that you

were whoring around with Dax Townsend in New York when it was supposedly a very demanding launch weekend?" he laughed.

"Whoring? Excuse me?"

"The tabloids can't get what's behind closed doors, but they sure did capture a budding romance!"

So many thoughts flooded my head, sporadically in partial statements: Coming from the biggest gigolo I've ever known.—Are you jealous?—Why can't you just ask me first?—You humiliate me on live radio and television?—I was blindsided!—Why did Dax agree to the radio segment?—What good did that do?—Have you even considered Alex in this?—It's none of your damn business!

But I knew that nothing I said would make a damn bit of difference.

"Goodbye, Andrew."

ALEX

I STOOD IN LINE AT the convenience store counter waiting to pay for a Diet Coke, when the cover of *People Magazine* caught my eye. It was my favorite of all the tabloid magazines, the only one I believed when it came to facts about celebrities and their lives. I always browsed the covers of the latest editions, but I felt a sudden knot in my stomach when I got closer to see this week's cover. Were my eyes playing tricks or was I actually looking at a snapshot of my mother linked arm and arm with Dax Townsend, known to just about everyone on the planet as a former NFL superstar? Squinting my eyes and keeping one foot planted on the ground, I lunged toward the magazine display and lifted one from the rack.

What? I studied the picture. Surely the magazine would

print their names. If it wasn't my mother, the look-alike certainly resembled her well. But if it was her, why hadn't she said anything about spending time with him outside the campaign. And the trip to New York was already two weeks ago. She'd been home for thirteen days and I hadn't heard one word about Dax in conversations about the launch party in Manhattan.

I was used to people recognizing my mother as a local news person, but that seemed small-town compared to this exposure in *People Magazine*. As I approached the register, I tossed the magazine onto the counter and paid for it along with the drink. Back in the driver's seat of my Honda Civic, I sifted through a couple of pages before pausing to stare at a half-page dedicated to a portion of *Star Tracks* titled *Exploring the TOWN*.

"Oh. My. God," I cringed. Three different pictures of my mother toting around New York City with the very famous former Arizona Cardinals player on what looked like three different occasions, boasted three different captions detailing their whereabouts, as well as their assumed association, including my mother's name. I dropped the magazine onto the passenger seat only to trade it for my cell phone, which I used to log onto the Internet. In a matter of seconds, I had info on Dax Townsend at my fingertips.

There was so much I was trying to keep straight as I tried to skim and become more familiar with a man who had only been a public figure until a few minutes ago, when he morphed into my mother's personal friend. I looked at the time on the car radio. Three-fifteen. Mom might be sitting behind her desk at the station, able to receive a call between news briefs. I tried her cell.

After two rings and a caller-ID view, she answered her phone. "Hi, honey!"

"Mom! Have you seen this week's *People Magazine*?"

"No," she said. "You sound frantic."

"Mom! You're *in* the magazine. Three times," I empha-sized.

She whispered into the phone. "What? No way."

"On the cover, too."

"If the pictures were taken during the campaign launch in New York, remember that photographers had three days of shooting throughout the course of all the events. And we're both representing the Phoenix campaign, you know that. Hang on, I'm pulling it up now," she paused. "You know that public exposure at a national level is different than the local market we're used to."

"Mom, I get all that. It's just—the pictures make it look like you're hanging out by yourself with him. Like on a date. Away from the campaign."

"I can't see what you're looking at exactly, but I just found a picture online. And your dad said he saw some pictures, too."

"You obviously know him pretty well."

"Honey, I really don't know what to say." Another pause. "There isn't much to tell, but we can talk about anything you want when we sit down together tonight. I'd rather be together with you than on the phone."

The line stood quiet.

"Alex, you're okay with that, right?"

"I guess," I answered flippantly.

"Honey, what's wrong? Are you mad at me or embarrassed by the pictures, or what?"

"Mom! Forget about it. We'll just talk later."

"I'm sorry we have to leave it like this right now, but I have to be on the air in a couple of minutes."

"I know."

"Sweetheart, I love you. I'll explain everything later. In the meantime, try to relax about the pictures. You know how the paparazzi tend to sensationalize and make things look like they aren't."

I wasn't sure I really wanted to know the answer to the question I was about to ask, but I asked it anyway. "Just tell me if you were alone with him or if those pictures don't show the other people with you guys?"

After another pause, she confessed. "Yes, we spent some time alone together exploring the city, but not that much."

I was mad but I wasn't sure why. I don't really care much about who my dad hangs out with, because he sees new people all the time. But my mom is different. I've never really seen her with anyone besides my dad. Being with Dax Townsend was weird and cool at the same time. Maybe that's why it was so hard to believe.

MARLEY

I'M NOT EXACTLY SURE WHAT happened during our late lunch, but when Rachel and I walked out of the restaurant and back to my car, I felt lighter. As in, less burdened by made-up scenarios—not that they'd be gone for good, let's be real—but in the moment, I felt freed. I noticed a significant change, as if the heavy thoughts that caused my shoulders to tense had flown the coop. The apprehension I'd felt about the possibility of having a real interest in Dax was lessened by simply saying it out loud. All I had to do was say the words to loosen up about everything?

"You've been unusually irritable since you came back from New York. I chalked it up to the extra workload for the campaign, but maybe all along, it's been about Dax," Rachel said.

"I haven't been irritable," I barked, slightly miffed that she was right.

Even though Rachel turned her head, I still noticed her eyes roll.

"Have I really been that miserable?"

"Let's just say you haven't made any new friends lately."

She was right and I knew it.

"Hopefully, that won't be the case anymore," I said confidently.

"Why? You're going to walk into the station with me with your head held high and confess to to the world that you're ready to rumble with Dax Townsend?"

"Don't be such a brat. I'm still a little sensitive."

"A little?"

"Okay, a lot. Which is why I need you to be nicer to me."

"Marley, I can be as nice as you want. But girl, if you don't get over whatever's holding you back from seeing him again, you're going to miss out. He's Dax Townsend, for chrissake! If you don't want him, there are plenty of women waiting in the wings!"

Ouch. Now she's got me wondering why he'd want me instead of them. Damn. I went from all pumped up to fizzled in a split second.

"I know you hear me. Are you coming back in or not?" Rachel asked, getting out of the car and walking toward the station's back entrance door.

I put my window down.

"Not. I told Alex I'd meet her at home."

"Thanks for lunch." She half-waved, half-smiled, and then she was gone.

Something felt seriously wrong. I pulled forward past the loading docks, beginning a three-point turn to leave the lot. As I approached the back entrance door again, Dax was perched on the steps with his arms crossed, flaunting a confident smile and determination that would stop anyone. Is he really even there? I tried focusing my eyes. I couldn't think of a single reason for him to be at the station.

How much time would it take to calm down? Every single time I see him, my heart races like a hummingbird's. I felt myself take two very deliberate deep breaths before I slowly pulled the car in front of the landing dock. Shockingly, he opened the passenger door and got into my car.

All I could do was smile a silly close-lipped grin. And breathe.

"Where should we go?" he asked.

He was definitely asking the wrong person. I was having a hard time thinking clearly, forget about remembering nearby landmarks, and—I was supposed to meet Alex. I was mute. I couldn't speak. He got out of the car. My neck lost a bit of control, bobbing to look through the passenger window. Where was he going?

My door opened.

"Why don't we trade. You take the passenger seat."

I still hadn't said a word, but moved like I'd been hypnotized.

The air was quiet except for the changing car gears and outside noise. I glanced at the digital clock on the dash. Exactly six minutes passed before he pulled over into a metered parking spot in front of Heritage Park.

My door opened and Dax took my hand, guiding me out of the car toward a slatted bench on the grass.

"This is a first for me, you know?"

I wrinkled my face, unsure what he meant, sure that my words were still mixed up inside my head. I turned away.

"I've never had to work this hard to get a beautiful woman's attention."

Whether he meant to do it or not, his comment relaxed me.

I spoke, but dammit, I was stammering with excuses and hand gestures, repositioning myself on the bench and wishing I'd worked harder on my hair.

I felt his hands on my face cupping my jawline and comforting me with his gentle grasp. He kissed me softly, dropping his hands to mine.

"The rest of my day is free," he said. "If that works for you."

I nodded in agreement.

"Marley, talk to me."

He gave me a reasonable time to answer, but I wasn't prepared. I couldn't use the same story I'd told Rachel. He'd think I was nuts.

"I know you remember the fun we had in the city. I thought for sure you'd want to see me again when we got home."

"I did. I do. I—"

"You're seeing someone . . . ?"

"No. No. I'm not. That's not it at all!"

He looked at me patiently, but I knew he needed to hear me answer.

"I have issues, Dax," I said with tentative puppy-dog eyes. "I'm not sure if you know what you'd be in for."

He stood up from the bench and laughed. "You think I don't know that?"

Way to make a girl feel better! I cringed.

"Everybody has issues, Marley. The biggest one we can work on right now is getting you to realize that I just want to spend time with you."

I heard him. He looked so sincere. I wished I didn't feel so pathetic.

CHAPTER 5

MARLEY

EVER SINCE ALEX CALLED WITH questions about Dax, I've been anxious to get home and defend myself. But several hours had passed and Rachel exhausted most of the emotional energy I'd stored. Not to mention, the time I spent with Dax in the park. Now that I'm a block away from clearing my name with one of the few people who matter to me, I wish I had more time to prepare my story and squeeze in a nap.

I don't know why I'm hesitant to face my sixteen-year-old daughter. She's spent countless hours through the recent years reminding me of her right to privacy, her ability to choose appropriate friends, her need for independence. She's pointed out my tendencies to overreact and judge based on first impressions and appearances. She's gone out of her way to prove herself trustworthy and honest. Obviously, there's only one way for me to handle this.

I'll give her a taste of her own medicine. I'll march right up those stairs and explain that my friends are my business and she needs to respect my decisions. How was I supposed to know that photographers would be interested in Dax Townsend's New York companion? Or that any pictures would end up in one of the largest entertainment magazines in the world? The photographs might appear suspicious, but they have no merit whatsoever on what actually happened in New York City. It was a huge event, with sponsors from all around the nation and superstar spokespeople with tremendous notoriety within their fan bases. It seemed surprising that photos hadn't surfaced earlier with all the social media feeds spewing facts and fiction across the globe in nanoseconds.

Come on, this is a charity with goals of going global in a very short period of time. It's a big deal business that could change the rules for every doctor in America who prescribes medication. In fact, the new relationships I established during that trip were nothing more than professional. I was photographed with dozens of people that weekend, simply because of the event publicity. It's not my fault that the three chosen pictures place me smack in the middle of a hand-holding session with a very attractive, super sexy, incredibly fun, and well-known sports legend.

I turned off the ignition and pushed the garage remote to lower the door. My forehead hit the top of the steering wheel and I tightly gripped the sides. Maybe thirty seconds had passed before I lifted my head to the darkness that now surrounded my vehicle. Did I actually need a sign from the universe to remind me that I couldn't spend the rest of my life hibernating alone, avoiding my future? The crazies in my head continued. That's usually the case. I knew my body was still capable of moving and I didn't need to be roused by someone else to release my grips and peel my body away from the driver's seat.

I don't know if it was for show or if it was the real deal, but the light in Alex's window wasn't on when I pulled onto the driveway. Of course, I pondered a number of different things. She could be intentionally avoiding me. Maybe she's watching television with the lights off. She could be on the telephone or surfing the web. Maybe she's actually asleep. If that's the case, then I just won the award for *More Time Granted* and our conversation can wait until tomorrow. Fingers crossed. A wave of relief passed through my body, exiting at the tip of each finger and a deep exhale.

I smelled Iris' tea in the air as soon as I opened the door. I could see the back of her head as she watched television behind the closed lids of her eyes, as she did each and every night. I quietly released my bag onto the seat of the dining room chair. The blanket that usually covers her until she turns in for the night was still folded on the arm of the sofa.

Alex startled me. She must've been laying with her head on Iris's lap, jostling her enough to rouse her when she sat up. They both looked at me with curious eyes, neither one anxious to do the talking. I owed both of them an explanation, but I was still sorting out my emotions.

I managed a weak, "Hi."

They responded with an echoed reply.

"Give me just a couple of minutes, would you? I'll be right back." I still hadn't decided what to say, and I hadn't counted on Iris being part of the confessional.

They both turned to face the TV, resuming their posts until my return. I was out of time, out of sorts, and way past making excuses for myself.

I changed my clothes and wrapped my pajamaed self in my huge chenille robe. I knew it couldn't camouflage my existence in the room, but it brought me comfort and a sense of protection. It's one of the awkward things I do in uncomfortable situations.

I'll put that on my very long list of personal things to fix later. But for the moment, I had to address the topic of Dax Townsend, my NYC campaign colleague extraordinaire.

"Why don't you two tell me what you'd like to know." I said, taking a seat on the other couch, pretty sure they'd already shared their own conversation about what they think went down in NYC.

They smirked at one another. Was Alex trying to hold back a smile? What the hell? Had they put their heads together to formulate some sort of interview? Or worse, an attack?

Iris spoke up first in a very matter-of-fact tone that didn't surprise me—for a couple of reasons: she always has something to say and generally, there's no fluff about it.

"Your daughter would like to know if you and the very famous Dax Townsend hooked up?"

"Grandma!" Alex shouted, embarrassed and giggling.

I nearly spit out the tea I'd just sipped. It would've been a perfect time for an out-of-body experience, just to see my reaction to the question. How could I explain a relationship that I, myself, didn't understand? The only thing I knew for sure was that I'd been avoiding Dax since New York. Seeing him today felt good, but I wasn't ready to tell them yet.

I simply said, "That's none of your business."

Alex jumped right in. "I told you, Grandma. I knew she wouldn't tell us."

Iris smiled.

I took another sip of tea and shrugged my shoulder as we turned to watch TV in silence.

THE NEXT NIGHT, ALEX SNAPPED a picture of me, dressed in the plum colored evening gown I'd chosen for the Phoenix launch party. The angled cap sleeves transitioned into sleek descending lines that joined a beautiful side ruche and flowing ruffle detail that nearly touched the floor.

"Now put on your shoes and turn to the side."

"Stop," I laughed.

"This is the first time I get to see you go out on a date."

"It's not a date."

Is it a date? I didn't want to put too much thought into it, but I couldn't put the breaks on my wildly creative mind. Eight hours ago, I planned to drive to the event alone, walk into the ballroom alone, and return home alone. After spending time with Dax at the dress rehearsal this morning, he offered to pick me up. Does that count as a date?

"When a guy invites you to go somewhere with him, it's a date, Mom," Alex informed me.

I heard whistling through the doorway, getting progressively louder as Iris got closer to my bedroom.

"My my, Marley. You look absolutely stunning," she said, nearly insulting me.

"You sound surprised, Mother."

"Darling, you're so sensitive," she brushed me off. "But, you're certainly dressed to impress tonight."

"Grandma, will you take a picture of me with mom so I can post it online?"

"Doesn't that go against your policy, Alex—no public display of pictures of you with your parents?" I asked.

"I know, I know," she said. "I'll make an exception for tonight."

"Is he bringing you a corsage?" Iris joked.

I couldn't bring myself to reply appropriately to her sarcasm with Alex in the room.

Iris nuzzled herself next to my window and lifted the covering enough to secure a clear view of the car that pulled into the driveway.

"Marley!" she yelled in an emphatic whisper, covering the window again.

I raised my eyebrows when we made eye contact.

"Dax Townsend is accompanying you to the event? He's your date?"

"Yes," I nodded, sensing an opinionated tone.

"Seriously?"

"Yes, what's the big deal?"

Both Iris and Alex looked at me with wide eyes.

I returned a look specifically at Alex.

"You may not post pictures of me getting into his car, driving away in it, or anything else that you might find interesting to capture as I'm leaving. That wouldn't be fair to him, or to me."

"I won't," she agreed.

"Now, if you two would like to meet him before we leave together, pick your jaws up off the floor, get yourselves together, and meet me downstairs. Try not to look too starstruck. All he's done to make you two ogle over him is catch a few footballs."

"I don't give a damn about football," Iris said. "I just want to see him up close and personal. Who wouldn't, with that physique?"

"Mother," I paused. "Tonight, he's just a regular guy, okay?"

"And he's a part of the campaign you're doing, so you'll be seeing a lot of one another," Iris pressed.

"Yes," I said, reaching the bottom of the staircase and checking my lipstick in the hall mirror.

The doorbell rang and I looked behind me to make sure the natives were ready.

"Hi," I smiled. "Would you like to come in?"

He stepped into the foyer wearing a perfectly fitted suit, sans the coat. He stood with confidence but not arrogance; his polished shoes glimmering in the dimly lit room. He reached his hand toward Iris, and she grasped it with both of hers, looking directly into his dark eyes.

"Iris Christopher," she introduced herself with a smile.

"And this is my daughter, Alex," I said, moving things along. "Shall we go?"

"It was a pleasure meeting you," Dax said to them.

He guided me down the walkway with his hand placed gently in the nape of my back. He opened and closed the passenger door for me, then rounded the car to take his place behind the wheel.

"Marley, you really look beautiful."

He sounded sincere. I felt a hint of embarrassment and giddiness, though still a bit awkward.

"Thank you. You look great, too," I said. "It was nice of you to pick me up."

How was it possible that I hadn't been on a real date since before Alex was born? My mind raced. What had I been waiting for? There must've been someone I've gone out with over the years. Why was this so hard for me?

"You're quiet," Dax said. "Are you anxious about tonight?"

"No, not at all," I shrugged. "This is my home turf, not like the New York launch party."

We drove the short distance with comfortable conversation, arriving at the parking garage two levels below ground.

"Well, this is it," he said. "This is the event that officially kicks off the campaign in Phoenix."

"I'm pretty excited. We've worked a long time preparing and most importantly, we can get started on educating the public."

Dax gave a subtle smile.

"How do you feel about being such a recognizable public figure in all this? There won't be many people who haven't heard something about your story."

"Well," he paused. "The reason I agreed to the campaign was not only to share my story from an athlete's perspective, but as Colton's father, sharing his story. He had to make choices about prescription drug use and he did things without talking to me, like most kids that age. In his case, performance enhancement was his focus. And now, of course, I want to make sure he doesn't overuse his pain meds. Fortunately, he figured things out pretty quickly and the car accident probably put things into perspective. But we know that's not true for everyone and there are a lot of prescription drugs being misused."

I kept my gaze focused through the front window.

"Ever since I heard your speech in New York, I've been inspired by your courage. I'm not sure many people would speak so transparently about anything that personal."

My voice stopped, but my thoughts continued. Would I ever get to a place in my life where I could just be me? Without worrying how I'd be judged?

———

"WHY DID YOU SUGGEST THE garage instead of valet?" Dax laughed. "You're that excited? Or maybe, you're not ready to parade around with me by your side."

The comment took me by surprise. Did parading insinuate a date like Alex said or was he simply referring to our partnership in the campaign? I did what any respectable woman would do when thinking quickly and cleverly didn't seem to be working, I avoided the questions and dug deep into my purse.

"Of all the things I . . . wait, here it is. Just a minute." I pulled down the visor and reapplied my lipstick, for the obvious and sole purpose of stalling. By the time I finished blending, blotting, and haphazardly tossing the tube back into my purse, Dax had meandered to my side of the car and was leaning on the opened door.

"Would you like to take the elevator ahead of me, and then I'll follow on the next one?"

I couldn't tell if he was serious, but my facial expression told the same story.

"I'm not kidding," he paused. "If you want to go first, without me, I'm fine with that."

Can't he just let this go? "Of course not, Dax." It felt weird calling him by his name. "To be honest, my daughter joked that you bringing me here was a date and I started to explain that it's just work—" he cut me off.

"So, it's not a date?"

I felt my chin drop enough to separate my lips. "I . . . don't know. Is it?" Insert immediate eye-rolling at self. That was a dumb response.

With an outstretched hand, he pulled me from my seat to a standing position next to the car. After a simple smile, he said, "We don't have to give it a name."

I bit the inside of my cheek.

We traveled two floors to the ground level when the elevator doors opened to a lobby laden with what looked to be a smattering of supporters, press, and vendors. We managed to step out of the elevator relatively unnoticed until attention was drawn toward a man yelling my name in the crowd. He was also waving his arm above most heads.

"Flick, hi," I said as we approached close enough to speak rather than yell. "Is everything all right?"

"Oh, yeah. Fine. I just saw you as soon as the elevator opened and I thought of something I wanted to tell you." He eyed Dax. "Hey, man. Flick," he cocked his head, "from the station."

"Yeah," Dax said, shaking his hand. "I'm pretty sure we've met before. Good to see you."

"Anyway, Marley, I'll catch you later," Flick said. "I thought you were alone."

"You know what?" Dax looked at me and winked. "I need to touch base with someone before we go over the program. I'll just meet you inside." He flashed a peace sign with a partial wave. Maybe he really had something to do or maybe it was his way of giving me space.

"Sure," I agreed, going along with it. I turned back to Flick. "You sounded pretty determined to get my attention." I intentionally averted my eyes toward Flick when I felt them wander in Dax's direction.

Flick chuckled first. "Any chance you've talked to Andrew about our run-in?"

I didn't like the sound of that. "No, he hasn't filled me in, but when you say run-in, what do you mean? Should I be concerned?"

"Ah, no, nothin' like that." He brushed his hand in the air. "That guy kills me every time I see him. He's just so damn calm and cool."

"Yep," I whispered sarcastically, "that's Andrew. Calm and cool."

"Obviously, you know him better than I do, but he seems like a good guy."

"You're probably right, Flick. He's a great friend to a lot of people. So, what about your run-in?" I checked the time on my phone.

"Okay, yeah. I was out on location ready to shoot a segment for the four-o'clock. All of a sudden, Andrew walked up to the van, talked for awhile, and then asked me for a ride to his house when we finished up."

My face wrinkled for a quick second before I returned to my in-public-persona. "That's odd, right? Where was his car?"

"Huh—you really haven't heard this yet?" Flick looked surprised. "I thought he'd tell you right away."

I shrugged. "You know how things get, schedules are crazy, he's busy."

"Anyway, I was working with the new kid, Sawyer Finn, on a breaking story and we weren't far from Andrew's house. He wanted Andrew to give him the exclusive on the story, but Andrew didn't want it in the news."

I shook my head a couple of times. "Wait, you lost me. I'm not following."

"Sorry. Some crazy lady got into Andrew's car and took off with it. He was only out of it long enough for her to slide over to the driver's seat and take off."

I rolled my eyes, not surprised that Andrew would have a woman like that in the passenger seat of his car.

"No, seriously. She stole his car and then, like a minute after we pulled up in front of his house, she pulled up next to the curb." Flick was so delighted with his story and himself that his smile and laughter continued.

"You're right," I agreed. "That's strange. I'll have to ask Andrew about it and get more info on the lady." I wondered if she could've been the same woman Iris mentioned from the text on Andrew's phone.

"Yeah, let me know what you find out."

"Sounds good, Flick. I'll do that," I waved, back-stepping toward the ballroom. "I'm sure we'll touch base again before the end of the night."

Dax greeted me at the double doors with a tall glass of sparkling water on ice. "You're up in the first ten minutes. You may want something stronger later." His hand guided me to the table we'd share with six other people.

I smiled softly and received one in return. "Is this considered parading around together?" I whispered.

I THINK IT STARTED WHEN I was about seven years old. It finally dawned on me that Iris never had any interest in the outside world while she was immersed in a show. Home and office were one in the same, our house looked like a costume design shop from the front door to the back, down the hallway, and hanging from the doorjambs everywhere in between. Cheap stainless steel clothing racks lined the small foyer and at least two sewing mannequins displayed pieced-together scraps that would eventually manifest into creative genius.

I've always been amazed by my mother's creativity; her ability to construct art from scraps because of a vision she sketched onto a spiral bound scratch pad. Another one of our noticeable differences: her ease with charcoal and colored pencils versus my frustration with anything abstract. Important documents such as medical records, insurance papers, photographs, or anything that most people kept in safe places, were strewn haphazardly; she'd refuse to locate them in the midst of her work. On the other hand, if you requested sketches from her earliest shows or even a few minutes of her time to talk about *the industry*, she'd find time to spare.

For each of her traits that have sparked my admiration, it seems that there have always been more that aggravate me. Like hearing the phone ring and not answering it. Her music blared in the background; typically heavy metal and lewd lyrics.

"Mom!" I'd yell, hopscotching through patterns on the

floor, dodging pin cushions, and heaps of fabric. "Mom!" I'd yell again, finally reaching her by the back door screen, smoking a cigarette.

"What is it?" she snapped.

"The phone keeps ringing. Aren't you going to answer it?"

"Marley—why does it bother you so much?" she asked, sliding her feet off the kitchen table and squishing out her cigarette in an overflowing ashtray.

"Don't you wonder who's calling you? What if someone needs you or it's an emergency?"

"If you're that curious, then you can answer the phone. But let me tell you something . . . " She turned my chin to face her gorgeous green eyes. "If you answer the phone and someone asks for me, I'm not taking the call."

"But what if they need you?" I interrupted.

"Marley, I don't answer the phone when I'm working. I'm not going to start just because you can't stand hearing it ring. If someone needs me, they'll wait. If they can't handle waiting, they'll find someone else."

I nodded, but I didn't really understand. On one hand, I was excited to be in charge of answering the phone. Right away, I scrounged up a couple of note pads, sharpened three pencils and sat them on the table next to the phone in the living room. On the other hand, I couldn't understand why she didn't care about being needed. At the time, it was the only thing I wanted. Even now, my intense craving to be needed is a powerful force.

So, I woke this morning to the vibrating sound of my cell phone on the nightstand. Isn't that a glorious irony? Not the peaceful morning declaration from happy birds chirping outside my window, or the smell of hot coffee brewing downstairs, but the damn phone that I can't seem to detach from my being. I glanced at the digital clock. Thank God for the glowing red hue, since I quickly noticed the lack of natural light behind the shutters. I panicked that something horrible had happened. It must've, because no one would be calling me at this hour, especially on my day off. I grabbed my phone and squinted my eyes.

Text message from Andrew.

ARE YOU UP?

I managed to respond.

NOT REALLY. U OK?

The phone vibrated in my hand. What is up with him? It's six forty-five in the morning.

I HAVE AN IDEA. CAN WE TALK?

My sleep had come to an end. I was waking for the day.

WHEN?

He returned a quick text.

NOW. I'M OUT FRONT.

I pulled the covers over my head. This is what my life has come to. My mother, with all her worldly possessions, lives downstairs in my guest room, my ex-whatever-he-is still wreaks havoc on my life, and my high school daughter must think we're the craziest people she's ever met. Perfect. I've managed to create the exact image I grew up trying to avoid.

WAKING UP WITH A SUDDEN burst of irritation is never a good omen, at least for me. I predicted that I might not fully recover for hours. Or days. Just as my forehead tipped backward under the shower head, I heard Iris call my name from somewhere in my bedroom. All I wanted was a small ten-minute window of time to myself, when no one talked to me, asked me anything, or needed me to do something. I didn't answer her.

"Marley!" she said sternly, this time standing a few feet from the shower door.

"Can it wait?" I begged.

"Do you have any idea what you're doing?" she said, as if it was a reprimand.

"Not now, mother."

"It's obvious that you don't want to talk to me, but I sure hope you're getting your head on good and straight before you let this go any farther."

After a thirty-second silence, I heard my bedroom door close heavily. Either Iris walked out, or secured the location, preparing herself and my room for interrogation. I didn't know what happened. She hardly spent any one-on-one time with me when I was a kid, during the years I really needed her; when I wished she was more like other moms. Now it seemed that she just couldn't refrain from meddling in my daily life, unless, and only if, she wasn't preoccupied with her own. Apparently, her calendar was wide open today.

I towel dried quickly, wrapped myself in the robe that hung on a nearby hook, and proceeded to the holding cell. Iris wasn't there. I really expected that she'd be in the room waiting for me. She wasn't.

I took my time getting dressed and drying my hair. I sauntered down to the empty kitchen. Including the shower, it'd been about forty minutes. Where was everyone?

"Mother?" I called, on my way to her room. Empty.

"Alex? Andrew?" I continued, in and out of each room like a hamster in a familiar maze.

I pushed open the door from the house to the garage. My car hadn't moved. Once I pressed the remote and the garage door had risen halfway, there was enough space to see that Iris's car was parked, but Andrew's car was nowhere in sight.

"Where did they go?" I asked into the open air. Even more strange, Iris should've still been asleep. She never gets up this early.

"Damn!" I whispered under my breath. Sitting down on my back bumper, everything seemed to be coming together. Iris wasn't worried about me. Her ranting had nothing to do with me at all. She needed me today, and in the midst of all this morning's chaos, I was distracted enough to forget the promise I'd made to her. So instead of kindly reminding me, she pulled out her typical passive-aggressive weapons, didn't think twice about what might have seemed off with me, and got someone else to do her dirty work. A knight in shining armor to the rescue again, this time, with the help of her impressionable granddaughter, who will hear all about her mother's transgressions throughout the entire ride to the airport. I hope you have a fabulous trip, Mother.

ALEX

THE BELL RANG THROUGHOUT CAMPUS and students scattered in droves. Like a flash mob dance, they reached into their pockets or purses in one choreographed motion, retrieving their cell phones and dialing into the world of instant communication. Text messages, phone calls, video chats, music playlists—all available within seconds, linking them to their alter-egos, their authentic off-campus bodies.

The fingers of my left hand linked with Toby's and I scrolled down the list of missed calls with my right. He asked if I wanted to hang out at his place.

"I would, except my mom wants me to meet her in a few minutes."

"That's weird. Why?" he asked.

I shrugged my shoulders. "I'm not sure, she just sent me a text."

"How long do you think you'll be?"

"I don't know. I have a ton of homework anyway, so why don't I just call you later. I probably won't have time to hang out."

Toby leaned me against the drivers' side door. He kissed me softly, then walked away with a small smile and tipped his chin.

I smiled back, relieved that he didn't pressure me to change my mind. I returned a text saying I'd be there in a few minutes.

MARLEY

"IT'S BEEN AWHILE SINCE WE'VE had the chance to sit down and talk together—alone," I said, welcoming Alex inside the frozen yogurt shop on Third.

"I know. But, we don't really meet up in the middle of the day, either. Is everything okay?"

"Honey, it's fine. There are just some things I want to run by you and I didn't want to wait until tonight."

We sampled different flavors, laughing and making faces, finally creating our own masterpieces and sat at a small rectangular table next to the window.

"Lay it out, Mom. What's the deal?"

I smiled. "Where would you like me to start? The topic choices are: Grandma, Dad, or Dax."

Alex let out a big smile. "Definitely Dax!"

I responded with a big smile of my own. "Dax isn't really an issue, but I feel like he's a factor. Does that make sense?"

Alex raised her brows.

"He's not an issue because everything is still new and we're just starting to get to know one another. But, since he's the first person I've really had any interest in—in a very long time, I want you to feel like you can ask me anything."

"So you're trying to say that you really like Dax and you don't want Dad or Grandma to mess anything up with him."

I shook my head. "How do you make everything sound so much easier?"

"It's a gift. How else can I be of service? And don't think I'm completely oblivious, Mom. When Dad spends the night at our house and then all of a sudden disappears for awhile, I know what goes on between the two of you."

"Don't go making assumptions, Alex. You know your dad and I have been good solid friends for years. We just aren't meant to be a happily married couple." I could say it out loud as many times as I wanted to, but I was only fooling myself. Even my own daughter figured out the convoluted mess that Andrew and I created. The on-again/off-again hook-ups didn't pan out well—no matter how things evolved with Dax.

Alex savored a spoonful of fro-yo. "Now Grandma."

I sighed. "Ugh, Grandma."

"I think it's time for Grandma to move out of our house and annoy someone else." I looked for a reaction.

"I wondered how long it would last," she said.

"Hey—you didn't think I could handle living with her?" I

was slightly offended.

"Honestly, Mom, I didn't think she could handle living with us."

We giggled.

"That's probably why she's gone so much. Whether she's on vacation or staying at her boyfriend's place, she still lives in our house. I just feel like we need our space back. Just you and me. No more extra drama. Not Grandma or your Dad."

"I get it," Alex said. "I mean, Grandma doesn't bother me, you know that. I've always loved spending time with her. But, you two are different."

"We only have a few more months together before you head off to college, and selfishly, I want you back to myself."

"You're going to have to split your time between me and Dax," she nudged.

"Don't do that, Alex. I'm not going to let my first relationship in a million years come between you and me. But I have no idea how to talk to your Grandma about this."

"When do we call Dax and tell him about the commotion he's caused in our family?" Alex laughed.

⸻

I HAD NO IDEA WHERE the week went, but I was keenly aware of how tired I felt. I walked past the bouncer at eight-forty, knowing that I'd have about twenty minutes before Rachel showed up—promptly at nine o'clock.

Marco and Iris had vacationed through small oceanfront towns for twelve days before returning home. If he wasn't committed to his work at *The Lounge*—as owner, early evening dance teacher, and occasional bartender—I'm sure Iris would've been perfectly happy staying away from home for much longer; oh, how glorious that would've been.

The climate inside our house was extremely peaceful while Iris was away for nearly two weeks, but having her home again seemed good for Alex. Oddly, they developed a bond that my mother and I were never able to get quite right. I've found them laying in one of their beds together, looking at magazines, chit-chatting, laughing about something in a scene unfamiliar to me. Don't get me wrong, Alex and I share a similar closeness, but it's something that I regret never having with my own mother. We never gave ourselves a chance; maybe I never gave her a chance. So sometimes, it's hard for me to see Iris adoring Alex as much as she does, although I wouldn't want the alternative.

Talking to Marco was on my to-do list before meeting up with Rachel. I'd taken a seat in front of his counter and he acknowledged me by touching my hand and combining a wink and nod before getting back to the couple he was speaking with when I arrived.

The Lounge catered to every age group, depending on the night, and Marco spent a great deal of time welcoming his guests and making sure they were enjoying themselves. However, the over-thirty crowd paid him a bit more attention than the college kids. Tuesdays drew a low-key group, mostly under fifty years old, interested in a pair of acoustic guitarists. Marco greeted me with one of his typical gestures toward customers, hardly singling me out as the daughter of the woman he sleeps with. He placed a glass of my favorite wine in front of me, keeping up his conversation with the couple down the way, and continuing to make contact with other patrons.

I realized that I may not get any one-on-one time with him tonight. Fine. I should just ask my mother anyway. My questions are really more for her, but sometimes its easier to get answers from other people. Since Alex has gotten very good at communicating with Iris, maybe I should get her to ask for me.

Another cop-out. I felt myself deflating. It happens when I realize that my mother still has power over me. I scoped *The Lounge*. Where was Rachel?

I saw a woman walk in, but it wasn't her. I checked my watch and looked up again. It was nearly nine. She'd be here soon. Wait, that's Andrew. What was he doing here? I inched up my hand to grab his attention, not wanting to alert anyone else. Was he looking for me?

Our eyes met, but he turned away and put his arm around the shoulders of the woman who walked in first, directing her away from the bar. What the hell? He's never blatantly ignored me before. You've got to be kidding me, Andrew. I deflated a bit more and turned around to grab my glass from the counter before schlepping myself to a small table in the back corner of the room.

I had a one-hundred-eighty degree view of the place, with the acoustic team on the small stage adjacent to my seat. I scanned the room but couldn't find Andrew. I didn't see the woman anymore, either.

"Thank God!" I said to Rachel when she slid into the chair across from me.

"I literally just bumped into Andrew as I was coming down the stairs. He looked at me really weird and didn't say anything. But it looked like he was with someone. Did you guys get into a fight down here?"

"No. He did the same thing to me. I mean, we didn't get close enough to talk—or fight, but he purposely ignored me."

"Weird," Rachel said, not overly interested in Andrew. "I saw Marco behind the bar, so your mom must be home?"

"Yep. If you want to hear the details, I'm sure she'd love to tell you."

A young cocktail waitress knelt down in front of our table. She looked to be in her early twenties with long gorgeous auburn hair. I'd seen her before but her name tag reminded me to call her Lacy.

"What can I get for you ladies?" she smiled.

I ordered another glass and Rachel chose a new wine that she'd read about in a restaurant review.

Lacy took two napkins from her beverage tray and laid them out in front of Rachel and me. It wasn't until after she walked away from our table that I noticed handwritten words on my napkin.

"Look at this," I said to Rachel, positioning the napkin between the two of us.

"Not tonight. Doing research. Call tomorrow," Rachel read out loud, a puzzled look on her face.

"That's Andrew's handwriting," I said.

"I will never understand you two," Rachel said. "Do you even have the slightest idea what he means?"

I thought about it for a few seconds. A message like that helped me justify the way he made me feel when he ignored me.

"Actually, yes," I said. "I think I know exactly what he means, but he's still a jerk for treating me that way."

AS FAR AS ENERGY EFFICIENCY during an Arizona summer goes, it's just common sense to keep draperies closed during the day if you're away from home. I understood. And over the years behind the news desk, I've reported dozens of stories related to energy-saving tips and strategies. It's not for a lack of knowledge, but a simple selfish preference that keeps me from following the same advice I share with viewers. Natural sunlight invigorates me and I don't want to live without it.

It's the first thing I do when I get out of bed in the

morning. Before going to the bathroom or preparing the coffee pot, I open the shutters in my bedroom and look out the front window. From the upstairs vantage point, I imagine what my neighbors are doing in their homes. I don't spend a long time perched behind window screens and shutter slats, but the routine has become typical each morning. Downstairs, a similar action takes place, opening the living room shutters that face the street, then the remaining downstairs windows in the family room and kitchen, peering into the back and side yards.

During the days that Iris traveled with Marco, the window coverings remained open throughout the day and into the early evening, pleasing to me as I returned home. When Iris was home, I'd return each day to some shutters open half-mast, and others closed entirely. Maybe it's just another frivolous issue that we can't seem to agree on; her reasons trumping mine, though my reasons should trump hers. After all, she's living in my home. I'm no longer the child, hypnotized by her omnipotence.

"What's the big deal, Mother?" I recalled blurting out in frustration. "Why do you insist on closing up this house every day? Sunlight is nourishing and radiant and you're putting a barrier between us and the outside world."

"It's too much, Marley," she declared. "It's just too much. And, I don't *close up the house*, you're being dramatic. I just tone it down. Go," she shooed me. "—stand over by the window. You can still see as much when the shutters are completely open, but it's not so bright and glaring. A slight tilt takes off the edge."

"Takes off the edge," I remembered mumbling under my breath. I walked away from Iris that afternoon, exasperated by her explanation.

What did she mean by that, I pondered, *takes off the edge*? My memory rolled back to Alex's first year of middle school.

Academic expectations had increased considerably and peer pressure began showing it's true colors. Andrew wasn't much help guiding me to make a decision on how Alex's change in behavior should be handled. He said he'd do whatever I wanted him to do, but that meant that I'd have to define the specifics.

I spent weeks reading books and research about adolescents and related *trouble* topics. My relationship with Alex had always been open and honest, but I sensed the uncomfortable presence of stumbling blocks wedging between us. Alex continued to answer questions, but she rarely initiated conversation like she used to.

"I think I know how you might feel," I'd said to her. "When I was your age, I remember having so many questions about things that I never wanted to discuss with my mother."

Alex remained silent.

"Questions weren't the only things I didn't want to talk about. I remember feeling stressed out."

Alex changed her posture and looked over at me for a couple of seconds before turning away again.

Did that mean I was hitting on a meaningful topic?

"Do you feel like there's a lot you're trying to manage?" I paused, hoping that Alex would eventually say something.

"I don't even know if I can explain it, Mom. I just feel like I'm always on edge."

I scrunched my face. "Help me understand what that means."

"I'm not sure," she said meekly. "Almost like I'm nervous or something, but I'm not. Maybe irritated or short-tempered, like I'm grouchy or bothered, but not angry. I can't really describe it." She put her head in her hands.

"I think I understand," I said, scooting closer on the couch and guiding Alex into an embrace. I hoped to comfort her, but I didn't really know what to do next.

She spent the next couple of weeks in tears every couple of days. Sometimes we'd share conversation, but often, Alex seemed so distraught that expressing words seemed utterly impossible. When I finally made the decision to seek the opinion of a psychologist, I learned that getting Alex scheduled to see a pediatric specialist would take weeks. I made the appointment, and spent those weeks experiencing life through the eyes of my distraught teenage daughter. My heart broke through each of her struggles.

I wasn't naive enough to believe that Alex was the only teenager in the world tormented by physiological changes, but I began to question how many kids were actually evaluated for emotional stress and treated by a professional. Maybe we'd be able to get through this phase before the appointment date and Alex would be back to normal in a few more days. I hoped so, because not only was Alex changing every day, but I felt different too. It affected both of us. Neither of us slept solidly through the night anymore or woke in the morning feeing rested. The mother of the anxious and agitated teenage daughter felt the effects of a parent's concern for her child: always on edge. We were in jeopardy of emotional upheaval. How we handled it together, with a little help from Andrew, seemed critical if our hopes for peace and healing were to be fulfilled.

———————

I HAVEN'T LIVED IN THE house on Coconut Trail in eight years. It's Andrew's house now, no longer the home we shared as an unconventional family. It's the place where Alex visits when she spends time with her dad and it's the place where Andrew sleeps when he's not staying overnight God-knows-where.

I'm not sure exactly how it happened. It was a gradual process; one that kept heaving in both directions like a tug-of-war, until I committed to a purchase and the county recorder made my new home official. Our home, which Alex and I nicknamed, *The Owl's Nest*, has been occupied by the two of us since the beginning of the transition, and now, by my mother, who wasn't going anywhere soon.

Iris fell in love with the view of Camelback Mountain and the hills of Paradise Valley. Her beloved hiking trails would be easily accessible at any time of day. It sounded fine at the time, knowing that my mother and I would likely occupy the general living space at opposing times and that Alex would not only share one-on-one time with both of her parents, but her grandmother, as well.

When Rachel and I parted ways, I got into my car feeling relieved. I'd spent a few minutes (okay, at least a half hour) telling her more details about how I spent my free time in New York City. Yes, some of it included time with Dax, but, I relished in a good portion of my free time alone. Sitting outside a coffee shop with an hour to myself, listening to city sounds, watching people and meditating in the midst of my own thoughts presented a calmness in me that I hadn't felt in a very long time.

Until tonight, I hadn't completely told my New York play-by-play to anyone. Sharing my experiences gave me an opportunity to process my thoughts more clearly, since I was forced to put them into words. I knew the power of saying words out loud, but more often than not, it felt more natural tucking them away in my mind. I'm so thankful for Rachel. She's been a wonderful friend; someone who encourages me, gets things out in the open, rather than letting me struggle with confusion and resistance.

When my car turned onto Coconut Trail, it was as if it was driving on autopilot. I would've parked in the driveway, but I didn't recognize the car already parked there. Did it belong to the woman from *The Lounge*? Immediately, my mind went racing with possibilities. What time was it? I looked at the clock on my dash. Only eleven forty-five. The light was on in the front window.

I continued driving slowly down the street and turned around at the end. As I approached Andrew's house again, I turned off my lights and parked across the street about two houses to the west. I felt nervous. What was I doing? His front door opened. I had to stay put. I only wanted to stay there for a minute, until my head cleared. Now, I was stuck for longer than I'd planned.

Andrew walked out the front door and down the cement steps with an attractive woman, smiling and flirting. She was too far away for me to compare her to the person I'd seen with him earlier. I didn't want to watch, but I had trouble turning my head. Please don't see me, I begged. He opened the driver's door and she got inside after giving him a dramatic hug and kissing him with his face in her hands. "Oh my God," I said. "I did not need to see that."

She backed out of his driveway, thankfully, directing his attention to whatever she was saying from her window. He waved goodbye and went back inside. As soon as the front door closed, I watched the light go out in his front window and I turned on my car. I felt nauseous.

As I drove down Coconut Trail and flicked on my head-lights, I caught myself having a conversation with Andrew in my car, knowing full well that he couldn't answer any of my questions.

Why did it have to be tonight? On the one night that I wanted to have a conversation, you had a woman at your house? The more I talked, the angrier I felt. If I hadn't just left Rachel, I'd give her a call, even though she hated my relationship, or whatever it was, with him. She'd be able to talk some sense into me. Twelve o'clock. She'd still be up. Maybe that's what I needed. A quick reality check.

I was already inside my house, laying flat on my bed, when I picked up my cell phone to call her. It rang in my hand. Caller ID flashed Andrew's name on my screen. Should I answer? I was still upset with myself and with him. Would he be able to tell by the sound of my voice? I accepted.

"Hi," I said, attempting to sound upbeat.

"Are you home yet?" he asked.

"Yeah. It's midnight," I reminded him.

"I saw you, Marley."

Crap.

Silence.

"Did you need me?" he asked sincerely.

Why does he do that? Of course I needed him. Was this the time to follow up with: only on my terms, only when I feel like it, only when I get to decide?"

"No, I'm fine. Really. When I saw that you had company, I realized that it can definitely wait until tomorrow."

"Usually you call me. It's not very often that you show up at my place on a whim."

"I know. When Rachel and I left *The Lounge*, I should've just come home."

"Well, I wanted to check with you, since it was a little awkward."

"We'll catch up later, okay?"

"I have some things I want to talk to you about anyway," he said.

I'm not sure I wanted details. I hung up the phone and looked at the picture of me and Dax on *Page Six*. There was a lot for me to sort out before seeing him face to face.

ALEX

IT SEEMED LIKE A LONG shot at first, but the buzz on campus was spreading wildly, creating the illusion of immediate acceptance, only making me more curious. I knew that a first impression would either give it merit or shoot it down with a vengeance. While not many people on campus were willing to stand up for something that might make them look like a fool or draw negative attention, it was typical for peer pressure to set in before weighing the outcome of actions.

Sitting fully clothed on the toilet seat in the girls' bathroom, I scrolled through my email. I went back to the invitation I received on my iPhone before school. It'd been nearly five hours since it landed in my inbox and I'd heard dozens of people asking about the website all morning.

DOGEAR WANTS TO YOU TO SUBSCRIBE

I signed in and went directly to the invitation. Maybe I'd missed something. I navigated to the *DogEar* profile page and clicked on the INFO bar. There it was—the brief paragraph, ABOUT *DogEar* and how it could be used as an anonymous opinion sharing site for teens. Something about accepting the invitation felt risky, like it would give away my identity, but was there really any harm in receiving the posts? I wanted to read everyone else's opinions, but knew myself well enough to know that I probably wouldn't add to the dialog.

Although the blog address was public and available to anyone interested in reading it, it wasn't advertised or made readily available through search engines using keywords or topics. Additionally, posting a comment directly to the site would require an approved username and password, available only with a registered school ID. Subscription would ensure that I would be updated instantly through my account whenever a new post or comment would be published on the *DogEar* page. I'd use an administrator's username and password to add new posts on the blog. Bold, capital letters explained a short *NO TOLERANCE* policy on profanity and direct criticism toward users. Inappropriate language would result in blockage from the site.

I did it. I clicked on the blue rectangle with white letters, confirming my subscription to *DogEar*. Within seconds, I scrolled my phone screen reading anonymous opinions from fellow subscribers. In response to the day's question: *How important is high school dating?* There were already more than fifty replies, with around ten waking hours left in the day. The bell rang, snapping me back to reality.

I ran to my next class and slumped in my seat, transfixed by my thoughts. The classroom was unusually silent when the teacher stood at the front. I sat up a bit taller and tried to focus on the test papers being handed down each row.

MARLEY

I RETURNED FROM WORK DISCOVERING a mobile-mini storage container parked on the driveway, without any prior knowledge of it's arrival. I parked on the other half of the driveway, since the monstrosity was on *my* side of the garage.

"Is that thing full or empty?" I growled at the big tin shed.

I barged through the laundry room, opened Iris's bedroom door, only halfway; but wide enough to peek inside the room and gaze at the astonishing amount of clutter. The room was packed full and stacked nearly to the ceiling with boxes and a whole slew of oddities.

"My God. What happened in here?"

Since no one was there to answer, or for that matter, explain the purpose of the metal dumpster in the driveway, I continued stewing about all the ridiculous things that had been flooding my mind the past few days. It was unlike me to lose sleep or wake in the middle of the night with anxiety about troublesome issues. Lately though, I'd been staying up late and waking too early, unable to find the required balance needed for making sound decisions and enjoying life.

I closed Iris's door and went directly upstairs, leaving my cell phone on the counter in the kitchen. I curled up on my bed, fully clothed, surrounded by decorative pillows and a chenille throw. I knew that an afternoon nap of ten minutes or two hours would surely destroy any intentions for going to bed at a reasonable hour. But, it was too late to change my mind. My body gave in to the contours of the mattress and I was asleep within a minute of daydreaming.

I ASKED FOR ASSISTANCE FROM the front desk security guard who happened to be standing adjacent to the parking lot when I pulled in. He had a tendency to sneak in a smoke around the time I arrived each day and I was hoping to catch him outside the lobby at just the right time. I flagged him toward my car.

"Mornin', Jim!" I called, slowing to a stop. "Everyone knows what you're up to when you disappear, you know."

Jim put up his hands. "You caught me, officer."

"Can you meet me at my car when you finish up? I've got too much for one person to carry inside today."

"I'd be happy to, Ms. Marley," he smiled, turning back toward the building to crush the last of his smoke into a soda-can ashtray.

By the time I parked and made my way to the passenger side, Jim reappeared.

"Special day today?"

"What do you mean?" I asked.

"It isn't like you to bring two coffees to work, ma'am," he said, nodding toward the two occupied cup holders in the console. "And that looks like a dozen donuts to me," he smiled.

I gave him a puzzled look. "It isn't my birthday, if that's what you're asking. But, I guess you could say it's turning out to be a special day." I hadn't given it much thought. In fact, my plan to stop for donuts and coffee on the way to the station wasn't really a plan at all. Everything fell into place, but I still felt anxious. Talking to Rachel would settle me down.

"If you don't mind just putting those on my desk, I'll handle the rest," I said.

"No problem," he said, inching ahead of me to hold the door open.

"You're a kind man, Jim," I said, rushing in to find Rachel.

I stepped past the front desk, but was called back by the receptionist.

"Ms. Christopher?" she called.

I stopped abruptly, cocking my head toward her. "Yes?"

"These are for you," the young girl said. "I'll bring them to your desk, if you'd like. You look like you've got your hands full."

I was stunned by the beautiful floral arrangement. "Thank you, yes. I'd really appreciate that."

"They're gorgeous, Ms. Christopher."

"They certainly are! Were you here when they were delivered?"

"No, ma'am. They were here before I arrived."

Interesting, I thought.

I was welcomed by the two iced coffees Jim delivered, the

over-the-top arrangement of tropical flowers, and a stack of scripts for the day. My briefcase and purse fell to the floor behind the desk, and I dashed around the corner to Rachel's editing booth. I tapped the pads of my fingers on the glass door to get Rachel's attention. She flipped the headset microphone away from her mouth and held up an index finger.

"Ugh," I sighed. I'd waited just about as long as my body could wait. If Rachel didn't hurry up, I'd have to restrain myself from pulling open the glass door and ripping her from the chair. I went back to my desk to pick up the coffees, and returned at the exact moment Rachel walked out of the booth.

"What's wrong? You look like you're ready to jump out of your skin," she whispered, putting her arm on my shoulder as we walked to the center of the newsroom. Rachel stopped suddenly. "What the hell?" she asked, motioning toward the colorful flowers towering over the top of my cubicle. "Where did those come from?"

"I know!" I exclaimed. "That's exactly what I need to talk to you about!"

Rachel's wide-eyed expression didn't need any words.

"Just a second. I brought food," I said, rounding the corner to display the box of donuts. "Pick what you want and then I'll put the rest out for the crew."

We walked into Rachel's editing booth with coffees and donuts in our hands. The door hadn't been shut for two seconds before I hit the gavel and the discussion commenced.

"You are going to flip!" I declared.

"How long are you going to make me wait? I just saw you yesterday," Rachel pleaded.

"It feels like so much has changed since then. You, of all people, know how long this has been going on with my mother!" I began with my best hushed yell.

"What did she do now?" Rachel cringed.

"For starters, there's a mobile storage unit on my driveway with all her worldly possessions. I was just getting ready to suggest she find somewhere else to live."

"There's nothing wrong with that. It was supposed to be temporary anyway."

"Rachel! You're supposed to be my voice of reason."

"I am. I'm trying. I'm supposed to help you see things from both sides, right?"

We paused enough to scarf down half-a-donut each.

Swallowing my last bite, I continued. "Alex said she's fine with it, but—"

Rachel slowly swiveled her chair to face me directly. "Alex? You've discussed it with her already?"

I couldn't tell if Rachel's feelings were hurt that she wasn't the first to find out, or if she thought Alex should be left out of the decision making.

"I didn't really have a choice."

Rachel looked confused.

"I don't want her to think I'm keeping things from her," I paused. "They really enjoy each other. It's weird because Alex and I are so close. And she's close with Iris, but I don't really mesh when the two of them are together."

"What?" Rachel squealed.

"You know how things have been."

"Wait. I'm still stuck on you actually considering not throwing her out."

"Why?"

Rachel stood up. "Okay, stop right there." She slowed her pace. "I remember you telling me very explicitly, not that long ago—I may remind you, that you've never had any kind of good, normal relationship with Iris. Now you're wavering?"

I stood to face Rachel. "That's what I mean. In the midst of dealing with Andrew, and now Dax, plus everything else I have going on, I don't know what to do anymore."

"Then let's stick with what we know for sure. Who are those from?" Rachel whispered, pointing to the bouquet on my desk.

CHAPTER 6

MARLEY

THE CLOCK AT THE BOTTOM corner of my computer screen said six fifty-five. I'd been off the air for twenty minutes, hibernating at my desk. Thankful for small miracles, I noticed that I was alone in the newsroom, finding comfort between the walls of my small cubicle. My head felt full, almost excruciatingly clouded by thoughts I couldn't decipher. My hands held up the sides of my face, but it wasn't really up, it was lingering in the air above my keyboard. I think my eyes had been closed but I wasn't sure—exactly.

I reached into the small cooler under my desk for a bottle of water. The news room lights were dimmed and I panned the area for evidence of life. Everyone was tucked into their personal spaces and the television screens that bordered the room ran stories from other stations, though the volume for each screen was muted. It was quiet. Almost lonely. Oddly unusual.

Nearly twenty-four hours since Andrew shunned me at *The Lounge*, a fleeting thought reminded that the situation was still bothersome. I looked at the three portable walls of my cubicle and smiled at the absurdity of my life. The pin-cushioned surfaces showcased the handful of snapshots that defined the last fifteen years.

I focused on a picture of Andrew and me. I was nine weeks pregnant with Alex but we were the only two people in the entire world who shared that secret. We were committed to one another; believing in a union held together by a love that we thought was solid, a clear vision for our future that we expected would last forever, and an agreement that we could remain strong without signing our names on a marriage license. It all seemed so simple, yet now, has proven to be anything but simple.

Why couldn't we make it last? Would we have tried harder if we'd gotten married? I wanted to throw a dart at the picture but I couldn't even muster the courage to take the picture off the board, let alone damage it. I peeled a yellow note from the stack on my desk and pressed it over our faces. It was all I could do. Covering it up seemed to satisfy my irritation—at least for the moment. Way to go, Marley—that's the way to call it quits. I cowered, feeling ashamed at the ways I'd averted control over my own life.

It sickened me, browsing the other photographs that decorated my space. "Iris, what have you done to me?" I whispered. She stood in a picture with Alex, wearing a leopard print top and a flower in her hair. For years I've blamed her for my unwillingness to commit to Andrew or anyone; my inability to responsibly separate from him. If she would've exposed me to a life full of love and loyalty to a partner, maybe I never would've ended up this way.

Finally, my eyes rested on a picture of my beautiful

daughter, Alex. Matted in a five-by-seven frame, I picked it up and brought it closer to my eyes, feeling joy and pride. I lifted the sticky note covering the picture of Andrew and me, just enough to examine my own face; the face that once reflected optimism, excitement, and happiness. I covered myself up again, acknowledging that the face reflected in a photograph taken more than a decade earlier rarely appears in the mirror anymore. I caressed Alex's face with my thumb and smiled, desperately desiring that she feels more love from me than I ever felt from Iris. God, I hope so.

Seven thirty. What to do? Back on the air in two and a half hours. Am I prepared, I wonder? I felt like I could walk out the door and not care about the consequences. But who am I kidding? I know that's not an option, nor am I willing to take any chances. Look at my life. It's void of risks. Void of commitment. Void of certainty in so many ways.

I know what I'm full of, though: fear, anguish, guilt, and failure. I have one best friend. I have a mother who is present but self-centered. And an ex-something who is the father of the one and only person who gives me purpose outside of my work. Self-talk was not going well.

I had to get out of here, clear my head, get something to eat, and prepare to host the late night news. I'm reminded of the viewers. Many of them have been loyal to the station for years. I'd bet that some of them feel like they know me and might even say they like me, though what they see of me is only a sliver of who I really am. I'm having trouble liking myself at the moment and I don't like feeling this way. I rarely allow myself to spend time wallowing in these thoughts, but avoidance hasn't been working well, either.

My cell phone chimed, signaling a text message from Andrew.

HEADING TO THE RADIO STATION. HAVE TIME?

Immediately, I perked up and replied to the text. If I could just talk to him and find out what the message on the napkin meant, then I could get last night out of my mind. On the other hand, if the conversation didn't go well, then I'd still have to pull myself together for the newscast.

PERFECT TIMING

Sometimes, I have no self-control with him. Grabbing my make-up bag, I hurried to the bathroom and touched up my face before letting him in the back door.

He pulled a chair up to my desk to munch a quick dinner. I cleared a space for food and was startled by his question.

"What's this all about?" he gestured with his chin.

"They're beautiful, aren't they?" I asked, not expecting an answer. "They're from my campaign partner."

He raised his eyebrows. "They look like more than a typical co-worker gift. Something going on between you two?"

"Andrew," I sighed. I didn't want to try explaining or justifying, fumbling over clumsy words. I couldn't have a conversation about Dax with him.

"Actually, I was pointing to the yellow paper over our faces in that picture."

Damn.

"I was having a moment."

"Anything we need to talk about?" he laughed.

I smiled and looked away, catching Alex's picture in my view. It was obvious that his joking nature was missing the emotional struggle I tried so hard to rationalize.

"Not anymore. Why'd you want to talk to me here?"

"I thought we could talk about last night."

"I couldn't figure out your note."

"That woman, from *The Lounge*," he said, turning his body

toward mine. "She's actually Toby's mother."

I felt disgusted. "Gross."

"No, wait. That's what I wanted to explain. She's in a bind."

"Oh, that's great," I said sarcastically.

"What I mean is, I've been worried that Toby might be bad news for Alex. But from what I can tell, he seems like he's trying to help her."

"What does that mean?"

"It means, she's going through some stuff, and he's trying to be there for her."

"And how do you fit into all this?" I wasn't sure what he was trying to say.

"I guess I'm trying to be a friend. She doesn't seem like she has too many."

I shrugged. "That's funny, Andrew. You've never been the philanthropic type."

"I know, right?" he agreed.

We parted ways with enough time for me to stroll around the back parking lot, collect my thoughts, and wonder if it was possible for people to change.

IRIS

THE RECEPTION AREA SEEMED INTENTIONALLY pleasant, I thought, noting the updated wall paint and framed artwork. It had been some time since I'd stepped into a doctor's office, but I didn't remember anything so sanguine. Three inspirational quotes hung intermittently around the room. The remarkably smiley woman seated behind the desk took her time with me, explaining the necessary paperwork including HIPPA laws and insurance details. I took the clipboard to an armchair at the end of a row. Attached to a long silver pull chain a black pen dangled, it's cap replaced with an artificial daisy. The pen slid off the board bungee*ing* slowly, just inches from the auburn stained concrete floor. Though uncommon for me to pay attention, I took notice of the three other people in the waiting room. I guessed I was the youngest in the room.

To my right, an elderly woman leaned with a noticeably curved posture. A walker positioned in front of her Easy Spirits served also as her purse holder. Sliced and repurposed tennis balls gripped the walker's front legs and a Kleenex box stood at attention in the front basket. A presumably older man sat next to her wearing boxy cover-up sunglasses over prescription lenses. Are those really necessary indoors?

Another woman sat to my left, her skin the color of whiskey, sun-kissed and tough. The young woman who'd brought her into reception said she'd be back in thirty minutes, leaving her with a grocery bag jingling with the sounds of plastic pill bottles and loose papers.

A nurse opened the waiting room door, calling the name of the woman with the walker. It snapped me out of my contemplative state and I began filling out the required paperwork. From my bag, I pulled out the stack of envelopes held together with a rubber band and hoped to quickly find the details about my new Medicare policy. I wasn't comfortable with a geriatric classification.

I completed the clipboard contents and watched a few minutes of the midday news before a different woman, whose smile trumped the receptionist's, called me to the back office. Beginning with the usual intake procedures and typical small-talk, I began feeling restless. "Is the doctor running on time today?"

"Yes, ma'am," she smiled again. "I'll share these numbers with him first, he'll take a look at your chart, and it should be just a couple of minutes."

"Great," I huffed.

Dr. O'Malley ambled into the room, followed by the smiling nurse. He reached out to shake hands and introduce himself and his nurse, Brenda, who nodded and smiled responsively. He sat in an armchair and prepared his iPad. "Why don't we start with you. What's been going on?"

Another burst of irritation wrenched in my gut. A short conversation took place in my mind before I could put words together for the doctor. I'd just spent a significant amount of time explaining everything in writing with a flower-topped pen and hoped by now, the doctor could simply handle the issues and send me on my way.

"Well, it's been awhile since I've seen a doctor, but I think everything I've been feeling lately is probably typical for someone of my age."

"Let's see," he said, scrolling over a couple of pages on his iPad. "You're sixty-five. Tell me what seems typical for someone of your age."

Again, I grumbled. You've got it all there in front of you. Read it, I thought. My legs dangled from the exam table and I felt my arm brace myself. "For starters, my back and shoulders kill me, seems like every day, all day and night."

Dr. O nodded. "Do you experience that type of pain in any other parts of your body on a regular basis?"

"Yes, I do. But my back and shoulders seem to be the worst. If I've been up and around for most of a day, then my ankles and feet occasionally bother me in the evenings."

Nurse Brenda sat at the desktop computer, recording information for the doctor.

"Tell me about other things that make you uncomfortable."

I began with a laugh. "How much time do you have?"

Dr. O and Brenda smiled. "We have plenty of time. Go

on," he nudged.

"I didn't write it anywhere on your forms, but I recently moved in with my daughter and granddaughter. I was really excited about it, and in a lot of ways, I'm happy about it, but I feel a bit more stressed, maybe anxious, than I used to. And I've been more tired lately."

"And how long have you been living with them?"

"About three months."

"And is this a new town for you or have you always lived in the area?"

"Not too far away. But downsizing to one room has forced most of my things into storage. I'm kind of living in limbo."

"Explain *limbo* a little more for me. Do you have plans of moving again soon?"

I shrugged. "I'm not really sure. It was supposed to be short term. But it's fine—and I love spending more time with my granddaughter. I guess life and age are just taking a toll."

Brenda typed furiously; her French manicured nails crisply clicked each key.

"Any other noticeable physical or emotional changes that are bothering you?"

I shared a few more accounts before Dr. O began his exam. He gave verbal cues and I obediently followed his lead. Occasionally, he spoke words in a code understood only between he and Brenda, who noted each and every comment in my file.

"Here's what I'd like to do," he said, retrieving his iPad from the countertop. "There are some tests that I'd like to run, with your permission, and once you've completed those, I'd like to see you again to discuss results."

"Okay," I said hesitantly. "What are you suggesting?"

"Initially, I'd like to run some blood tests." His eyes scanned the screen, "Has it been awhile since you've had your blood drawn? I don't see anything here."

"At least a couple of years."

"Okay, and then I'd like to write you prescriptions for a bone density test and a sleep study."

Astonished, I blurted, "Geez, if I knew you'd want me to do all this, I might've waited a little longer."

"Well, like I said earlier, these tests are only to be completed with your permission. However, I highly recommend that you make appointments at your earliest convenience. The more we understand what your body is doing each day, the better I can prescribe treatment for you."

"So that's it? Today was just a meet-and-greet?" I asked, hands open in front of me.

Brenda's face was obstructed by the computer screen, showing no effort to make eye-contact.

Dr. O held his iPad behind his back and poised himself stoically. "In part, yes. I like to take the time to get to know a patient and his or her concerns before jumping into any significant treatment. On the flip side, I recognize that patients often come to see a doctor after putting off signs and symptoms for lengthy periods of time, hoping to get immediate relief."

"Thank you!" I concurred with a subtle grin.

Dr. O handed his iPad to Brenda and crossed his arms. "So before we conclude, please tell me what you were hoping for when you made the appointment to see me."

"Honestly, Doctor," I rubbed my fist to my forehead. "I'd love to get a heavier-duty pain relief, or a sleeping pill, or even something along the lines of anti-anxiety. I'm just at my wits-end and need to try something different before I go crazy!"

Dr. O took a seat in the armchair next to Brenda, whose typing proficiency seemed equivalent to that of a seasoned court reporter.

"I hear what you're saying and I sense the desperation in your voice. I'm not comfortable agreeing to all of those requests at this time. We really need to examine the results from the tests I recommended so that we know exactly what to treat and how best to treat."

I involuntarily bowed my head.

"In the meantime, though, let's start with one thing at a time. That way, if you experience any side effects, we can attribute those to the one change, rather than guessing among a host of new medications."

I lifted my head enough to look at the doctor. I could see one of Brenda's eyes peering beyond the screen frame.

"Of the three: body pain, sleepiness, and stress, which bothers you the most?"

I thought about the question heedfully, taking longer than my usual impulsivity.

"Let's start with the aches and pains."

Dr. O put a hand on each of his knees. "We can do that." He spoke directly to Brenda announcing a name and dosage that she added to the file. He took a moment to explain when and how much to take daily, insisting diligence with evening administration only, as not to impair my daytime driving. He suggested over-the-counter pain relief during the day for now. "Okay," he took a deep breath. "Do you feel good about the plan?"

"I do, thank you. I don't feel good about what comes with the territory."

The doctor shook my hand again, wishing me the best for pain management, and encouraging me to follow through with the additional tests. He left me in the room with Brenda.

"So before you go, I'd like to set up your next appointment."

"How long do I have to get those other tests done?" I asked.

"Well, that's completely up to you, but the sooner the

better, of course. However, since he prescribed the pain medication, he'll need to see you again in six to eight weeks to follow up specifically with that." Brenda waited patiently with a smile. "What day of the week is best for you?"

ALEX

"I'M GOING TO BED EARLY. Goodnight, Dad," I leaned down to kiss him on the cheek.

I headed upstairs feeling the weight of my task resting heavily on my shoulders. I fell onto the bed and grasped at the hairs on the front of my head. I never thought this would be so hard. It sounded fun, but now I realize that it's so much more than that. It's pressure. Rolling myself into a sitting position, I reached over to the side table and grabbed my laptop.

My room was lit only by the hue from the computer screen as I began to write. I knew the importance of choosing words carefully. The school newspaper column had become a phenomenon throughout campus. Topics resonated among my classmates; experiences that they could relate to and talk about together. I knew that without the column, it was very unlikely that many of them would strike up a conversation and speak honestly. It seemed to be the talk around campus, as students received a digital notification about a new post, either by text or in email. Still no one knew my identity, and I intended to keep it that way.

In order to take on the position, my dad signed a permission slip for me to write as a ghost columnist. I never told my parents that *DogEar* had gone live or that I was the only contributor to the postings. I didn't want to hear opinions from seasoned radio and news people. I wanted this to be my own thing. But tonight I felt alone. Really alone, as I tried to sort through the drama of my own life and separate it from what I'd write for the column. It would have to be approved by my mentor and journalism teacher, Eve Kingston, but upon acceptance, the prompt would be posted online, for all the world to see.

My cell phone buzzed from somewhere on the bed. I checked the lit screen and read Toby's name across the top. Not now. I had so much to do and I was exhausted. If I answered the phone, I could be talking for an hour. We'd been dating for five months, beginning at the end of last school year. This year, our senior year, Toby played varsity football and led the in-crowd in whatever direction he wanted to sway them. Sometimes, with his witty sense of humor and perfectly squared jawline, he'd think of the most unlikely of adventures and steer the group to follow. In most cases, he'd get the majority of them to do whatever he proposed. He took pride in his *talents*, as he liked to say.

I backed myself up to the headboard, resting the laptop on my thighs. I can get this done in an hour, I thought, setting a reasonable goal and trying wholeheartedly to believe it was true. My phone buzzed again and I could see the screen without even picking up the phone.

"Hi Toby," I said quietly.

"What are you doing?"

"I'm just trying to finish some homework," knowing that it wasn't entirely a lie.

"How come you didn't call me back?"

"It's been seven minutes."

"I've been waiting to talk to you all night."

"Me too," I agreed. "I just have a lot to do, and with everything we need to talk about, I don't really have time to get into it tonight. Can we just wait until tomorrow?"

"I guess. I don't want you to be mad at me."

"I'm not." I wasn't angry, but I was definitely confused and disappointed.

"Alex, I just didn't think you'd think it was such a big deal. So, I promise you'll never have to see that again."

"Toby," I sighed. "I can't talk tonight, okay?"

"Fine. I'll see you tomorrow."

I hung up the phone feeling indifferent to him being frustrated with me. I didn't want to get deeper into anything, and the more I'd try to ease his mind, the longer the phone call would last.

"Tomorrow," I whispered.

MARLEY

IT WAS MY DAY OFF and I planned to stay away from work. Not only was it a twenty-five minute drive from home and off the map compared to my errand-running radius, I tried to wipe the stress of work from my mind. When I work, I'm focused and dedicated, I enjoy the crew, and the best days are when I can spend time with people outside the station—the ones we tell stories about, the public. I love writing and speaking and being on camera. But on my days off, I'm reminded that life goes on without me, whether I'm actually present in it or not. The laundry has piled up, the refrigerator is bare, bills need to be paid. When I'm at home, I feel behind and pressed for time, sometimes overwhelmed with lists and things that will never be completely done.

Today, my mind is heavy. I'm not ready to tackle anything on the to-do list. I called Rachel and made plans for lunch. She was working on a tight schedule, so I offered to pick her up and we drove to a nearby sandwich shop.

"Give me the lowdown," she said, sliding into the passenger seat.

"On what?"

"On Dax," she smiled, with her body turned toward mine. She was already raising her voice and talking with her hands.

I laughed, knowing she was excited to hear anything I'd be willing to tell her that may have transpired since we last talked.

"I will, I will. You know that."

"I only have an hour, Marley. Start now so we have enough time."

"What are you so worried about? We have plenty of time!"

"I'm not sure an hour is enough time for you to tell me everything," she smiled.

"You know pretty much everything," I said with a grin.

"Why didn't you just come out and say you were looking for an excuse to come to the station today?"

"What? I'm not looking for an excuse. I want to have lunch with you and just hang out with someone I don't actually have to talk to," I admitted.

"Marley, seriously."

Thank God we came to a red light. I needed more than a second to look into Rachel's eyes. "Why are you saying that?"

"Because Dax is at the station this morning preparing for a segment with Chris Dalton. He's going to co-host with him on the Friday night football highlights."

I felt my face change. I was smiling.

"Are you saying that he was here this morning, or that he's still there now?"

"When I came out the back door, he was still inside with Chris."

Green light.

"Honestly, Rachel, I had no idea he'd be at the station. I didn't even know he'd be working with Chris."

"I'm rea-dy," she sang. "What's going on?"

Two minutes away from the restaurant, I started speaking

the thoughts that had been trampling my mind for days. "You, more than anyone else, know how much emotional trouble I've gotten myself into with Andrew over the years."

Rachel nodded.

"Here's what I know. I went to New York for a national campaign kick-off, doing my job as a spokesperson for Arizona, and looking forward to a couple days away from home. I knew it would be fun, I'd meet a lot of people, get by on minimal sleep, and take in a few sights. What I didn't know, is that a terrific guy, who happens to be a hero in this city's public eye, would catch my attention as equally, I think, as I caught his. I had no idea that we'd spend the last two days of the trip together without a care in the world about who saw what. And, maybe most importantly, just a couple of thoughts about Andrew slithered themselves into my head during those two days. It was the first time in a really long time that I felt free of him."

After ordering at the counter and taking a table near the window, Rachel took her turn. "Marley, I have to say, as much as I was really looking forward to hearing more about you and Dax, and believe me, I still do, I think I'm still processing what you just said about Andrew."

I felt myself smile again, but this time, it was that uncomfortable smile that I make when I'm a little embarrassed.

"I know you guys have hooked up here and there over the years, but seriously, you didn't really think it would just continue that way forever, did you?"

"You know, I never really gave it much thought—probably since I didn't want to consider any alternatives. I mean, he's Alex's dad, we get along fine, we can still do things together and be around each other without too many issues. I've always liked him fine. I mean, we're friends, you know?"

"But the way you're talking, it sounds like he's always been in the back of your mind. Is that why you haven't really dated?"

All I could do was shrug my shoulders. Maybe—if neither one of us ever settled down with another person. I don't know.

Rachel noticed that I'd slipped away in my thoughts for a minute. She snapped her fingers in front of my eyes. "If you've spent the last fifteen years thinking about Andrew and then you spend two days with Dax—nearly forgetting about Andrew, then I'd say that something pretty significant happened in New York."

"He took me to a place I've never been, Rachel, socially and emotionally. He's absolutely unbelievable." My gaze drifted away from Rachel, but my words never left her. "I'm just not sure if I can handle someone who seems so unflawed."

AS THE GARAGE DOOR LIFTED, I peered into an empty garage. I took in a deep breath, anticipating the joy of being in my own home, alone, at least for a little while.

Iris left this morning on a day trip with Marco, who seemed to be turning into a little more than the *man of the hour*. I, for one, am a bit surprised that their chemistry is still yielding a positive reaction. I can only recall two other times when Iris fell deeply into a relationship with a man. But, I would be remiss if I didn't also mention her short attention span and many infatuations with men for small, even undetectable, windows of time.

I tossed my purse onto the kitchen island, nearly knocking over a cup of room-temperature coffee. That damn cup greets me from the same place every time I come home from work. Stained with the outline of my perfectly painted lips, the first and only sip I take before I setting it on the counter each morning, leaving it to fend for itself until I get home.

It's irritating, really. Same action, same result, every single day. Why do I do it? I have no idea. I placed the cup into the microwave, set the cook time for one minute, and headed upstairs to change clothes.

Although it was only one in the afternoon, I slid off my clothes and let them drop to the floor where I stood. I pulled back the top layers from my bed and laid down on my back. The shutters were drawn, but a fraction of light peered through the slats. Iris must've come in and adjusted the lighting. "Stay out of my space, Mother," I grumbled.

At one twenty-five, I stretched my body, from fingertips to toes, separating and curling each digit, becoming more aware of my surroundings. I could hear the voice of my yoga instructor, cuing me and placing gentle reminders into my stream of thoughts. I'd checked out, unexpectedly. For the last twenty-five minutes, my mind reflected on time spent with Dax in Times Square.

He'd been so easy going, so non-threatening. We didn't make formal plans to meet up once we returned home, but—where would things go, I wondered? It was a strange feeling; one I hadn't really felt since I met Andrew so many years ago.

At the risk of sounding arrogant, the truth is, men aren't shy about approaching me. I'm convinced it's because they recognize me from the local news. That type of attraction isn't appealing to me in the least, but some guys are just googly-eyed over *famous* people. That's where my thoughts go first, and I've admitted to Rachel in the past that it's hard for me to change that assumption, put forth effort into getting to know a guy, take his interest at face value, and give him the benefit of the doubt.

My cell phone rang. I could hear it from upstairs, but I wouldn't get to it in time. I gave myself another ten minutes before heading downstairs. The message was from Andrew and he'd asked me to call him. He was already scheduled to have dinner with Alex. I hoped he wasn't calling to cancel; I knew it would disappoint her.

"Yeah, I'll be there tonight. I just wanted to give you the heads-up on something I'm working on," he said.

"With what?" I asked, starting the cook time on the microwave again.

"So, I've still been keeping an eye on Toby."

"Did something happen?" I blurted. I don't know if I've been secretly hoping that Andrew would find something we could use to sway Alex away from Toby, but suddenly I was listening very intently.

"I'm not exactly sure," he began. "It's kind of confusing. Are you doing anything else right now?"

"Andrew, don't do that to me. I hate it when you patronize me! I'm hearing every word you're saying!"

That is one of the things, among several others, that he does—that gets me fired up immediately! Now, he may have a point sometimes, but not all the time. I'm notorious for multi-tasking, a skill for which I believe is extremely valuable. But occasionally, I focus on a particular task more-so than another, and lose track of what someone might be saying to me. In this particular case, I was following along swimmingly.

"I stopped by *The Lounge* for lunch and on my way out, I caught a glimpse of Toby in the alley by Marco's back door."

"Strange. Especially in the middle of a school day. And Iris is out of town with Marco today, so that makes me wonder, too."

I leaned back on the couch with the phone on my chest after finishing up the conversation with Andrew. Alex walked in thirty minutes later.

"Are you okay, Mom?"

I stood up and walked toward her as she rummaged

through the fridge for a snack. I kissed the top of her head and my mind flashed back to the days when she wore two French braids in her hair and ate toast soldiers with cream cheese and strawberry jelly after school.

"Your dad's coming for dinner tonight," I reminded her.

"I know. Have you ever thought about drinking iced coffee?" she asked, smirking and gesturing toward the cup on the counter that always turns cold and never gets finished.

IRIS

"WHY DO YOU WASTE SO much of your time and energy judging what I do?"

It wasn't unusual for me to blurt out a first response, but pouncing on Marley in front of Alex was very unusual for me.

Eyebrows raised, Marley turned from straightening the mess on the coffee table and asked Alex to give us a few minutes.

Once we heard the sound of Alex's door close upstairs, Marley stood very close to me, making eye contact to emphasize her intentions.

"Believe it or not, Mother, your poor choices in behavior are becoming quite apparent to Alex."

"Is that so?" I snarked. I looked at Marley with a sharp stare.

"Yes, it is so," she confirmed, adjusting the volume of her voice to reflect a whispered shout. "What you do in your every day life when you're living on your own is your business. My opinions about what you've done and when you've done them haven't mattered—until now, because you're living in my house. And since you're here, dancing around all of our lives in your carefree glory, I will have you know that my opinions will be made loud and clear."

I dismissed Marley's heated expression with a wave of my arm and puff of air through my lips. I returned to stirring a pot on the stovetop. The room remained awkwardly quiet for nearly a minute when I made the next move. "I thought you would've outgrown this by now." Without turning, I could feel the emotion stirring in Marley. A slight smile presented at the left corner of my mouth.

"And what is that supposed to mean?" The sound of Marley's voice was getting louder and closer to me with each word.

In a slow motion pirouette, I faced her and tasted the sauce from the stirring spoon. "This is clearly about you and not about Alex. Since you were a child, I encouraged you to spread your wings and discover the world according to your interests. I can honestly say that I never discouraged you from trying new things, even when I knew you'd be unfulfilled."

Marley's expression teetered somewhere in between irritation and pity. The passive-aggressive reflection of charitable behaviors from mother to daughter were nauseating. "Oh for heaven's sake, Mother. You are really taking a leap into the deep end today."

"That's fine, don't give me any credit," I said, shrugging my shoulders. "This isn't about that, anyway. You didn't let me get to my point."

Marley took a deep breath. "I didn't realize there was a point."

"For the sake of your fragile mood today, I'll tell the rest in short form."

"That would be wonderful," Marley said, under her breath.

"You and I are vastly different from one another in many ways."

Marley hooted in response. "That's where you're going with all this?"

"My turn or yours?" I glared.

By a gesture of her arm, Marley suggested that I continue.

"And by those very differences, the most stifling barriers have been built between us. Yet you, unlike me, are the one who views a difference as a flaw."

"Oh no you don't," Marley began. "You are not going to turn all of this on me. It's not my fault that your moral compass isn't calibrated to meet *normal* standards."

"And by *normal*, you mean the same as yours?"

Slightly raising her voice, she replied, "By *normal*, I mean behaviors that I wouldn't mind my daughter learning from you, rather than the exact opposite."

"So in simpler terms, you think I'm an unsuitable influence on Alex because she's getting to know me on a daily basis instead of only when you see fit?"

"That's right."

"And in other words, you don't feel like you're in control of Alex anymore because I'm here now and she's exposed to ways that are different from yours."

Marley's frustration was heightening. "The last thing she needs is for people to find out about the things you do and how you live."

"Excuse me?" I declared. "We won't take the time to debate my life according to how you see it, but I will say this: your daughter will be judged on her own performance and merit, not mine, not yours, or anyone else's. If you hadn't been so insecure all your life, you would've realized that a long time ago. If I'm that embarrassing to you, then we're a long way from becoming friends."

"Friends?" Marley asked. "You've never wanted to be my friend, mother. You've spent your life doling yourself out to everyone but me." She walked to the base of the stairs and paused before she looked back.

I cocked my head to the side, making eye-contact with Marley. "We were just starting to get somewhere and you're walking away from the same conversation we've never been able to finish."

"I really don't know if it's possible to finish it. I don't think we can finish it. Nothing is ever going to change."

I gave one response before Marley approached the staircase. "That depends on both of us."

She looked back at me.

"You've never asked me why, given our history, I'd do something completely out of character and ask to live with you and Alex."

Marley took a seat on the bottom step, crossing her arms. "Why, Mother, do you suddenly want to share living space with us?"

I leaned on the wall adjacent to the staircase. "When Alex was born, she became the center of your world," I paused. "In glimpses, I saw examples of your attention and presence dedicated to her, that I couldn't give you."

"Yes," Marley nodded with a sarcastic expression. "That's what she deserved from her mother."

"I know we can't go back, but who knows how long we have together in the future."

"Suddenly, you're philosophical?"

"What I'm saying is, I'd like to spend time with both of you, be present in your lives, maybe mend some of our wounds."

Marley stood. "From a person who uses words to make a living, I'm at a loss for them at the moment."

"I just want you to know that I'm here, with you and Alex, by choice—not necessity."

It was a step in the right direction.

MARLEY

I PULLED INTO THE PARKING lot of the seemingly busy coffee house, sighting Andrew's car parked and unattended. By the time I turned off the engine and grabbed my purse, he'd arrived at my door before it was open.

"Hi," he whispered, guiding me into the restaurant with his arm around my waist.

"Hi," I said suspiciously, tilting my head toward him and surprised by his gentle affection.

"I already have a table for us," he announced, taking me past the hostess station to the last booth in the corner.

"Are you alright?" I asked. "You look edgy."

Ducking his head beneath the Tiffany-style lamp above our table, he leaned over and looked me straight in the eyes. Anger emerged in his face through his serious eyes and hushed tone. "Marley," he began, gritting his teeth and taking in a deep breath. "Obviously, things have been strained between us, but I don't want our differences to get in the way of what I have to tell you."

Our differences, that's one way to describe the past months, I think.

"I know you're on a time schedule, with your next segment in two hours, but this couldn't wait until you got home. I'll tell you as much as I know now, and we'll fill in the blanks later."

"What is it?" I ask matter-of-factly. I wracked my brain with a plethora of possibilities, but this felt dramatic, even for Andrew.

"Marley, something has happened."

"Just tell me!"

He spoke softly. "I think Alex might be in danger, but I'm also concerned about you and me."

"You're not making any sense," I said, leaning closer to him, trying not to attract the attention of anyone else. "What do you mean by *danger*?"

"Are you ready to order?" the waitress smiled, with perfectly straight white teeth and the apparent inability to sense the difference between the right time and the wrong time to interrupt a conversation.

"We'll need a few more minutes," I reported. "I'll just wave to you when we're ready."

She nodded and smiled again, backing away from our table.

"What has gotten you so worked up?" I growled.

He leaned even further over the table. "Marley, this is serious."

"Just tell me what this is all about, so I can understand. You're talking in circles."

Andrew took one of my hands in his. "Alex is in trouble."

I felt my head droop and my eyes cringe, but I had to hear more. Holding my head up with one hand on my forehead, I needed Andrew to tell me everything.

"She's fine, but I left her at home because I thought we should talk without her first."

"What? Why isn't she at school?" I yelped.

"Marley, the school did random drug testing and she tested positive for marijuana."

I gasped. "No, she didn't. There's no way."

"Yes, she did," he paused.

"My God, Andrew, she's a baby. And she's a good kid. We would know if she was taking drugs."

"Her school counselor called me today and—"

"Wait. Why did you get a call? No one called me," I argued, taking my phone out of my purse to check the recent call list.

"Mar, I have no idea. We can dive into that later. Right

now, I just want to talk about Alex."

"How could I miss the signs? She's an athlete, Andrew. She's an excellent student. How long has this been happening? I'm the spokesperson for a drug abuse awareness campaign!" I felt myself getting angry for all of us.

"Take a breath. Blame whoever you want later, but right now, we need to focus on the safety of our family."

"You said that before, but what does that mean?"

"I don't know yet. When I first got the call from school, I didn't believe it either. It doesn't make sense. Alex swears she hasn't even tried marijuana. To be honest, Mar, I think she's telling the truth."

"I agree with you. We hear all about false positives, right?"

"That's what I said too, and when I mentioned the possibility to her counselor, she told me that they run a second test before alerting parents, just to make sure that it's a true positive."

I closed my eyes. "And the second one came back positive?"

"Yes. But, teenagers can be assholes and it's possible that Alex took something from one of them and didn't even know she took it."

"Andrew! You know as well as I do that a bong or a rolled and twisted paper are obvious giveaways, and she'd have to consent to smoking it."

"Those were the olden days, Marley. Think about it. Marijuana is available in so many forms now. They even use it in foods. Hell, there's a whole line listed as *edibles*. They look normal, like brownies, cookies, shit like that, but they have weed in them."

"You can't just walk into a store and buy this stuff," I argued.

"I know, but shouldn't we take her word for it until we get more information?"

"She tested positive twice. Whether she knew what she was doing or not, she's got it in her system. She's sixteen years old, Andrew."

"After begging me to believe her and by the way, she's an emotional wreck, I told her I wanted to see her cell phone. She handed it over willingly, Marley. No hesitation."

"And?"

"I scrolled just a bit and found a questionable text message sent three days ago."

WATCH YOUR BACK. EYES ARE ON YOU.
GET YOUR BOYFRIEND TO PAY.

"Oh my God," I gasped. "Who was it from? What did she say about it?"

"She claims to have no idea who sent it or what money they're talking about. Toby told her not to worry about it."

"Why didn't she tell us? Didn't that message scare her? It scares me!"

"I asked the same question. She thought it was just a prank and had planned to tell us if she got another one like it."

"This is the twenty-first century. Can't we find out who sent that text?"

"I tried. Not surprisingly, it came from a disposable phone."

"What are we going to do? My God, she's going to the game tonight!"

"I'll handle Alex until you get off work. I'll keep her with me, away from the game, and I'll make contact with Toby."

I picked up my cell phone and began dialing. "I'll call Rachel and tell her we have an emergency."

"No," he insisted. "I really don't think you should draw extra attention right now. You need to be seen on the news just like you always are. Do your show and we'll deal with Alex when you're done."

I put down my phone hesitantly. "Andrew. This is our daughter. She just got busted on a second positive drug test and has a threatening text on her phone. I haven't even talked to her or given her a hug or asked her how the hell this could be true! You want me to go back to work and continue business as usual?"

"Can you do it?" he asked.

It was an unreal experience. I had so much to process emotionally. "I'll leave as soon as I'm off the air, and I'll meet you at your house."

Andrew reached across the table and took my hand. "I'm sorry I had to tell you this in the middle of a shift, but I really thought you'd want to know. I knew you'd be pissed if I waited."

"Yes, I absolutely want to know. I just can't believe it. And I'm ticked that no one from the school called me."

Andrew waived the waitress back to our table. "We just need two black coffees to go."

Coffee would be good. I took my head in my hands and felt Andrew slide into the booth next to me.

"Marley, you've always been able to put on your work face even when you didn't want to. Tonight, you march right in there and do the same thing. You have to. And when you're done, Alex and I will be waiting for you."

ALEX

I CAN'T BELIEVE I'M BEING treated like a prisoner in my own home. Never in my life have I lost phone privileges—until today. I literally had to hand over my phone before taking up temporary residency in my bedroom until *later*. Whatever later means; the point when I'll be forgiven for my so-called infractions and invited to join the land of the living. Who knows?

My head hung over the side of my twin bed, both legs dangling off the other side. I caught a glimpse of my backpack on the floor near the door. Suddenly, I captured an out-of-body vision, a cartoon-style lightbulb appeared above my head. Jumping to my feet, I tackled my backpack and reached inside for the laptop. "Yes!" I cheered for myself. Why hadn't I thought of it sooner? It didn't take long to power up but, "What? You've got to be kidding me," I grumbled, noticing very quickly that a wireless connection was no longer available.

"Dad!" I yelled from my position on the floor, followed by a few more drawn out name-calls but he didn't respond to my exclamations. I pulled open my door and stomped into the hallway. "Dad!" I shouted again. He appeared at the foot of the stairs without a word, just tipping his head to make eye contact with me.

"I can't get Wi-Fi!"

"Right," he said matter-of-factly, and walked away from the staircase.

I growled under my breath, "This is so stupid!" From my bedroom window I noticed the sun going down. I was sure he'd keep me here until my mom could either come get me or until she'd be home from work and he could take me home.

If I couldn't search the internet for information about false positive drug tests, at least I could write a blog post about it. I brought the laptop onto my bed, resting it on a hard covered book and began typing a new document. Typically, I write both sides of an argument, but without the help from my online resources, I only had my personal experience to report. I made a separate list of questions I wanted to be sure to ask at the end of the post.

1. *Did you know that your high school require athletes to take random drug tests?*

2. *What consequences are enforced when a student tests positive?*

3. *At what point does the school contact parents?*

4. *Do you think it's fair to test high school students for drug use?*

5. *Are there certain drugs that should be tested more seriously than others?*

6. *Does a student have the right to contest the results?*

I heard a couple of soft knocks at the door, but Dad opened it before I even took the computer off my lap. "What're you up to?" he asked, leaning on the hinge side of the doorjamb.

"Just writing," I shrugged.

He sat on the side of my bed. "I talked to Mom."

"And," I questioned, lifting my eyes to meet his.

"She's coming over after the broadcast. She wants to be here when we talk."

"Okay."

"Listen," he said, gently grabbing my calf, "why don't we get something to eat and just hang out till she gets here?"

"You're allowing me out of my room?" I asked, sarcastically.

"If you want to come out. Or, I can bring you something and you can eat in here by yourself."

I smiled. "Dad . . . I swear, I have no idea why I tested positive. Twice."

"We'll figure it out, babe," he said. "Let's wait for your mom."

The doorbell rang when we got to the base of the stairs. Dad answered the door, but I arrived just after him. When I saw Toby standing on the welcome mat, I didn't know what to say.

"Hi," he sounded surprised. "I've been calling you all afternoon," he said. I wasn't sure if he was irritated that I hadn't called back or if he was genuinely worried.

"Hey, Toby," Dad started. "Thanks for stopping by."

I cringed. What a weird feeling. I didn't even know what to say to him, but even stranger than that, I didn't know what he'd heard. Were rumors already starting at school? Was anyone else sent home with positive drug test results? I guess if anyone tested positive earlier in the school year, I never heard about it, so it's possible no one knew it happened to me. Right?

"Yeah, sure," he hesitated, taking just a couple of steps backward.

"C'mon in," Dad said. "Have a seat." He directed Toby to the couch.

What was going on?

"Alex, you can join us. Or not. Completely up to you," Dad said.

"Did you ask him to come here?"

"I did! We need to talk about that text you got and I thought face-to-face would be best," Dad smiled.

I lowered myself into the couch across from Toby. Listening to my dad talk to my boyfriend was not incredibly comfortable. Toby kept his cool and came up with a few possibilities about pranks, typical high school shenanigans, but nothing that worried me. He said he'd gotten one text, as well, but nothing since then. He didn't seem worried. I really wasn't, either.

I stood at the corner of the front window and watched Toby get into his car. He must've checked his phone or messed with the radio because he didn't dash away in any kind of hurry. I took a step back when I saw him look back toward the front porch. Why didn't I want him to see me?

"Ready?" Dad asked.

"Where are we going?" I wondered.

"I don't know. You don't even need shoes. Just get in the car, we'll get some fresh air, and grab something quick. We'll bring it home and eat in front of the TV.

I opened my window and slouched in my seat, just to the point where the seatbelt rested on my neck. I wasn't sure if Dad really believed me. Was he just being cool until he and Mom could ambush me together? With the way the tests came out, I'm not sure I'd believe me either.

"Do you have any idea when I'll get my phone back?" I knew it was a pathetic plea, but still worth a shot. I couldn't even look at him, but I knew he wasn't ready to hand it over yet.

"I'm not sure you realize how serious it is to get a text like the one you got."

"C'mon, Dad—not the text again," I huffed.

We pulled into the northwest parking lot of a popular intersection. "You pick the place, I'll get your dinner," he offered.

Unfortunately, I felt sick to my stomach and nothing sounded good.

MARLEY

I WASN'T SURE IF I could hold myself together through the broadcast. My head felt heavy and I wiped my palms on the sides of my pants. With just over thirty minutes left until I'd sit in my chair behind the news desk, I prepared for the stories, but what I really needed was a genie in a bottle offering a single wish. Just one wish. I wanted Alex's situation to magically disappear.

I must have looked terrible because the look on Rachel's face was concerning. Rather than whispering to her in my small cubicle, I gestured for her to follow me inside the editing booth. Once the glass door was closed and locked, she sat down on the chair next to me.

"What was that all about?"

"I don't even know where to start. I have so much to deal with before I can fill you in on the latest Andrew report. I just need to get through this broadcast and go home."

The studio was barren except for the sports and weather guys, my co-host, Ripley, who thought he was God's gift to evening news, and a couple of camera and tech support people. Even the lights in the news room were dimmed.

I took Rachel's hands in mine. "Can you promise me something?"

"Anything, yeah, of course! You know that."

"If I look like I'm not going to make it through a segment, make sure Ripley covers for me. Don't let the camera catch me in a moment of weakness."

"Marley, what happened?"

I couldn't bring myself to confess Andrew's full disclosure, but I really wanted to. "It's just something with Alex."

Rachel cringed.

"Andrew said she's fine. She's at his house and I'll head over there when I'm done here." I returned to my cubicle, the five-foot space I could call my own in the heart of the news room. I didn't even have privacy when I talked on the phone, since the cube walls stood as high as my shoulders when I sat in my chair. Fortunately tonight, I was nearly alone in the faintly lit room. I stared at the picture of Alex that was tacked onto the wall with a push pin. "How did this happen to you, baby girl?"

"Five minutes 'til air," Rachel whispered, peeking over the makeshift wall. She knew I was disconcerted and probably didn't want to smother me, but since I'd decided to go ahead with the show, it was her job to make sure I could follow through.

"In five, four, three, two . . . " the floor manager prompted me.

As soon as we were off the air, Rachel stood at the podium with my purse. "Go. Take care of Alex, and call me whenever you want to talk. Anytime. Really."

"Thank you," I mouthed. I didn't have the energy to speak. I could feel the tears beginning to melt from my eyes and I wanted to get out of the studio as soon as possible. I needed to get to Andrew's and see Alex. I knew I'd feel so much better after holding her tightly in my arms. There must have been some mistake. She's too smart to do something so stupid!

I called Andrew from the car. "I'm about ten minutes from your house."

"Take your time. We don't need another incident to deal with tonight."

"I know you're trying to keep me calm, but I've waited long enough to see Alex! You've had all afternoon with her."

"And she's right here waiting for you. She's on the couch in her PJ's, not going anywhere. By the way, Iris called when Alex didn't answer her calls. I didn't give her any details, but you'll have to figure out how you want to handle her."

"Dammit—you've been called twice today about our daughter! Last time I checked, my phone still works!"

"See you in a few," Andrew said calmly, and I threw my phone onto the passenger seat.

When I pulled into his driveway, I shook my head in dismay. The outdoor lights were on and the front yard was well groomed. The television illuminated enough of the family room to see them sharing couch space, comfortably slouched in their positions. On the outside, the scene looked lovely, but as much as I needed to see my baby, I wasn't looking forward to going inside.

Andrew met me at the door with a drink. I inhaled deeply and slowly shook my head.

"Mom?" Alex called out from the couch. "Aren't you coming in?"

"I'm here . . . hi," I smiled, stepping through the threshold. I dropped my things on the edge of the couch and sank into my daughter's space. I felt some unexpected tears drizzle from my eyes as I hugged her lovingly. The smell of her hair and body hadn't changed; she still smelled like my little girl. Her skin felt good. Wouldn't something seem different if she had drugs in her system?

I sat back a few inches, holding her shoulders with both hands. As we looked at one another, I wanted to believe that Alex had been truthful; completely honest about everything, without holding back to protect herself or anyone else. "Why don't we start from the beginning," I said, sliding off my shoes and cozying into the couch. "And before we even get to you specifically, can someone please explain the random selection for drug testing at school? I cannot believe this is happening without parent consent!"

"You actually did consent to it when you signed off on my athletic contract," Alex shrugged her shoulders. "It's not really any big deal. They just call you up to the P.E. office, you take the test, turn it in, and you're done."

I looked at Andrew for guidance; some kind of save. He was sitting on the coffee table with his legs between both of us. I was already behind the eight ball, unaware of my piece in all of this. Did I actually give consent for random drug testing? I sign things all the time for Alex, but do I read the fine print? Not to mention, my daughter looked completely unaffected and nonchalant. Finding the right words in response to every part of the conversation was going to be an unbelievable challenge for me. I'd have to find some way to keep my emotions in check.

PART 3

"I used to think the worst thing in life was to end up all alone, it's not. The worst thing in life is to end up with people who make you feel all alone."

—Robin Williams

CHAPTER 7

MARLEY

I HATE WAKING UP WITH this much anxiety. We're doing something today that I've never considered doing until three days ago. We're installing software on Alex's cell phone that will track all texts, emails, and photos, sending them to a website that Andrew and I can monitor in real time.

Of course, she's extremely upset about this change. I assume that her anger stems from a desire for privacy, but I know that she's still processing the fact that she tested positive for marijuana, still swearing that she's never tried it, and seemingly unaffected by a threatening text demanding money. It's a lot for anyone to grasp, including her parents, especially in such a short amount of time.

I'm not sure how long we'll enforce the use of the software, but for now, we're taking every precaution to keep her safe and make ourselves more aware of her social interactions. I hope she understands why we've decided to go this route. My travel schedule, in the next thirty days alone, will keep me away from many of her day-to-day activities. Andrew can't be with her all the time, and I never count on Iris, especially when I really need the help of someone responsible. Andrew and I agreed, however, to ask for assistance from Rachel if we needed her. She's so good at digging for information faster than anyone else we know.

I looked at the clock, noting exactly the same time I wake up each work day, yet my body feels like I haven't slept more than a couple of hours. I shuffled my way across the bedroom into the bathroom. Without intentionally looking at myself, I noticed my poor posture in the mirror. I really wanted to put on my robe and snuggle back into bed with a good book, but that was absolutely impossible. I knew that I wouldn't be spending a day like that until after the initial months of the T.A.D.A. campaign.

I changed my mind. I wasn't ready to shower.

I hadn't really talked to Alex about the drug testing results since we were at Andrew's, she has a whole lot going on in her head right now, and she just found out about the new phone surveillance. Even though morning isn't her best time of day, I wanted to try to get some time with her before school. The only way she'd get face time with me tonight is if she watched the evening news.

I opened my laptop to check emails and briefly viewed the headlines for the day. Feeling overwhelmed by the quantity of mail in my inbox, I scanned the addresses to see if there were any of immediate interest. I nearly jumped out of my seat when the stereo started bellowing downstairs. The floor beneath my seat suddenly vibrated to the beat of the Eagles' Hotel California.

"What the hell?" I said under my breath. I slid my chair backwards and headed downstairs. "Mother!" I yelled, pacing room by room, yet she was nowhere to be found. "Mother!" I called out again, getting more frustrated by the second. I noticed that the back door was open, but the screen was pulled shut. I stood at the threshold shaking my head in disbelief.

I let myself onto the back porch and she still didn't acknowledge my presence. With her hands immersed in a very damp flower bed, her face was protected by the brim of her floppy, yet stylish, hat. She wore a long cotton sundress, but covered her shoulders with an unbuttoned linen shirt. Completely inappropriate words ignited my mind, but for the sake of our neighbors and the reputation that I wanted to keep, I was able to muster a loudly whispered, "Mother!" as I put my bare foot into the potting soil where she was planting.

"Good morning, dear!" she said whimsically, burying my foot under the soil and patting my ankle.

"Mother," I said again, squatting down in front of her. "What are you doing?"

"My darling, I'm planting your spring flowers. If you weren't so uptight, you'd see it for what it is. I'm doing work that you have no interest in doing. I know you'll enjoy sitting on your porch and admiring your yard in full bloom."

"Yes, I will," I blurted in a not so kind manner. "But I don't enjoy being blasted out of my chair by the blaring of stereo speakers notched into the red zone at this time of day!"

"Lighten up, Marley. If your plate is too full, then maybe you should take a few things off. Give yourself permission to do something you enjoy each day—and I'm not talking about work."

"Where did that come from? I just came out here wondering why you were supplying the entire neighborhood with music from the 1970's at this time of day."

"No you didn't," Iris said, finally stopping her work and looking at me. "If that's true, then you would have turned off the stereo before you came stomping out here. You were ready to start a fight because you're tired, stressed, and pissed off about what happened with Alex."

I wasn't ready for that. I didn't have anything planned as a rebuttal. And, I wasn't ready to talk, either.

"I'm not stupid, Marley. And, I'm not a novice to what unplanned circumstances can spring on a person."

I stood up slowly and turned away from her. I needed to get ready for the day.

Alex was standing at the screen door. "Morning," she yawned.

"Hi, honey," I said, linking my arm in hers as I went back inside. "Let's make some breakfast."

———————

SOMEWHERE IN BETWEEN MY COLLEGE graduation and fortieth birthday, I transformed into a full-fledged adult, completely unaware that this crazy metamorphosis was happening to me. Distorted memories flashed in my mind as thumbnail-sized pictures, torturing me with discrepancies between then and now.

Not only has my role in life changed, but so has my mother's. She gave me life in this world, but honestly, the woman was irrational. Maybe I never realized the depth until she moved into my home, but for my own sanity, I had to figure out a way for her to live somewhere else.

"Please, please please, answer the phone!" I clenched my teeth, hoping Rachel would pick up.

"Hey, Marley," she said.

"Thank God!"

"What's going on? Where are you?"

"You are never going to believe the filth I just witnessed!" I said, deliberately slowing my words.

"Give it to me. I hope this is about Iris because you know she just cracks me up."

"You've got the first part right, but I don't think the rest is very funny!"

"Come into my office and tell me. I love to see you this heated up," she said, assuming I was still in the newsroom.

"I can't. I went home to get my lunch and my mother was *with* Marco on my living room couch. I will never be able to un-see that."

"No, she wasn't! As in *with* with?" Rachel blurted with excited amazement.

"That's exactly what I mean!"

"It's nice to see that she's still enjoying life, Marley."

Not the response I was looking for. "Yeah, it's great. But she needs to find another place to rendezvous besides my house!"

"What did she do when she realized you were home?"

"She didn't realize I was home. I just grabbed my lunch and got back in my car."

"So they could still be . . . ?"

"Ugh! I don't even want to think about it. I'm almost back to the station. I'll be at your office in five."

I pulled through the gate at the entrance of the parking lot, turned the corner and proceeded under the covered parking area. Taking in my surroundings, I felt a little disappointed. Is this what it feels like to make it in the professional world? Why don't I feel more accomplished? I'm a well-recognized local evening news anchor in a huge market, with a designated parking space. I'm launching a huge campaign for the network to raise awareness about prescription drug abuse, I have a beautiful daughter now in possession of two positive drug tests on record, and a mother who is draining every bit of my patience.

What's not to love?

I grabbed my lunch from the passenger seat and grumped back into the station, disgusted by the back-door entry that no one outside the business knows about, reminding me of yet another misconception regarding the glamor of life in television.

Rachel slid open the glass door of the editing room when she made eye-contact with me in the long hallway. Leaning into the metal door track, she tipped her head with a sly grin and flipped up the mouthpiece, headphones still resting on her ears.

"What?" I snapped.

"Have a seat. You've got to let this stuff roll off your shoulders more easily. You have far more pressing issues to worry about."

"Easy for you to say. She's not your mother."

"You're right. My mom's vacationing at a nudist resort in the Bahamas for three weeks."

"Ohmygod, I completely forgot! At least you don't have to watch her. It's one thing for a grown woman to live a promiscuous life of adventure and it's another thing to witness her in action."

"Are you going to be ready for the campaign promos?"

"When are we doing those?"

Checking her watch, and double checking the time on the newsroom clock, she said, "In about thirty-five minutes."

"I just need to eat and scan some smut on *Page Six* of the *New York Post*. I'll feel better when I read about someone else's life being more screwed up than mine."

"It's not that bad. Don't forget the good things you've got going for you."

"She's really wearing on me. I've got to find her a new place to live, and frankly, I don't care what it costs me. My mental health is more important than an extra few bucks in my checking account."

"I've never heard you say that, Marley. I'm proud of you."

"What do you mean?"

"You sound like you're finally getting a grip on how much you can handle and what you're going to do about it."

DAD KNEW. UGH . . . THE WORDS I hated hearing from my daughter. If he knew about it, then I have two questions: Why didn't he tell me? And furthermore, why did she tell him and not me? I don't know which question is more infuriating.

"It's not that big of a deal. I had some coding questions, and you know how good he is with computers. It's not like it was a big secret or anything," Alex said.

Oh, really? "I can imagine that a project of this size has taken you weeks, at least, to plan and execute. I feel like you've had adequate time to mention your position as the single ghost columnist for your school newspaper, at some point during the process."

"I guess," Alex shrugged, continuing to work on her laptop.

Now what? Trying to sound more genuinely interested than outwardly devastated, I asked, "Can you show it to me? Walk me through everything you created?"

"Sure, Mom. Just a sec."

More waiting. I checked my phone after hearing an email notification. From Rachel, nothing in the subject line. I opened the email to find contact information for a licensed counselor. Really? I slid my readers onto the mid-section of my nose, clarifying the font. The name looked familiar, but I'm not sure how or why. I highlighted and selected the counselor's name, pasted it into my web browser, and viola! Harper Havens, focusing on interpersonal therapy and stress management for women. Like a filmstrip in my mind, images flashed from the segment interview I facilitated on-set several years ago.

"Okay, ready?" Alex asked.

"Yes—yes I am. Let me just send a quick reply to this email." I sent Rachel one word, then I realized that I just put my daughter on hold for meaningless sarcasm. Sometimes I felt like smart phones should remind the user to be smart instead of acting so stupid.

"So basically, the site is a platform for students from our school to have conversations about student-interest or campus-related topics. Things they like, don't like, want to know more about. They can write and share freely, as long as the dialogue isn't harmful to others or name-specific. Each user has a registered ID, but the screen name can be something more cryptic; a way to have an identity without being recognized. The user decides on an alias or a more obvious screen name."

I was in awe of my sixteen-year-old baby. "You did all this?" Her ideas had come to life on the World Wide Web and I knew nothing about any of it. In fact, I'd still be in the dark if it weren't for that damn spyware we put into her phone.

She smiled, the same beautiful smile since the permanent teeth came through. "It's cool. I got a little help here and there, but the ideas were mine. I've been learning this stuff since I was twelve, Mom. It just seemed to make sense."

Twelve. It was only a few years ago, but as I noticed her perfectly applied makeup and the animal print bra strap peeking out from the neck of her sweatshirt, it seemed like a lifetime ago.

"Can I set up an account so I can keep up with the column? This is amazing!"

My girl chuckled. "Actually, no. Student IDs or staff ID numbers are required, so that everything can be tracked. But, you can read it anytime. You just can't post your own comments or respond to any that are there."

Exhale. I'm relieved that access wasn't denied by my daughter. "So that means someone from the school staff is reading and checking the site all the time?"

She was clicking and double-clicking, moving and rearranging all the while that I talked to her. "Actually, since it's linked through the online newspaper, the advisor is technically *in charge* of the site. But, several of us are supposed to monitor and report if we catch things that appear harmful or inappropriate. We're not allowed to address the person directly."

"I agree with that completely. My guess is that you want to remain anonymous and not get yourself into a situation that could lead to dissension."

Alex nodded, keeping her eyes on the screen. "I wasn't sure how long it'd take to get this up and running, but it's been fun."

I studied her for a few moments, intent on *her* project. "Do you ever comment on the site?"

"Sometimes."

"Does anyone know it's you?"

Alex pierced her lips, squinted one eye, and scrunched her nose. "I haven't told anyone my screen name, if that's what you're asking."

"O-kay," I said in slow motion.

"Are you asking me to tell you?"

"Well, if you're willing to give me access to your sign-in and password, then I'd find out eventually."

Alex slid the sticky notepad toward the laptop, and grabbed a pen from the canister. She wrote the information in perfect penmanship. "I can change this at anytime, so keep it safe, and don't share it with your viewers," she teased.

"I'm so proud of you," I said, going in for a hug.

"Thanks, Mom."

I left Alex to continue her work and looked at the email again. Phoning Rachel was faster.

"Good. You got my message," she greeted.

"I did. Now tell me why you're getting involved. You've got your own teenager to worry about."

It was quiet on the line for a second or two. "Just a minute, okay?" Rachel said. A bit of commotion was followed by calm. "What are you saying about Morgan," she asked in a lowered voice?

"I'm just saying that our girls are teens, of course they will have things they need to work through. Especially our girls, who live part time with a mom and part time with a dad. I just don't think Alex needs counseling right now. She seems to be doing fine."

Rachel howled in laughter. "Just when I thought you were ready, you're still resisting. I didn't send the counselor information for Alex. It's for you!" she blared.

I walked myself rapidly to the back porch, sliding the door behind me and bringing my voice to a near whisper. "Me? What do you mean, me? I don't need a counselor. Why would I need a counselor?"

"Hmmm, how many reasons would be sufficient? You've got a list a mile long and most of the reasons have something to do with the people in your life that you're closest to, aside from me, of course. Just the ones that make you crazy."

"Seriously, Rachel? Suddenly, I've graduated from needing counseling to needing it *because I'm crazy*?" I felt a whole lot of eye rolling and head shaking coming on.

"You know that's not what I meant."

I couldn't come up with a single appropriate word in response.

"Marley, you're one of the smartest women I've ever known. This shouldn't be a surprise to you. If you're honest with yourself, you'll agree. It's time."

"Good night, Rachel." And that was that.

———————

THE FAMILIAR SCENTS OF BREAKFAST ascended the staircase and wafted under the doorway of my room. First and foremost, the identifiable smell of bacon prevailed. Eyes still closed, my senses heightened. I envisioned waffles and hash browns stacked beneath a tower of foil-covered foods, lying in wait for the last egg to poach. I snoozed my internal clock for ten more minutes when I'd rise from a cozy slumber and join the chefs downstairs. Alex and Iris made weekend breakfasts a regular tradition, quite differently than when I was a teen.

"Just in time!" Alex announced, catching a glimpse of me at the base of the stairs while gracefully executing her kitchen duties. She positioned a plate on the table for herself next to a tall glass of orange juice and took a moment to admire her work.

"Help yourself, sleepyhead," Iris said.

"Everything looks delicious!" I pulled my disheveled hair into a ponytail. I could nearly taste the maple syrup as I drizzled a thin line into each square of the waffle, careful not to miss a single one. I'd repeated the same ritual for as long as I could remember, though waffles had become less frequent and more of a splurge. When I sat next to Alex, I noted that she'd done the same. Out of curiosity, I took a peek at Iris's plate. Was she still doing it, too? Aside from the extra pats of butter that took over the top layer, she also trickled syrup into each square.

"So what's the plan for today?" I asked.

Alex shrugged and chewed at the same time, suggesting she was open to suggestions.

"I was thinking about going over to my storage unit, if either of you would like to join me," said Iris.

"Really? What are you looking for?" Marley asked.

"Actually," Iris said, pausing to finish her bite. "I'm sorting and getting rid of a few things."

I swallowed hard, holding back a sarcastic laugh. "My mother. The queen of holding on to treasures of all kinds. I'm having a hard time believing that you're even thinking about purging, let alone actually following through with the idea. You just finished filling it with the leftovers from your mobile storage unit."

"Thank you for your vote of confidence," she sneered. "If you must know, I've been thinking about it for quite some time, and really, since I've been living here with you two, I haven't had a need for much of what I've been storing. I certainly can't take any of it with me."

"Where are you going?" Alex said, squinting her eyes. Had she missed a conversation?

I smirked in the background, giving Iris a chance to explain herself.

"It's just a phrase. I'm referring to a long time from now, you know, after my time here is done."

"Grandma! Eww."

"I'm happy to go with you," I said. "Are you thinking of getting rid of the unit entirely?"

"Well, eventually. For now, I was wondering if any of the furniture in there could be sold. Online maybe?"

"I can take pictures. It's easy to post things for sale online. We can set up an account just for you, Grandma."

"What are you going to do with the things you wouldn't necessarily sell, but don't need anymore?" Marley asked.

"Like things you consider trash?" Iris glared.

"More like donations: clothing you haven't worn in years,

holiday decorations, stuff like that."

"We'll have to see when we get there."

I looked at the clock. I figured we'd get to the storage unit in an hour and a half or so, after breakfast and a bit of cleaning. We'd probably spend at least two hours there, maybe three. On the drive home, I'd mention the date planned with Dax later tonight.

He took me by surprise when he showed up at the station to do a pre-taped interview with sports commentator, Chris Dalton. Once their camera stopped rolling, the two spent the next twenty minutes catching up off-camera in Chris's neck of the woods. I figured that he'd stroll by my desk, close enough to wave on his way out, but he actually approached me directly, pulling up a chair to propose dinner out for Saturday night.

I agreed, and then Dax raised his brows curiously. He plopped his palm on my desk with a smile; a few heads turned in our direction.

"Good. I'll pick you up at seven."

I expressed a pleasing smile. "Perfect," I said softly.

We arrived at the storage unit just under an hour after finishing breakfast. With precise right, left, right turns, Alex opened the combination lock on the unit door as fast as any kid with a school locker.

"We're in," she announced, lifting the door to roll on casters.

"You've obviously been here recently, Mother," I declared, noticing far less quantity than the last time I accompanied her. At least three months had passed, but I had no idea she'd been here without me.

"Let's just stick to the furniture today," Iris suggested. "We can carry each piece out to the drive, take a picture of it, and Alex can handle the technical stuff. Maybe you two can help me with a price range and we'll go from there."

Alex and I inched a rolltop desk toward the door. We remembered it being extremely heavy from the move into the storage unit, but at that time, we had the help of a wheeled dolly and a couple of guys who helped with the move.

"Can we take this thing apart so it isn't so heavy?" Alex asked.

"I'm sure you can," yelled Iris from deeper in the unit. "But I have no idea how."

Alex wiggled under the leg opening, able to unscrew two bolts that held down the top from underneath. I lifted the lid and found one bolt on each corner, both loosely fastened. Standing one at each end, we lifted the roll-top and carried it to the drive. All by itself, it was still quite heavy.

We returned to the base and carried it using full strength, positioning it as close to the top as possible. Together, we lifted the top onto the base to take the picture and a standard sized photograph floated to the ground. Alex scooped it up and stuffed it into her back pocket without giving it more than a glance.

"What is that?" I asked.

"It fell out of Grandma's desk."

"Can I see it?"

"Yeah, sure." Alex pulled it out without pausing to take a closer look.

I studied the picture quizzically.

"Mom!" I called. "Is this me?"

We approached one another, meeting near the middle of the poorly-lit unit.

Iris held it farther from her face, trying to focus on the yellowed paper. To no avail, she walked toward the sunlight; both Alex and I by her side.

"Yes, of course that's you." she said.

"Then, who's holding me?"

Iris smiled. "All those years ago, there were a lot of people around; all the time. We were enjoying life and living it to the fullest," she laughed. "I'm sure we'll find a lot of things in here from back then. It's part of the reason why I want to go through this stuff. If I can't tell you the stories, then you'll never know what you're looking at."

I began to feel a bit nauseous by Iris's sudden sentimentality. At a young age, before I even realized what my mind would remember, I had a keen sense that I wasn't my mother's first priority. I had no interest in rummaging through the past.

YOU HAVE NO IDEA HOW much time I've spent imagining myself in different outfits to find just the right one, sitting at tables we might share together in different restaurants, rehearsing conversations we might engage in with one another over dinner or drinks. If that's any indication of how long its been since I've actually been in a respectable dating relationship, then you'll understand completely when I tell you that I was wrong on each and every account—at least in reference to Dax.

I'd pushed him off as long as possible and I needed to give him a chance. Even in the midst of everything that had been going on with Alex and my mother, there was something about him that I just couldn't dismiss.

We agreed that he'd pick me up at my place, so I was compelled to chat with my daughter before he arrived.

"You've been a little giddy each time we've talked about him," I said, hoping to gauge an appropriate starting point for our conversation.

Of course, she smiled before any words made their way out of her mouth. "How can I not be giddy, Mom? He's kind of a

VIP and everyone knows him."

I tipped my head toward her. "Everyone might know his name. They know how he played football. Those things don't have anything to do with who he really is."

"You know what I mean," Alex said.

"I just wonder what you and I should clarify before I leave with him tonight."

"What do you mean?"

"I'm talking about discretion."

"The night he picked you up for the Phoenix launch party, you made your expectations very clear."

I laughed, and she was right. "You know as well as I do that I don't have much control over media photographers, but I'd like to think that my own daughter won't be posting references on social media about her mother's whereabouts, her company, or distorted cell phone pictures."

"Just so we're clear, you're referencing tonight and any other time you're with him, right?" Alex asked.

"Of course and exactly," I answered, smiling.

Alex began laughing hysterically.

"What is so funny?"

Once she settled herself, she said, "You're being so weird, Mom! He's just a guy. You're the one who's forgetting that you're both allowed to have a life."

"I really hope he turns out to be who I think he is," I admit. I scrunched my face at nearly the same time the doorbell rang.

"You look great. Don't worry about a thing! Where are you going, anyway?"

"I'm not telling you," I grumbled, omitting the fact that I didn't have a clue where he was taking me.

"C'mon. Dax doesn't want to hang out with a grouch. He's a football superstar, remember? He can get any girl he wants."

"You're not hel-ping," I sang.

Alex ran ahead of me and put her back against the front door. "I'm just kidding. He obviously wants to spend time with you, or he wouldn't have done everything he's done to get your attention. Now put on your game face and have a good time," she ordered, putting her finger up to her lips and silencing me until she made it upstairs.

I opened the door and greeted Dax. He looked fantastic in crisp denim jeans and a tight black t-shirt. I must've smiled because he returned one and said hello in a voice that resonated in me like comfort food.

"Hi," was all I could reply, trying to tone-down my grin.

Once in his car, he adjusted the air conditioning and backed out of the driveway heading somewhere that made no difference to me. I was nervous, but more excited and content than anything else. Being with him felt comfortable. He was down-to-earth, easy-going, gentlemanly. Our conversation was light, but I'm a little fuzzy on the details.

"And, we're here," he announced, turning off the car.

I looked around, counting three horses in an area off to the left, and a gravel path on the right, leading to a restaurant over-looking the city. The strapless dress, bolero sweater, and heels I wore would've been a great choice for a different date. But, as my daughter emphasizes to me on a daily basis, I need to *relax and go with the flow*." Dax appeared at the passenger side, opening my door and extending his hand.

"You look stunning," he said.

"Thank you," I laughed. "I think I picked the wrong outfit for tonight."

"Why? Are you worried about your shoes?" he asked.

"Not really."

"Then, let's go," he said, whisking me away from the car and over to the path. "Have you been here before?"

"No, but I've wanted to check it out."

"Good. We'll check it out together," indicating a first for him, too. He moved his hand from my lower back to my hand as we walked in together claiming our reservation for two. We sat across from one another at a quaint table next to the window, where the sun set in our midst and the city lights resumed their place in the night sky. We were the last to leave; my body intoxicated with a peaceful excitement and a hunger to learn more about the real Dax Townsend.

As we drove home, my mind wandered. My brain created a checklist between Dax and Andrew. I didn't want to compare them, but it seemed that my head was doing the work on its own. Dax noticed when I shook my head, trying to erase the etch-a-sketch image and clean the slate.

"Marley?" he sounded concerned.

"I got caught up in my thoughts, but I'm back now," I smiled.

He drove the rest of the way with his left hand on the wheel, holding mine with his right. The light on the front porch was lit, and my teenage girl was waiting for me on the couch when I came inside.

"Fabulous?" she asked nonchalantly.

"Fabulous," I replied, plopping down next to her, sharing her bowl of popcorn, so thankful and relieved.

ALEX

IT DIDN'T SEEM TO MATTER how early I woke up to get online and check the feed, I always felt ten steps behind. Consistent sleep deprivation would only make my life more difficult and I was already beginning to feel the effects. Lack of sleep had always affected my moods, but over the years I've learned to mask the fluctuation. It wasn't a risk I was willing to take—yet, at least. Six o'clock in the morning was the earliest I could handle, unless I changed my bedtime. The window would have to be altered on both ends if I wanted to commit to a change, but staying up late worked better for now.

I'd kept up with the daily routine, first reading the newsfeed from comments posted after I powered down for bed. I knew I wasn't alone as an early reader, based on the number of commenting peers who were obviously doing the same thing. That didn't include the silent observers who never posted anything, but stayed in the loop by reading everything on their screens.

I wanted, *needed*, a few more minutes in bed, choosing a small screen over my laptop. I reached for my cell phone on the nightstand. Logging in took a matter of seconds; not long enough to focus my vision through sleepy eyes. Nevertheless, I powered through the blurry terrain, eventually retrieving the most talked about topic on campus, the *DogEar* post of the day. I propped onto my elbow, bringing the phone closer to my face. Each day recorded an increased number of responses, growing in popularity and interest.

Last week, the *Los Angeles Times* revealed that drug deaths have exceeded traffic fatalities for the first time. Does this fact impact your beliefs on drug use?

I promised myself that I'd never comment on a *DogEar* post until at least noon. Why? For no real rhyme or reason, except for a whole host of random thoughts: not appearing too eager, weighing my thoughts against others, giving myself time to decide whether I'd post an honest answer or a comment that might trigger more discussion, simply responding to someone else's comment, not looking like *one of those* who always has something to say or likes commenting first; typical teenage logic.

Noon came and went, but I wasn't sure if I was ready for complete honesty and full disclosure. It was no secret that plenty of peers took pills for a wide range of things from sports injuries to mood stabilizers and ADHD to anti-some-thing-or-other. I wasn't ready to post about random drug testing in schools. I couldn't even answer for my own drug test results, and the difference between legitimate prescriptions and unprescribed *legal* drugs was more than a one-answer question. Some pills carried less stigma than others, while sports injuries seemed to hold a high esteem; something that was hard to comprehend. Were athletes placed on the same level as heroes and philanthropists? I made my decision. I wasn't ready for honesty, but I was willing to comment by way of a newspaper article quote.

> Not all drug use is illegal and dangerous. Unfortu-nately, drugs used responsibly, under the care of a physician, still fall into the same category as those used in unintentional drug overdose, coined by the media as *Pharmageddon*.

I read it twice, looked away from the screen and then read it a third time. Once I clicked SHARE, I knew it was out there. I could delete it, but everyone who'd already commented would read the response in their notifications anyway. The comment didn't point directly at me specifically, but I wondered if people would respond.

Before the end of the school day, just two hours after my posted comment, another thirty comments followed. Some people agreed, others fessed up to a genuine fear, and I knew there were many opinions that readers would never write.

On our way to dinner that evening, I focused on the road,

trying to decide if I wanted to tell Mom about the online discussion. After all, as a local ambassador for drug abuse education and prevention, she'd probably have a few insights for sharing in such a large forum.

Over fried rice and orange chicken, we talked about the day and ate with chopsticks. Mom asked a million questions and wanted to know how people responded. "You're practicing reporting skills," she approved. "Anything you say should stand alone, without a hint of opinion, affirmation, or disapproval. Your comments are your own, though, separate from writing as the page developer?" she smirked. "If your opinion is important to you, then it shouldn't matter whether others agree or disagree. I wouldn't want you to refrain from sharing. Isn't that one of the reasons you wanted to create this page?"

I signed in to the site again after dinner. The discussion was still growing. My opinion was just one in a hundred or so. Tomorrow would present a new issue. I'd have to choose a position and whether or not to share it publicly.

MARLEY

I BARRELED INTO THE HOUSE with both arms full of groceries, including the margarita mix I planned to use as soon as possible. The door from the garage into the house dumped me into the laundry room and then the long hallway.

It registered that Iris's door was open. I was in a hurry to unload and yelled, "Hello, Mother," and continued toward the kitchen. I didn't hear a response, but didn't really expect one, either. Iris had withdrawn a bit since selling some of her things from the storage shed, spending more time closed up in her room. She's very good at pouting, and since I may have snapped at her recently, I decided to let her sulk in solitude.

I came through the door with another load of groceries, this time noticing a large brown box resting on the edge of her dresser. "Mother?" I called, but again, she didn't answer. I peeked around the half-closed door, still holding my grocery bags. I could see the light on inside her walk-in closet, along with several larger boxes stacked along the perimeter of her room.

I tossed the bags onto her bed and stepped into her closet. She was kneeling on the floor, placing shoes into a larger box. "Mother?"

"Yes," she said without looking up at me.

"What are you doing?"

"It can't be too hard to figure out, Marley. I'm packing my things."

"Since when?"

"You haven't been very forthcoming lately. And furthermore, I didn't ask for your approval."

I wanted to stand up for myself; justify my recent behavior. I wanted to tell her that she was overbearing and it was an adjustment for all of us to have her living in our house. I wanted to tell her how disappointed I've been in her, that she wasn't helping me out as much as I'd hoped she would. But she was right. I haven't been open to conversation. She doesn't need my approval. And, my expectations for her were probably unrealistic, since I never actually sat down and discussed them from the beginning.

I squatted down a few feet from where she was sitting.

"It's time, Marley. You have a teenage girl who needs your full attention when you're home and you've been distracted with me here."

I'd attributed my recent moodiness to the extra work associated with the campaign. The trip to New York kept me away for only a few days, but I still wasn't finished with research, promotions, and scripts. I felt like my mind had been reeling at warp speed during the last months of preparation. I filled each unaccounted moment with thoughts about my role in the campaign, frustration with Iris, concern for Alex, and possibilities with Dax. Whether I was at home or at work, in my car or elsewhere, I tossed around ideas. I kept my spiral notebook with me at all times to jot things down and try to make sense of things.

The absence of Andrew was likely affecting my moods, as well. At the beginning, when we established that we were pretty much done, but not ready to permanently split, I knew we couldn't continue living together. But we've been doing this on-again/off-again thing for years until fairly recently, and for the first time, I have a potentially real and legitimate interest in another man. All that aside, co-parenting is hard, no matter how you look at it. I wish it wasn't even a factor. But it is, and at least for a little longer, it will remain.

"You don't have to move out," I tried saying gently. Did I mean it?

She continued packing.

"Where are you going?"

"I found a nice condo a few miles from here."

"When do you plan on leaving?" I asked, startled by the fact that she already had an entire plan in motion and this was the first time I'd heard anything about it.

She braced herself on the closet wall and stood up, pushing the box of shoes past me and into her bedroom. "Hopefully, I'll be settled by the end of next week."

I followed her into the bedroom and picked up the bags of groceries. "What can I do to help?"

Iris shrugged her shoulders. "I think I've got everything covered."

"When do you want to tell Alex?"

"Why don't you just tell her for me. No need to make it a big deal."

"Let's eat dinner together tonight. I can make something special and you can tell us all about your new place."

"Marley, that's entirely unnecessary. You have lives of your own. I won't be too far away, but I'll be out of your hair. You've never approved of my ways, anyway."

She was right, again, but why does she always make me feel so guilty for having my own opinions? We don't have to agree on things all the time in order to carry on cordially.

As much as I talked about it, I wasn't sure she'd actually leave. It felt like it was time for her to move on, and probably time for me to face the facts. The only thing I could really wrap my mind around at that moment was sitting on the patio with an ice cold margarita.

———

I SLUMPED OVER MY DESK after completing a grueling hour of shooting and re-shooting promos for the campaign, allowing myself to fume over my mother. Rachel waved to me through the glass doors of her editing booth.

"Hi," I said, holding the sling-backs of my heels through my fingers.

"You look exhausted!"

"I know. The reality of my mother's new life plan is really bothering me, and I can give you two dozen reasons why, if you're really interested."

"Listen, we can talk about that later. Do you have time to sit for a minute?"

"Yeah. What's up?"

"You left your phone on my desk while you were filming in the studio. A notification came up from Alex's phone about a meeting with someone, only initials, and it seemed kind of cryptic."

"What are the initials?"

"They're JAC."

I thought about the letters, but nothing solid came to mind.

"Thanks for telling me. The way things are going, I may not have seen it for awhile."

Rachel handed over the phone.

I read the details for myself. "I really don't know what to make of it."

"I can't figure out if it's just Alex or a group meeting up."

"What day is today?" I wondered out loud, though I didn't need Rachel's help. It just took me a minute to focus. "It's Friday. There's a game tonight. Where are they playing?"

Using a second screen, Rachel looked up the high school's football schedule, verifying tonight's game at HOME, starting at seven.

"What time is it right now?" I asked. "If I remember correctly, the last concerning text she got was on a game day, too."

"It's almost five-thirty."

I had to be back on the air for the six o'clock broadcast.

"I'm going to try getting in touch with Alex right now," I said, leaving Rachel's booth and darting toward my cubicle.

My phone vibrated in my hand. Two missed calls, the screen said. Scanning through my incoming call list, I noticed that both were from Andrew. I pierced my lips, a bit surprised, since he rarely called during my shift. He left one message.

"Marley, hey. Uh . . . do you have time to meet me for dinner between your six and nine tonight? Call me."

That was strange. Maybe he talked to Alex.

I dialed Alex's cell, hoping I wouldn't have to track her down elsewhere.

"Mom?" she answered on the third ring.

"Hi, honey. How are you?"

"Fine."

"Hey, I just wanted to check in about your plans for tonight."

"Oh, okay. I'm surprised to hear from you this close to your show."

I paused, hoping to piece together a string of non-judgmental words. "Hon, I don't want to sound too overprotective, but I'm concerned."

"About what?" Alex asked. Her tone expressed a slight irritation.

"The text you got about a meet-up tonight. I can't make out who's going to be there."

After a slight silent pause, Alex tried to clear things up. "Oh, you're talking about the JAC meeting?"

"Right. Should I know those letters?" I asked, sheepishly.

"Mother, you're not still worried about me, are you? I know we never got solid answers about the drug test results or the weird text that Dad saw, but everything is fine now. JAC is the Journalism Advisory Council. It's high school kids in journalism from both high schools that meet up under the home-team bleachers during half time to just talk and introduce ourselves."

"Thanks, that clears things up."

"Hey, Mom, Toby's calling. Are we good?"

"As long as you touch base with me when you're leaving the game tonight."

"Promise!" Alex committed.

I called Andrew, hoping to keep it brief.

"I just wanted to tell you that I'm tailing Toby tonight. Something's off, and I'm going to be there to find out what it is."

"What makes you think something's off?" I asked.

"He was at the house with Alex and I told him that I'd seen him come out of Marco's office."

I closed my eyes. "And?"

"He tried to keep his cool and act like it was no big deal. But he doesn't know what I know."

"That you're just like him with your big talk and egotistical confidence?"

"I'll take that as a compliment."

I could almost see Andrew's big grin through the phone.

"So what'd you get out of him?"

"He said his mom borrowed money from Curtis, Marco's bartender, and he dropped off a payment for her."

"Did she verify that for you?" I pushed.

"I'm working on Cypress. In the mean time, I'm tailing Toby."

"Keep me posted. Alex will be at the game tonight and I don't want her in any kind of danger."

"I hear you," he stressed. "At the very least, I'll be nearby."

And that was that. What started out as confusion ended in confusion, for the time being. At least for the time being. I headed back to work; my head took over and completed everything on autopilot. I felt another transformation taking place, morphing into a new normal, again. I was not okay with it. Not at all.

CHAPTER 8

ANDREW

S PRING DAYS PROMISED MORE THAN great weather and predictably brought people outdoors. Flick was exactly where he said he'd be at the precise time I pulled up next to the curb. He wore an olive-colored bucket hat, carried a bag on his left shoulder, and a giant telephoto lens in his right hand.

"Anything yet?" I called from the passenger window.

"Nope," Flick answered, keeping his eyes on Toby, from his position behind a picnic table.

I pulled away to canvas the park from a different angle.

Toby greeted Alex with an affectionate hug; his face buried in the side of her neck, unusually gloomy. They held hands, strolling leisurely to the picnic dinner that Toby positioned on a couple of blankets in the grass. They sat together leaving the food untouched, waiting, it seemed.

I spotted Alex with animal instincts, drawn to her location

as soon as she arrived. I parked the Prius across the street and jaywalked to the park, concealing myself as best I could. My phone chimed with a text from Flick.

SURPRISE GUEST

I panned the park to decipher Flick's cue. "Son of a bitch," I mumbled, identifying Cypress as the mystery companion. Flick must've recognized her from the showdown on Coconut Trail. She shuffled to Toby and Alex's location and planted herself like dead-weight on one of Toby's blankets. Looking tense, she folded her arms around both knees and rocked back and forth.

I repositioned myself near a shaved-ice trailer. Plenty of kids milled around the front window with their parents. I figured it was a good place to go unnoticed, still aligned with Toby, Alex, and now Cypress.

They sat without words or eye contact for what seemed to me like ten minutes. Flick and I agreed that Cypress became fidgety when Marco approached their picnic area.

"Marco? What the hell is Marco doing here?" I brooded. Neither of the kids appeared as if it was a first-time meeting. Alex only knew him by name, I thought. My emotions escalated to intense concern. All I knew for sure was that Marco was a bar owner who came to the U.S. within the last five to ten years, and was involved with Iris at the present time. Now I questioned Marco's link not only to crazy Cypress, but to two high school kids. And not just any kids, one—my own daughter.

My phone chimed with another text from Flick.

SIT TIGHT. LET ME DOCUMENT THIS.
WALK AWAY IF YOU NEED TO.

Marco opened the lawn chair he carried into the park. He took a seat facing Cypress, Toby, and Alex, folding his arms across his chest. From my position, they all remained silent, until Toby looked at Alex. She handed him a small vinyl food cooler, which he held with both hands.

Cypress looked at Marco, biting her bottom lip. Even from my distance, she looked like she was trying to hurt herself, unrelenting with a strong bite. Alex handed the cooler to Marco, flashing both of his empty hands in the air, as if to say, *That's it.*

Marco stood, folded his chair, and flung the cooler strap over his shoulder. He left the park the same way he entered, appearing unaware of me on his left and Flick across the grass on his right. Cypress walked away from Toby, meandering to an open playground swing. She looked shockingly mellow.

Flick closed the trunk of his sedan as I pulled into the parking spot on his driver's side. He shook his head and flashed an amused grin. "Where do you want to meet? I'd say *The Lounge* is out," he couldn't contain his laughter.

"Yeah, you're right on that one. How about the station?"

Flick stopped laughing. "As in, my station? Marley's? The place of our employment? I'm not sure that's a good idea, bud. I have a feeling that Marley's gonna have a few words when she finds out what just went down. I vote for neutral territory."

"You just want to send me the pictures?"

Flick thought about it a minute. "You know what, just take the memory card. It was fun, but you probably have what you need." He opened the trunk and removed the card from the camera. He leaned in through the passenger window. "Good luck with this. I hope it's enough."

I pulled the cash from my wallet and handed it to him. "It's been a pleasure, man. I really appreciate this." I put the car in reverse, but called out to Flick one more time. "Dude, as much as I know you'd enjoy telling this story around the station, what do you say about giving me some time to handle everything with Marley first? Can you do that?"

"You betcha," Flick agreed. He pointed a finger at Andrew and clicked his tongue against his teeth.

IRIS

"SHE WASN'T SUPPOSED TO BE involved in this!" I roared when Marco closed the door to the car.

"My darling, how was I to know she'd attend the meeting? I can't control her whereabouts or the people she chooses as companions," Marco retorted.

I backed out of the parking space abruptly, nearly causing a side swipe with another vehicle. "Dammit!" I griped. "I'm so upset right now, I can hardly see straight. That's my grand-daughter, Marco. Where's your tact?"

He turned his head to the left like a marionette. "And how do you think I should have handled the situation?"

"Jeezus, I don't know. Ask her to leave while you handle the business, tell the kid it wasn't what you'd planned, make that crazy woman handle her own trouble instead of putting it on her son?"

"My love, it's easy for you to say. It hasn't been your money owed for more than a month. Business is business, and it can't continue without payment or consequence. You know that."

"Yes, I know that. But I also know that my granddaughter doesn't need to be caught up in any of this, including the fact that she now can piece together who you are, along with putting a face to your name."

"I don't see why that's a problem," Marco disagreed.

"And for that very simple answer, my dear, I bid you

farewell." I pulled into *The Lounge* parking lot, allowed Marco to kiss the top of my hand, and exit the car with a gentle smile.

"It's been a pleasure," he said, blowing one more kiss through the opened window. "I will miss you."

ANDREW

I HAD EVERY INTENTION OF driving straight to Marley's television station with the memory card from Flick's camera. I wanted to show her that I'd been right about Toby all along. But as the minutes passed at each red light, my surprise that Marco was involved turned to anger. And Cypress, damn! I knew she was off, I just couldn't put my finger on it.

Marley could wait. The truth wouldn't change whether I went straight to her or waited until after a couple of conversations. First, I needed to touch base with Alex. She answered after the third ring.

"Hey, Dad."

"Honey! I'm glad you answered. What are you doing?"

"Nothing, really," she said, taking a few seconds to finish chewing. "I'm just getting a quick dinner with Toby before we head over to the game."

"Oh, okay. I didn't know if plans changed."

Not the answer I was hoping for, but glad to hear her voice. She didn't offer any details or mention where they were eating, but I knew. Knowing she hadn't seen me was a relief and hearing her calm voice reminded me of her innocence. I wondered if she asked any questions about Marco or just believed the explanations Toby and Cypress gave her. She took after Marley when it came to giving people the benefit of the doubt, with the exception of Iris, of course. While Alex seemed to be her grandmother's biggest fan, Marley still believed that

her mother would never be more than a narcissistic, independent, self-centered woman.

I parked the Prius behind *The Lounge*, knowing the back
door would be propped open with a keg on a beautiful
afternoon like today. Four other cars sat haphazardly in the
alley. I entered without a knock or a smile, welcomed not by
Marco, but by Cypress, seated in a metal folding chair behind a
bucket of white bar towels.

"What in the hell?" I asked, pulling the sunglasses from my
eyes.

Cypress looked exhausted, still managing to look manipu-
lative.

"You're still messing around with this guy?"

"You don't know nothin' about me. You got rid of me too
fast to find out, you jerk." she sneered, placing the folded
towels across her lap.

Marco entered the room from the bar. "Well, look who's
here. Andrew Donovan, radio-personality extraordinaire. To
what do I owe this great pleasure?"

"You son-of-a-bitch," I growled, shaking my head in
disgust.

Marco took a seat behind the heavy wooden desk,
grimacing with one raised cheek, squinting an eye.

"I should've known you were bad news when you offered to
take Iris to South America with you."

"Who's Iris?" Cypress chimed.

Unsure if her inquiry stemmed from jealousy or curiosity, I
didn't really care. "You know what?" I asked. "I didn't come
here to talk about Iris. I came here to ask what kind of business
you do with kids."

Cypress closed her eyes and looked away.

Marco folded his hands. "Andrew," his voice condescending. "You must have me confused with someone else.

What are you speaking of?"

I placed my hands on the front of his desk, leaning in as far as I could retain balance. "You're dealing drugs and using this place as a front!"

Marco looked at me and then took a long look at Cypress. She stared back as long as she could, but knew she didn't have willpower to outlast Marco.

"Andrew, I provide services to my patrons, just as you frequent this establishment for food and beverages with the intent to receive the services you desire."

"You took money from her son!" pointing toward Cypress. "Don't sit there and try to deny it or twist it into some other bullshit story."

Cypress took a hard look at me. "You've never liked my kid from day one. You keep him out of it."

"So you're going to protect this asshole now?" I shook my head again. "I don't get you people. He screws you royally and then you protect him. Where's the sense in that?"

Marco smiled, seemingly enjoying the banter between Cypress and me. "And you think what you're doing is okay?" I asked him.

"Andrew, sit. Please," he gestured to one of the two chairs in front of his desk.

"I don't want to sit. I'm not even sure I want to know what you have to say, you piece of shit."

Marco responded in a controlled tone. "My final offer: you stop the name calling and vulgar assumptions or you walk yourself right out the door while you still can."

I hesitated for a moment, wondering if any truth would come from me staying to listen to another word of his exaggerations. "Fine. Here's an offer: Don't ever do business with my daughter present."

"How do you know about that?" Cypress snapped.

Marco glared sternly at her.

"What are you still doing with this guy?" I asked her. "He's no good. You could just walk away from him and this whole mess."

"No one's forcing her to remain here, Andrew. You're misinformed."

"Then tell me, Cypress, what's the draw? Why this guy?" I asked, hoping for a hint of decent reasoning.

She dropped her head, willing to confess the truth. "I borrowed money and I have to pay him back."

Marco rendered his hands like a magician who'd performed a tantalizing trick.

At least the story was consistent with Toby's. And that was all it took for me to recognize the end of my time in that back room of lies. I loathed Marco even more than when I walked through the door to his office. I needed to figure out the next best plan of action.

On my way back to the car I wondered if Iris knew the extent of Marco's business endeavors. And dammit, if she did, she will have hell to pay.

I left *The Lounge* and drove straight to the television station, calling Rachel en route.

"Hey, I'm on my way over. Can you slip out and meet me in the back lot without being seen?"

"Probably. What's up?" she asked.

"Just meet me in five and don't tell Marley. I'll tell you everything in the car," I explained.

I spotted Flick perched on the back bumper of the news van scrolling the screen of his cell phone. I pulled up next to him and rolled down my window.

"Hey, thanks again for your help earlier!"

Flick stood and approached my car, slipping the phone into his back pocket. "I love surveillance! I'd do it again in a heartbeat," he confessed.

Rachel descended the concrete steps from the back door of the building. Flick waved jovially, insisting that she join us.

"Hey, guys!" We chatted and caught up briefly before I took the lead.

"Where's Marley?" I asked.

"Actually, I don't know." She looked at the time on her phone. "She's cutting it pretty close." Her notifications showed three missed calls. "I don't know why I didn't hear the rings, but I missed two calls from her," she said.

"Okay, just give me a few minutes before you call her back. I have a hunch. I want to bring you up to speed and see if we can come up with some kind of plan."

ALEX

"YOU DIDN'T HAVE TO PROVE anything to me," I assured Toby, folding the blanket.

"I know. I didn't want you here for that reason."

"What do you mean?" I asked.

Toby scrunched his lips, trying to put together the right words. "It's just—I've been trying to be honest with you over these last months when you asked questions about where I was going or thought I was acting strange. But, I was trying to be *honest* without the whole truth. Does that make sense?" He carried both blankets and we strolled toward her car.

"I'm not sure," I said, leaning against the side.

"I just didn't want to mess anything up between us," he admitted. "I mean, look at you. Your parents are normal people with awesome jobs. And normal is just the beginning of how cool they are. I mean, I love my mom and all, but she's got some serious problems."

I reached into the car and turned the key just enough to start the radio. "They're cool?" I paused and looked in the direction of where we sat with Cypress. "You've been protecting me from finding out the ugly stuff, but you've also been dealing with everything on your own. I could've helped you, Toby."

He shook his head and repositioned himself at the rear of her car, plopping the towels on the trunk. "I appreciate what you're saying, but I just didn't want you in it. And then this morning, when I told my mom I'd help her for the last time, I had a really strong feeling that you had to be with us so I could have someone else there to hold my mom accountable."

"Accountable for what? I don't understand." After all the months Dad warned me that Toby wasn't a good influence, I felt validated for believing he was a good, responsible kid. On the other hand, I felt a hint of devastation that he hadn't trusted me with the whole story.

"To start, my mom uses drugs."

"What? What kind of drugs?" I blurted, suddenly wondering what might've been in the cooler I handed to Toby at the park.

"Pills. Legal, just not prescribed for her. And weed. Whatever she can get from that Marco guy. Her habit is expensive."

As the pieces started fitting together, I thought of my grandmother. I wondered if she knew about Marco's business.

"I mean, the pot is cheap because she got a prescription from her doctor for medical marijuana. She complained enough about lingering pain from an old injury and she made it sound pretty easy for her to qualify. It's the other stuff that gets out of hand. And that's another thing, Alex. Your mom is representing a huge campaign against drug abuse. I didn't want to risk getting you involved in anything that could potentially get her or you in the news for association with us!"

I knew the conversation would take longer than a few extra minutes at the park. "Where's your truck?"

Toby gestured across the soccer fields. "Over there. Why?"

"Can you leave it for awhile and just come with me?"

"Yeah. sure." He closed the passenger door and gently took my hand. "Are you mad?"

I exhaled a deep breath and backed out of the parking space. "Kind of. But not really at you," I admitted. "I have a lot of questions tumbling around my head and I'm not exactly sure where to start. I know I'm telling myself that I want to know the answers, but I'm not sure if I really do or not." The recent *DogEar* post came to mind. I never considered that kids would know about prescription drug use from their parents using irresponsibly.

The sun slid behind the peaks of South Mountain, just enough to sit comfortably outside the food truck on the picnic benches that overlooked the golf course.

Toby started to explain. "I finally got my mom to put my name on her bank account. The child support my dad deposits every month was getting used up to buy more pills before I got any of it."

"And that's why you got a job?" I cut in.

"Yes, partly. The more I thought about things, the more I understood that if I want to get out of her house as soon as I'm eighteen, I need money. And more than my cut of the child support."

"What do you mean, *your cut?*" I asked.

"So on a day that my mom was fairly sober and agreed to put me on the account, it gave me a chance to move some of the money into my own account. One that she doesn't have control of. I mean, she's not a junkie but she doesn't always make the best decisions."

My expression changed enough for Toby to clarify more.

"What I mean is that her head is clear enough to know that I'm still in the picture. My food and other things require money, so I have to make sure there's enough. If she has full access to every penny, there's a real possibility that she'll spend it all and nothing will be left for the things we need."

I had a thought. "That text I got about the money—it was real?"

Toby looked away. "Unfortunately, yes."

"So we really were in danger!"

"It took me by surprise," he said. "That's when I stepped in to figure out how to pay her debt. I'd never be able to forgive myself if something happened to you."

The more I learned, the more questions I asked. "Toby. Your mom is a professional woman. She has a job. She's responsible for it and for you, and she looks completely normal! She drives a car, I'm assuming, when she's under the influence of whatever she's taking?"

"Yes," he agreed. "I guess that's one of the reasons why there's even a need for a drug abuse campaign. She figured out ways to glide through her days looking fairly clear-headed. I don't think anyone has ever suspected anything."

I always considered T.A.D.A. as an effort designated for teens and college kids. But if what Toby said was true, I wondered who else I knew—disguising drug use like Cypress.

"Okay, that's the money part. But, does your mom ever talk about quitting? I mean, that's most important, right?"

"The only thing I know for sure is whatever Marco gave her the last time really kicked her ass and she didn't like how it made her feel or the higher price that came with it. So, I think she's done with that one. I hope she's serious."

"So what now? Your mom's obviously not ready to quit cold turkey and her funds aren't going to last forever. If you're serious about not paying any future debts, what will she do?"

"She's just going to have to figure it out. Without me," he claimed. "I'm glad you were here to see why I've been trying to protect you."

IRIS

LEAVING MARCO AT *THE LOUNGE* was easier than leaving other men in my life. From the beginning, I considered him temporary. He only became a comfortable companion after the dozens of hours we shared across the bar from one another. He listened to my day-to-day complaints and served each drink with an elegant compliment to lift my spirits. I knew he was in support of recreational drugs, but not the heavy ones. That was his choice and it never interfered with our time together—until now.

One afternoon, a cake stand adorned the center of the mahogany counter behind the bartenders' galley. Under it's lid were an assortment of desserts prepared by Marco himself for only his favorite customers. He asked me if I preferred chocolate, caramel, or double fudge.

"I'd probably go with caramel, but not tonight, darling," I'd said. "I have a curfew this week, remember? I'm on duty while my daughter is away on business." We exchanged smiles while I finished my second and final drink for that night—at least my last drink at *The Lounge*.

As usual, I left cash on the bar, swung my shawl across the back of my shoulders and blew him a kiss at the other end of the counter. He met me at the door with a small pink box.

"Please, take this with you for a late night snack. I cannot let you leave without promising to taste my work."

It was the first of many nights I returned home with

desserts in a small pink box. In a flash, the memories of taking them home and sharing with my sweet, innocent grand-daughter, Alex, startled me. We'd sat together on the couch with two forks, eating the delicious treats from the boxes before bed.

Only two miles from leaving Marco at *The Lounge*, I slammed on my brakes in the middle of the road, not thinking to pull off to the side. "That son-of-a-bitch," I realized. "Holy Jeezus, mother of God! I'm the reason Alex tested positive for marijuana! He baked with it and didn't warn me against sharing with her. I fed her the very thing I hoped she'd never touch."

The two cars behind me could not slow down in time. My car inched on the road, still in DRIVE, but I wasn't in control. One hit the rear of my car, trying to swerve, while the last one caused both of us to spin and buckle over the center median.

MARLEY

"RACHEL, I NEED YOU," I spoke into her voicemail. It felt like I was being forced to stop at every mile marker. Each inter-section donned a red light, an idle pause in my efforts to reach Iris at the hospital.

"Oh, thank God," I sighed, when Dax answered his phone.

"Marley, are you okay?"

"Not really," I said. "My mother was in a car accident and brought to the hospital by ambulance. I'm just pulling into the parking lot now, but I can't get in touch with Rachel."

"I'm so sorry." His tone was sincere and gentle. "Don't worry about anything. Focus on your mom. I'll find Rachel and tell her what happened," he promised.

I parked on the third floor of the parking structure. "Thank you, Dax. Tell her that I'll get Andrew to help with Alex, but if she can handle the station for the rest of the night, I'll touch base when I know more."

"Marley?" Dax said calmly. "Just call me when you know what you need."

———————

THE NURSE AT THE TRIAGE desk recognized Dax, more than willing to escort him to Iris's curtained bay. An elderly nurse stood inside the small space recording vitals and Dax peered through partially opened curtain. My face relaxed and I slowly stood. The triage nurse left us in a comforting embrace.

Iris was covered in blankets from toes to neck, connected to machines with wires in every direction. I sat in a bedside chair, Dax in the remaining vinyl one. We whispered face to face, he caressed my cheekbone and I held his hand tightly.

"Everything she owns is boxed up in her room at my house, stacked side by side, ready to move to her new place," I explained. "She just told me about it. It was supposed to be a good thing."

Divided by two armrests, I rested my head on Dax's shoulder.

A police officer stood outside the curtain and a different nurse requested my attention. I gestured to Dax and he followed, both acknowledging a second officer once we rounded the corner to a small empty waiting room.

After the initial introductions, the on-scene officers explained Iris's circumstances from their perspectives and those of the witnesses who assisted in getting Iris emergency services. I was taken by surprise, as my initial assumptions never once presented the possibility of a heart attack behind the wheel.

Dax's cell phone vibrated in his pocket, but he stayed with me and let it ring.

The lead officer provided the report and contact information, then I borrowed Dax's phone to call Alex from the small waiting room.

"Honey, it's Mom. I'm using Dax's phone," I paused. "Listen, I'm with Grandma at the hospital." My sentences sounded fragmented. Each one seemed to be difficult to piece together the right way. Was there a right way, I wondered? Everything felt so wrong. And strange.

"Honey, Grandma's going to be okay. But, I thought you might want to come to the hospital?" My voice inflected a question rather than a simple statement.

As I spoke to Alex, Dax leaned his head on the wall behind his chair.

"She's coming," I said softly, handing Dax his phone.

"I can pick her up," he offered.

"No, she's already in her car. Thank you, though." I smiled. "Thanks for coming."

"I'm here for you. And I'm sorry for all this confusion with your mom, for the accident, the stress between the two of you lately."

I stood and took his hand, leading him back to Iris's curtained bay.

"I can stay until Alex gets here."

We returned to our vinyl chairs. "I'd really like that."

Hospital machinery throughout the ER pinged and beeped, though nothing seemed to jar Iris. Her position remained the same, no change in head placement or crinkles in her blankets. Her eyelids were shadowed gray and speckles of dried blood scattered from her widow's peak to above her right ear.

"I'm so mad at myself," I confessed to Dax, "for being mad at her right now."

He nodded without judgement and Alex gently pulled the curtain. Dax slipped out quietly, and I embraced my precious girl.

Alex scooted her chair as close to Iris's bedside as possible, even sitting on her knees to eliminate the extra space. She lifted the side of the hanging blanket to hold onto her grandmother's hand. She spoke delicately, as if she knew that every word was not only heard by her grandmother, but swallowed and digested as nutrients that would heal her ailing body.

"Where are her rings?" she asked me. "And the rest of her jewelry?"

I stood, locating the white plastic bag of Iris's personal effects.

"Everything's in here, I think."

It wasn't until Alex asked about Andrew, 'when he'd be there to see Grandma', that I realized I hadn't called him. For the first time in Alex's entire life, I didn't reach out to Andrew for help or a listening ear during a crisis.

"Actually, I still need to do that," I admitted.

A female doctor entered the bay. She asked lots of questions regarding Iris's prior health history, current doctors, possible disorders, prescription medications, and daily habits.

"And—you said she lives in your home?" the doctor clarified, when I wasn't able to answer some of the questions about my mother. It wasn't condescending as much as a painful truth. Even Alex could fill in most of the blanks when I couldn't.

"Mom, it's okay," Alex assured me after the doctor left the room.

It was true. But I knew that truth wasn't always easy. Nearly every news story I ever reported included elements of discomfort. Sometimes truth came with embarrassment, hardship, and feelings of failure. Very rarely did truth come simply, with no consequence.

IRIS

HORNS HONKED AROUND ME, I think. Only vague memories have returned. I'm told though, that the horn sound I recalled could've been from my own vehicle. My panic-induced heart attack took over without any regard for circumstances. Whatever happened inside my body presented itself very publicly just beyond the intersection. And as much as I love a good show, I've always preferred a role behind the scenes.

Alex told me that a particularly handsome paramedic returned to check on me the day after I was admitted to the hospital. Unfortunately, I was still sedated and unable to thank him for his efforts and generous show of compassion.

I'm sure you can imagine Marley's dismay when finally, I woke up enough to tell her I'd been seeing a doctor by the name of O'Malley. She'd spent nearly two days with Alex by my side before I gave in and confessed. At least a day was prolonged by Marley's lecture, followed by long periods of silence and sleepy eyes. You'd think she'd jump for joy with relief when I regained consciousness after an episode like that. To her credit, she was thankful and endearing for a few hours until my brain started firing properly. But she was at a sudden loss for words when the teensy bit of missing information about my visits with Dr. O was announced.

Even Alex cringed when Marley became unglued. Thank God, her cell phone rang. She was kind enough to give me a fierce stare before ditching my room for the hallway to take her call. Being able to communicate with another person void of words can be both a blessing and a curse. I made an accurate assumption that her *look* was more of a semi-colon and not a period. It was definitely not the end of her conversation with me.

Andrew took position in the room when Marley accepted Dax's invitation for dinner. "You gave us a pretty good scare, you know?"

"That's my job, as of late, isn't it?" I joked. "Marley is always waiting for my other shoe to fall."

Andrew gave Alex a ten-dollar bill, requesting a tray of snacks and drinks from the cafeteria. "Welcome back to the land of the living," he joked. "Iris, I know this isn't the best time, but I really need to talk to you about Marco."

I pressed the button to raise my bed into a relaxed seated position. I waved my fingers at Andrew, requesting that he hold my hand. "Go for it," I said. "I'm an open book."

"I talked to Marco a few days ago when I suspected he was dealing drugs and using *The Lounge* as a cover."

I lowered my chin marginally, but didn't want to speak for Andrew. I wanted him to continue talking.

"Of course, he didn't admit to anything, but he's not really who I'm concerned about. It's Alex."

"Alex? What worries you about Alex? She's wonderful!"

"Yes," he agreed. "That's not in question. It's just that—if he is dealing, and you knew about it—I mean, if he's your pick for a boyfriend, Alex can't hang with you anymore. Marley would literally have all our heads if she knew that we knew about Marco and that we still allowed Alex anywhere in his reach."

I straightened my body to sit a little taller and adjusted the pillow behind my back. Andrew was still leaning on the edge of my bed; I took his hand in both of mine. "Let me answer your questions. First, I knew he had connections, but I was under the impression that they were light-weight only. Stuff that doctors prescribe—nothing illegal, per se. But to be completely honest, I never introduced him to Alex."

"Anything else?" Andrew asked, listening intently.

"I took him to a park to 'pick something up from a friend' a few days ago. I waited in the car when he said it'd be quick. I parked to wait, and don't freak out Andrew, but I watched him meet up with Alex's Toby. And then I saw Alex. I couldn't believe my eyes when I saw her!"

Andrew's gaze widened, suddenly questioning something that hadn't crossed his mind. "Wait. Do you think Alex is buying from Marco?"

"C'mon, Andrew. Hell no, I don't think she's buying drugs. She's a good girl."

"Have you asked her? How can you be sure?"

"Because I know. I've been around enough drugs in my life, and people who use them, to know what Alex would be like if she were taking drugs. Besides, that's not the point. Alex stayed in the background. It didn't look like she said a word. What I'm trying to tell you is that when I witnessed Marco doing business with Toby and some older gal who was there, I was pissed! You don't cut deals with kids or around kids. They're not old enough to make informed decisions. And if self-medicating begins at an early age, there's a very good chance that things will only get worse."

"So we agree on that!" Andrew sounded relieved.

"Long story short, I dropped him off at *The Lounge* that day, told him we were done, and ended up here not long after that."

He sat up and stretched his arms, cracking the knuckles on both hands.

"Andrew," I said. "There's one more thing."

ALEX

I FELT LIKE I'D BEEN awake for hours. Memories from last night's dreams were clear in my mind, distracting my thoughts and affecting my focus. I had a job to do, a column to write; not a single extra moment to sleep. I only had one hundred fifty words to start a conversation. Worries about Grandma puddled in the front of my brain. I sat up in bed and propped a pillow behind my back. I adjusted my posture with the laptop in front of me and began to write:

For the first time in a long while, I felt alone last night. I kept thinking about the high school girl in the news. She didn't even live that far away. They said she had a lot of friends. She was smart and planned on going to college. Now she's gone, along with her dreams, because of pills that weren't hers. The rest of the story is starting to surface. People are talking about her inquiries, her innocent pleas for anything to help with headaches, sleep problems, focus issues, pain. She built up an arsenal that was supposed to heal whatever she was going through, but instead, caused permanent devastation. Her presence is lost, forcing a ripple effect of pain for the people who knew her and loved her—not to mention the effect on the rest of us who never even met her. Can you relate to her story?

Mom knocked twice before opening my door. She was wrapped in her fluffy robe, the one she wears a lot. She doesn't tie it at the waist, she holds it around her body with her arms, like she's cold—but I don't think she is.

"Good morning," she said gently, sliding under my comforter where the laptop had slept.

I closed the lid and leaned the computer against the night-stand on the floor. Scrunching under my covers, I rolled into her chest and we laid quietly for a few minutes.

"I think you should go to school today," she said.

I tipped my head to look at her. "Really?"

"Really," she assured me. "I'll be with Grandma all day. There's no sense in you just sitting in a dreary hospital room, letting yourself get behind on your work. You can visit her as soon as you're done with school."

I rolled back to my side.

"Do you feel okay with that?" she asked.

"I guess. As long as she won't be alone," I double checked.

Mom made me breakfast before school and Toby offered to pick me up. We arrived at school with fifteen minutes to spare, but neither of us had interest in milling around with the crowds in the courtyard. With the windows up and the radio low, we caught up on last night's events.

"My mom left around nine last night," he said. "She didn't tell me she was leaving and she was still gone when I went to bed. She was sound asleep on the couch when I got up this morning."

"Where do you think she went?" I asked.

Toby just shook his head. "Can't say for sure. I don't know. I feel like she's in a downward spiral."

I took his hand across the emergency brake.

"And if that's true, maybe I'm handling this all wrong," he said. "I'm not her parent and I don't want to mess up my future, but she needs help."

"I don't know the right answer," I admitted. My own parents have had their ups and downs. They seemed to make it through the hard stuff. Maybe Cypress will one day, I hoped.

"So about your grandma, your mom's hanging out with her?" Changing the subject made sense. Talking badly about Cypress wasn't good for Toby. It wouldn't help or change anything except make him feel worse.

As we walked through the lot onto campus, I checked my

phone. There were already dozens of notifications that comments had been written on the school site. "Yep, that's the plan. But I kind of wish I was there instead of here."

Toby put his arm around my shoulder. "What are you reading?"

I clicked off my screen and slid my phone into my back pocket. "Nothing, really. Just school stuff."

He led us around a brick wall adjacent to the library entrance.

"What are we doing?" I asked.

We stood eyes to eyes, Toby's hands holding my face. "I want to ask you something and I don't want you to be mad."

"Don't be weird," I laughed. "Just ask."

He turned to me, close to my face again. "I'm ninety percent sure that you're the ghostwriter for the *DogEar* column, but you haven't said anything about it. So—?"

I surveyed the courtyard. "I might be. What's the big deal?"

"Can you believe how many people are talking about it? Doesn't that surprise you?" he exclaimed.

"I don't know. I mean, people seem to like it."

"Alex . . . ."

I wasn't ready to say anything, but I had to. "Can you please promise that you won't broadcast my part in it?" I smiled the whole way through my rambled explanation. We walked back to the parking lot, away from passing students. The bell rang, declaring five more minutes to be seated in each of our classes.

"I'll keep your dirty little secret," he said. "But I knew that you were the only person who could pull it off and keep it under wraps. I knew it!" He punched his left hand with his right. "You're the smartest girl I know and you figured out a way to bring all these crazy different people together just talking about regular life. Do you have any idea how hard that is?"

I heard every word and I saw his excitement, but only one sentence engraved itself into my soul. I was the smartest girl he knew.

MARLEY

NOW SEEMED AS GOOD A time as any, I justified. What had been swarming in my thoughts for the past couple of weeks had now taken a front seat in my mind. I didn't know for sure, but I had a hunch that its priority skyrocketed because of Iris's unknown state of health. No matter what happened, I knew for sure that I didn't want to be deprived of the truth simply because I never asked her.

I took the photo from my purse and placed it in Iris's left hand. She lifted her arm toward her face, a slight smile forming in the corners of her mouth.

"You were the most beautiful child I ever saw until Alex was born."

Not the response I was expecting.

"I don't think it was a mystery to anyone that I wasn't overly fond of children in the first place." Her smile was fuller. "It wasn't that I disliked or loathed, but more that I never felt any particular need for them, to be honest. But you—"

For some reason, she had my undivided attention. In all my life, I didn't remember another genuine expression of endearment from her.

"You were different, Marley. Somehow we've made it to this point in our lives, but I wasn't sure how things would go," she paused. "From the beginning, I never felt good enough for you. You were always more than I would ever be in the most magnificent ways; I knew that from the moment we gazed into each other's eyes."

I didn't know if I should feel appalled, grateful, suspicious, regretful, or little bits of each emotion. Everything she'd said sounded heartfelt, I thought, but the words were like those of someone else's mother. Like the mothers of the girls I knew when I went to birthday parties or play dates, but not my mother. Certainly hidden cameras weren't poised to capture the hoax. I couldn't be too sure. I stood and peeked around the corner, observing a clear hallway except for a nurse entering the room next door with a rolling cart.

Iris's eyes began to close.

"Mother," I called mildly. "Do you need to rest?" I hoped she could stay awake for a bit longer.

"No, I'm fine." She raised her eyebrows and widened her eyes. I could see her pointed feet under the covers, stretching her legs. "You want details?" she asked, nudging the picture toward me.

"I do," I admitted. "Does that mean you're willing to tell me?"

Her lips curled upward. "You know what's funny about this picture?"

"No." It didn't look funny to me.

"For a couple of months before this picture fell out of the roll top desk, there was a man at *The Lounge* who seemed so familiar, but I couldn't place him in my memory."

Iris turned to face me.

"Take a very close look at this picture and tell me what you see."

I held it closely, though I'd examined it on several occasions before coming to Iris with it. I saw the same things I'd seen before. Two men sitting on a wooden bench, maybe a picnic table. A body of water was to their left and a toddler girl faced them with delicate light brown curls, wearing a seersucker sundress. She stood with a tiny hand on each of the men's knees.

"I see two young guys with me, maybe on vacation or at a lake."

"Let me see that again," she inquired. "Okay, yes, the one on the right. Look at him."

I examined the photo closely. "What am I looking at? Or looking for? Just tell me."

"Hmm," Iris grunted. "You don't see it?"

"Mother!" I felt irritated, on the road to frustrated; not my intended goal.

"This is obviously a very old photograph, but I finally realized that the guy on the right works for Marco at *The Lounge*. This is a picture of him when he was a much younger man."

"What?" I gasped, holding the photo much closer to my eyes. "Are you sure?" I held the picture closer to Iris, my index finger pointing to the man on the right. "This guy," I tapped the picture, "works at *The Lounge*? The only one I can think of that looks remotely like this guy is Curtis."

"I know," she nodded. "I could hardly believe it myself, but it's true."

"Did he recognize you?" I blurted.

Iris's sly grin appeared again. "Much to his chagrin, yes, we've made the connection."

That caught my attention. "What does that mean?"

"Wait a minute!" she demanded. "Before we go there, why don't you tell me why this picture sparked an interest for you."

My face must've scrunched into puzzlement.

"C'mon," she prodded. "You could've asked me anything about this picture recently, but you haven't. And you obviously didn't return or discard it, either." One eyebrow raised.

I swiveled in my very uncomfortable guest chair, squaring my body with poised posture. "Since I have very limited information about my childhood, once I knew it was me in the picture, I started imagining things."

"Like what," Iris asked.

"Like, did you take this picture? And who are these men—I mean who were they at that time of my life?"

She inhaled deeply through her nose, holding one hand across her tender chest. "No, I did not take the picture. In fact, I wasn't even there when the picture was taken."

The typical hospital sounds filled the momentary pause.

"Those two were best friends. They were both very dear to me. I trusted them with my life, and at that time, my life was you. It really was. When I couldn't handle the pressure of being a mother one-hundred-percent of the time, they helped me with you, even when I had to step away for awhile."

"You're talking in circles." I stood up and rounded the foot of her bed. "You're saying that Curtis from *The Lounge* and this other guy took care of me when you couldn't, and now years later, Curtis is here, and neither of you have mentioned a word to me, even though I see him working there on a very regular basis?"

"Yes," she paused again. "I never expected to see Curtis again. This picture was taken in Northern California, you know we lived there for a few years when you were young."

I nodded.

"But I took you with me and left my friends without a word. I just walked us away from everyone who mattered. You see, our very dear friend, Mack, the other man in the picture, was very ill and never told us what he was going through. One day, we found him dead, collapsed in a chair at the theater and it affected me deeply. I couldn't handle it. I had to get away from the people and places we shared together."

"I never knew. I'm sorry, Mom."

"Marley, this campaign you're working on—it's important

and I applaud the efforts."

"I don't understand," she shook her head.

"I'm not completely certain, but there's a good possibility that Mack had a hand in the timing of his death. I mean, yes—he was very ill, but he was also a drug user, and I knew that. I've just always suspected that he may have lived a bit longer without recreational intervention."

"And Curtis?"

"Mack's death and our sudden departure were very difficult for him. It was a long time ago. When he and I spoke at *The Lounge*, he made it very clear that we couldn't rehash the past. He looked angry, still unforgiving about how I disappeared with you. He and Mack cared for you with fatherly love."

"What does that mean?" I was shocked and disturbed.

"Marley, your father could've been any number of men I knew at that time."

"Mother!"

"I know that's not what you want to hear, and quite honestly, that's why I've never wanted to talk about it. *Who* fathered you never mattered to me, because I cared for them, and they cared for you. It was a different time."

I stood and turned away from her.

"Marley, please listen to me," she appealed. "I'm trying to explain in the clearest, simplest terms. The decisions I made when you were a child were because of my love for you. I made the best choices I thought I could possibly make at the time, for all the best reasons, which is what I'm doing now. You're entitled to disagree with me, but you know it's not always easing making decisions for the right reasons—even if down the line, we find that they were wrong. I will apologize if you need me to, but I'm standing firm in my decision, whether you like it or not."

"Knock knock," Dax announced, peeking in for a visit.

"Hey!" I didn't shout, but his presence was welcome respite, reminding me to pause. I needed his comfort, his steady disposition, his support without judgement. He'd become that person to me in different ways than the ebb and flow of life with Andrew.

"What a lovely surprise," Iris waved. "Come in!"

I was so angry with my mother, sitting at her bedside, listening to her memories of Mack, his life with addiction, how it all began in his early teens, and what he felt he needed for quality of life.

Then she told me her big plans and how we were going to make Marco pay.

After an awkward meeting when Curtis arrived later, we went over the details and put the plan into motion. Dax stood behind me, his hands on my shoulders. I wasn't sure if he was holding me down, providing a barrier between my mother and I, or if his touch simply brought the comfort I needed during another uncomfortable situation. We went along with it—we had to, for Alex, Colton, and every kid who faced a similar situation.

CHAPTER 9

MARLEY

THE NEWS STATION SET UP camp in the middle of the vendors, promoting the T.A.D.A. campaign. Literature pamphlets, swag bags, and window clings were available on the table, including a meet-and-greet opportunity with Dax and me, scheduled from eleven to noon. Flick would be there to film a clip for the evening news after shooting some promotional footage for the city event.

It was a beautiful afternoon for an outdoor event. *Rock The Block* was situated between First and Sixth Streets. Merchants lined the perimeter with shade tents over their goods, single performers meandered the streets making balloon animals, playing instruments, selling cotton candy, kettle corn, and lemonade. Food trucks were angled between picnic tables. Live bands were staged on each end of the block, scheduled throughout the day and into the evening.

Andrew's radio station set up with live streaming and plenty of giveaways. Staffed with interns for most of the day, three of the fan-favorite DJ's were scheduled for one-hour slots intermittently throughout the event. Establishing my whereabouts was important to the plan.

"You're doing great," Dax reassured me, noticing my forced smiles. With so much on my mind, leaving the hospital to fulfill the obligation was not an easy task.

"I don't like this at all," I grumbled. "Iris has this crazy hold on me even from her hospital bed."

Dax caressed my back, though public displays of affection were not yet fully public. "We can go back if you want to change the plan."

I breathed deeply, barely shaking my head. "No. We decided to do it this way. We're here . . . and there are so many people involved."

Flick parked the van behind the station tent. As he set up for filming, we strolled through the street, checking things out, saying hello to people who recognized us. We took a few pictures and made our way back for the official meet-and-greet under the tent. Much to my chagrin, at least two dozen people were already lined up, waiting for us to begin signing photos and handing out promotional merchandise. Behind sun-glassed eyes, my lids closed as I took in another deep breath.

"I guess that's what the presence of a professional athlete will do in a crowd," I joked, checking my watch.

Every place of business along *Rock The Block* had opened early with plans to stay open late. The Irish Pub positioned a crew on the front patio. They wore kilts and held tankards under the umbrella of authentic music that poured from the outdoor speakers. They flagged off an extended area for an outdoor beer garden. The art gallery offered mini canvas painting classes in the courtyard and the brewery sat in the prime mid-block location, adjacent to the news station tent.

Rachel showed up just in time for our scheduled event. She took charge of the people in line, generating conversations to pass the time and reaching out to the public on behalf of the station. She gave me a thumbs up and the wink of an eye.

"Did you see that?" I asked Dax.

"I did," he nodded. "That's good, right?" His gentle smile reassured me that what we were doing was important. One more hour and our commitment to the event would be complete.

Rachel continued crowd control through the last two people who stood in line to meet the faces of the T.A.D.A. campaign. She passed out consolation freebies with a smile to each person she had to turn away. I smiled and waved to a few folks who stuck around long enough to make eye contact and Dax seemed to satisfy most people with a simple grin and head-nod. She guided us away from the table and into Flick's van, poking her head inside the door after we took a seat on the bench.

"I know you're tired and this whole thing is making you nuts right now, but you were terrific."

"Thanks," I answered, rubbing my temples. "I really appreciate you being here."

"Flick will take you to your car," she said. "I'll swing by after the broadcast tonight."

After Flick loaded the back of the van and slammed both doors, he hopped into the driver's seat, swinging his body around toward us. "Wanna see what I shot?" he asked enthusiastically.

Dax looked at me, still sitting with my hands over my face. "Maybe later, man. We trust you completely, you know that."

"Yeah, thanks for everything today, Flick," I added. "You really came through for us."

"The pleasure was mine," he said, swinging back to the

front. "Now where'd you guys park?"

"We're actually really close, but Marley's exhausted and you getting us out of here quickly, really helps," Dax said. "My truck is in the lot just behind the pub."

"Not a problem. After I drop you guys off, I'll head back to the station and get started on the first round of editing right away."

Dax got me into the truck and met Flick at his driver's side window. "Touch base with me later if you need anything."

Flick put the passenger window down and turned up the radio. It was a good day.

IRIS

I'VE SEEN PEOPLE DIE. NOT instantly, of course, but at my age, it's inevitable. Unlikely, really—to have lived as long as I have and not known death in some way. I've never really been comfortable with that damn *circle of life* philosophy either, especially when a person's life seemed too short—like their circle wasn't actually a circle at all, but incomplete, a kaleidoscope of broken pieces.

As a child, I remember being told on two different occasions that a relative passed away. I didn't know either of them very well and never even witnessed a funeral until my early twenties.

I almost didn't go to Mack's funeral. After all, his lifeless body didn't respond to my touch, my voice, my desperate pleas. Knowing him taught me the importance of acceptance, that people have the right to make unpopular decisions, choices that could change relationships. He would always be with me, regardless of my presence when his casket lowered permanently into the ground, returning him to the earth.

I was emotionally drained, my body limp. The only thing I could move were my eyelids, keeping a rough estimate of time based on faint hues of sunlight and darkness tracing the outline of the window shades in our bedroom. Every ounce of energy was depleted from my body. The morning of the funeral, I woke up with my head on Mack's pillow. Our sheet wrapped around my skin, embracing me with the scent of his body.

Mack was significant to me, maybe more in my mind than reality. I've wondered over the years, how certain thoughts are remembered so clearly and others unfocused and hazy. Without a doubt, we were a couple at the time of his death, by our own definition, with an open relationship. We shared a mid-century bungalow with my little Marley. She reaped the benefits and consistency of male figures in her life. It was good.

Dr. O'Malley entered quietly after two knocks on the hospital door.

"How are you today?" he asked.

"I've never been one for nostalgia," I admitted, "but I seem to be making use of this solitude with memories from the old days."

Dr. O looked at me, holding his clipboard to the side of his body. "I don't see a problem with that," he smiled, raising an eyebrow. "Tell me how you're feeling, though, overall—head to toe."

"I'm tired. That seems to be common lately."

He nodded, waited.

"When I'm awake, I feel tired. When I sleep, I have these realistically vivid dreams as though I'm awake. It's very odd. I never feel rested."

"Iris, is your daughter coming in today?" he asked.

"I'd bet on it," I drooped. "She's been here every day. Do you need her?"

"Well, unfortunately, we've come to an impasse," he

admitted. "We've monitored and treated you for the heart attack. The pneumonia you've developed is improving, but still a concern if you want to proceed with chemotherapy. I can provide you with medication to help with calming and comfort, Iris, but I'm afraid that staying in the hospital is no longer necessary."

"You're going to discharge me?" I asked, as excited as I could muster.

"I'd like to discuss other options with your daughter. Discharging requires stringent care-taking duties and there are several facilities nearby that would serve you well," he explained.

"Not a chance," I scoffed. "How much time do I have?"

"Excuse me?" Dr. O looked up from my chart, held the top of his pen to his lips.

"I'm serious. How long do you expect me to live?" I pushed.

The doctor rolled the stool to my bedside. "I can't say, for certain. There are so many factors to consider. As long as the pneumonia improves and chemo can begin, we could have better information in about three months. I'm not comfortable with a solid timeline at this point."

I guess you could say I'm a pessimist. It's an awful word if you think about it, describing a person who typically assumes the worst. Then again, maybe I'm more of a cynic. That seems more like me, not really believing that certain things are even possible. Take Mack for example. After he died and after the time it took me to feel like I could function again, I never considered how I could stand up for him—to do something in his honor that would complete the fragmented circle of his life.

I knew exactly what Marley was doing as Dr. O spoke, carrying out the plan I helped her set in motion. Never in a million years did I expect that Curtis would make it possible for us to work together, with Marley—no less, to bring down a corrupted drug dealer. I should've known better when I met Marco all those months ago. His confidence and charm blinded me from seeing his true business goals. *The Lounge* was a front for his real love and his hunger for power and money was fueled by easy customer deals and prescription pill trafficking. I didn't get involved, because people do what they want to do. Far be it for me to have a say in his business. But my indifference changed dramatically when Curtis confirmed Marco's expanding business, dealing with kids. They were too young, too vulnerable, too naive. He knew I'd never allow another irresponsible and unnecessary death like Mack's.

It would all be fine. I knew it would. It had to be. A lifetime cynic has to tell herself that, over and over again.

CURTIS

I PARKED MY MOTORCYCLE ON the driveway of my rental, a single level adobe style house on the corner. The cool air conditioning greeted me with immediate relief from the summer heat. On the kitchen counter, I found exactly what I'd been promised: five hundred in cash and a prepaid phone.

The house was sparsely furnished, clean, and quiet. A large wood-framed clock hung on the accent wall behind the L-shaped couch. Thirty minutes to go-time. I made myself a cold sandwich and guzzled a can of soda before heading out.

What happened so many years ago became crystal clear again after starting to work for Marco at *The Lounge*. My modest career behind a corporate desk ended with a solid retirement package, providing a clear slate for relaxation and adventure opportunities, yet—not going to work each day felt like a waste of time. I learned quickly that total retirement wasn't for me.

Over drinks and games of pool with former co-workers a few nights in a row, we landed at *The Lounge*. Marco and I became fast friends, like comrades from a past life. Two polar opposites, our banter was easy going, welcoming, and eventually anticipated. I started showing up at *The Lounge* on my own, sitting at the counter bar, chatting it up with Marco or just stopping in for a quick bite from the kitchen after work.

After officially retiring, it was an easy transition from patron to bartender. I was comfortable there—low stress, different people every day, something to do—until the night that Marco introduced me to his lovely Iris. Her eyes spoke volumes, subtle intrigue peeked from the corner of her curved lips, though not a single word delivered from her mouth. She smiled without showing her teeth, and though years had aged her in real time, she was as beautiful as the first time we'd met. I recognized her right away. She didn't seem to notice.

After a brief introduction, I turned away awkwardly, continuing to work; the shock of seeing her unexpectedly triggered a racing heartbeat. It cannot be, I thought. Each subsequent shift at *The Lounge*, I anticipated the possibility of seeing her again. I had no desire to rehash the past or catch up as if a lifetime of distance and intentional dissolution were null and void. Mack was the person who'd brought us together. He was also the person responsible for abruptly severing our contact.

I banged on Cypress's door three times before she opened it, just enough to slip onto the porch and close the door behind her.

"What the hell are you doing here?" she demanded. "How do you even know where I live?"

"You're going to see Marco. He sent me for you."

"Like hell I am!" she blurted. "I'm not going anywhere with you."

Cypress yelled for help. I tried silencing her with a hand over her mouth and the other around her body, but she flailed and kicked around, requiring all of my strength to get her back into the house, wrestling her to the floor. I held her down with my knee while she thrashed and screamed. It wasn't part of the plan.

"Oh my God! Mom!" Toby gasped, high-tailing it down the stairs in response to her desperate pleas.

"Call the cops!" she ordered.

He was momentarily paralyzed.

"This is between your mother and me," I told him sternly. "Either go back to your room or take a walk."

"Oh my God!" he said again.

Maybe he was unsure of what to do, frantic to help his mom, or just plain frightened and unable to think clearly, but he ran full force, diving into me. His action set Cypress free, but I grabbed him and held tightly.

"Let him go, you bastard! You let go of my son now!" Cypress yelled, looking for something to grab or throw.

The room felt hot. Cypress was sweating, crying, out of control.

"Mom, call the cops!" He yelled to remind her. It seemed so obvious but no one reacted rationally.

"Right!" she turned in circles, looking for the phone. "Shit! Shit! Where is it?"

As soon as she rounded the corner to find a phone, I scooped the keys from the coffee table and dragged him to the front of the house.

"Get in!" I demanded. The key fob unlocked the truck doors and I tossed him across the bench seat. I got in behind him and peeled out of the driveway faster than he could attempt getting out on the other side. "Don't even think about trying to jump."

He pulled his cell from his back pocket.

"Give it here. You need to calm down and listen to me."

"Listen to you?" he exclaimed. "You're friggin crazy! You just attacked my mom. You're out of your mind!"

I grabbed his phone. "When I give this back to you, I want you to call Alex.

"What do you know about Alex? That makes no sense. Who are you?"

I drove in silence, making right turns at any red light we approached, just to keep the truck moving and him inside it.

He stopped dialing after three numbers.

"C'mon now," I glared, pulling the phone from his hands again, ending the 911 call. "I told you to call Alex. Don't mess this up."

"Mess this up? It's already messed up! Everything about this is messed up!"

By the time I pulled into the driveway, he still hadn't talked to Alex. I tugged on his arm and dragged him out the driver's side. I unlocked the door to the house, still holding him, and tightened my grip as his muscles clenched.

"Where are you taking me?" He wasn't yelling anymore, visibly shaken.

The door opened before I took out the key. Alex stood in front of Rachel and she jumped into the boy's arms. I pushed everyone into the house to get the door shut. They melted down the wall onto the floor, young emotions mixed with relief and uncertainty.

"What the hell is going on?" The kid wanted answers. "What about my mom?"

"They'll fill you in. I need to go," I said, making eye contact with Rachel.

"Got it," she saluted.

I left in the truck, returning to Cypress's house to trade for my motorcycle. I hoped she'd still be there, but the place was desolate.

MARLEY

DAX BACKED HIS TRUCK INTO my driveway. His arm rested around my shoulders and he kissed the side of my face before pulling the keys from the ignition. The sun was warm through the windshield, but comfortable, not blaring heat. We both slid out the driver's door. He opened the tailgate and leaned up against it, his face content while I entered the code on the keypad.

As the garage inched up, my legs crumbled down. Dax caught me in motion, rescuing me from my weaknesses.

"Whoa, it's okay," he reassured me. "I've got you." His muscular arms fully embraced me and I buried my face in his chest. Slow backward steps guided us to lean on the lowered tailgate. "I'm here. You're good," he whispered.

He helped me into the house, straight onto the couch and my face dropped into my hands; the sobbing flowed freely. My crouched knees became the basin for my tears as my arms wrapped around my legs. Dax wriggled his body as close to mine as he could, resting his head on my back, slowly caressing my calf; his silence a comfort.

We didn't plan to nap but an hour had passed. Dax was sprawled on the floor next to the couch. His eyes were closed and I could hear the muted exhales of his breaths. My body ached from the prolonged awkward positioning and I cringed, unfolding to stretch across the cushions, my arms extending above my head. Dax woke to my movements, the touch of his hand on my thigh felt natural, comfortable.

He leaned up on his elbow, his eyes meeting mine with a soft smile. "Do you want to do this another day?"

My hands instinctively ran through my hair. "Ugh. No . . . we have to do it today. I don't want her to come home to her room the way it is."

Iris's twelve-by-twelve square bedroom space was cluttered with packed boxes, leaving no room to walk around.

"Let's get her things to the storage shed so that I can prepare her room for when she comes home."

Dax repositioned and reached out to me. "Whenever you're ready."

I stood in the doorway of her room. The sheer curtains were closed as she liked them, pillows and blankets littered her side chair, strands of necklaces and costume jewelry scattered her nightstand.

"When do you think she'll be released?"

I really had no idea. Just a few days ago, her life was business as usual. She did as she pleased, often unpleasing to me, but a friend and confidant for Alex. Today, she lays in her hospital bed unsure of her health, surprising the rest of us with pre-existing concerns she never mentioned. I felt torn between frustration, fear, stifled love for my mother, and so many unknowns.

We loaded the back of Dax's truck, filling the bed with whatever Iris had packed in the boxes. I didn't look inside a single one. Our movements back and forth from the house to the truck were quiet, as was the drive from home to the storage facility. Dax pulled the truck forward so that the side was parallel to the door. I found the combination to the lock in notes on my phone and read them aloud.

He raised the door and I surveyed the space. Everything looked the same as the last time I was there. But I knew very clearly, that everything wasn't the same. My mother was not with me. Would she ever return to this space, I wondered? Would she ever peel back the lids of the boxes and squeal with excitement for the treasures she'd saved?

I shook my head in disgust. "I hate this."

"I'm with you," Dax said, facing me with his hands on my shoulders. His presence gave me strength.

"I know," I said. "Thanks for coming here with me," I smiled.

He lowered the tailgate and pulled a couple of boxes to the edge. The unloading was quiet like the loading we'd done thirty minutes before. Two boxes at a time, sometimes one, stacking and rehoming my mother's belongings. Would this be their final resting place? No, I wanted to believe it wasn't true.

Iris would be back to claim her things one day. She had to. We weren't done yet. Our mother-daughter tensions were still in full swing. It was too soon. She'd started reaching out to me for resolution but I hadn't gotten there yet. I never considered not having the time or a chance to resolve things with her.

"Can you take me to the hospital?" I asked anxiously. I put the last box on a stack of three others.

"Of course," he replied immediately. "Are you okay?"

"I don't know." It was an honest answer. My heartbeat accelerated. "This isn't what I pictured when I asked you to help me today. All of a sudden, I feel worried. Like I'm not going to have enough time to fix things with her."

Dax pulled the garage door down and latched it with the combination lock. He opened the passenger door and he helped me into the cab. My body was moving but it felt like my thoughts were a few steps behind. I was shocked into real time when my phone vibrated on the bench seat.

"Hello."

"Mom. I need you," Alex pleaded. Her voice was serious, void of tears, but direct and rushed.

I listened to every word she said, thankful for the update. My eyes closed in an effort to block out anything that could be a distraction, until I slipped out the passenger door and ran around the front of the truck. I gestured to Dax that I'd take the wheel and he slid to the other side. I knew exactly where to meet her.

ANDREW

"LET ME CALL YOU BACK," I said, setting my cell phone on the table next to a beer. I eyed Cypress from head to toe as she rounded the corner. "You look like shit," I laughed.

"Andrew!" she yelled. "Thank God." Cypress huffed in relief, entering the rear yard, finding me in a shaded hammock. After a glare, she rubbed under her eyes. "I wouldn't be here if I didn't need you."

My ego inflated quickly, she could see it in my face.

"Just shut up!" Cypress pierced. "He took my kid! I need you to help me get Toby back."

I rolled out of the hammock and took a chair next to her. "What? Who took him?" My hands held her knees. "You have to catch me up, Cypress. I can't help until you slow down and explain. Who has Toby?" I reached for my phone and rested it on my thigh.

"I think Marco has him," she started to cry. "His bartender guy came to my house. I don't even know what he wanted. I tried to talk to him outside but he pushed his way into the house." She wiped under her eyes. "We kind of got into a little—"

"Did he hurt you?" I interjected.

Cypress used the shoulder of her shirt to wipe her face. "No, I'm fine. I'll be fine. I just need to find Toby."

I listened intently.

"He must've heard us arguing and the next thing I knew, he was tackling Curtis."

I activated the home screen on my phone. "We have to call the police."

"No!" Cypress insisted. "No! Not yet! That's why I'm here."

I looked at her dubiously. "This is your kid. And Marco, for God's sake! C'mon! We have to call the police," I asserted, following her to the front of the house.

Barefoot, Cypress jumped into the passenger seat and I drove us to *The Lounge*. We backed out of the driveway as the sun shined brightly. The visor above the steering wheel barely blocked the harsh glare.

"I hate you, Marco—you son of a bitch!" she called out, venting anger and guilt. "In the months I spent justifying my actions and how they'd effect Toby, I never thought he'd be in danger like this." She reached around for her cell phone. The bare vinyl was a quick reminder that she left home with only her keys. "Dammit!"

The sun was close to setting, shining a peaceful combination of pink and purple hues behind the base of the mountains. Per Cypress's instructions, I parked in back. The metal door was propped open.

Wearing a pair of flip flops she found on the floor behind the seat, Cypress popped out of the car and into Marco's office.

I bolted in behind her.

He sat facing a computer screen. "You surprised me," he faced her smugly.

"Where's my kid?" she demanded, rounding his desk.

Marco stood up in defense of Cypress's accelerating hysterics. I held her around the shoulders when she lunged toward Marco.

He gestured to the chairs in front of his desk. "Why don't you calm down so I can understand what you're saying."

"You know exactly what I'm saying. I'm speaking God-dammed English, you son-of-a-bitch," she yelled. "You sent your lackey to my house and he took my kid!"

Curtis pushed through the flap door from the bar into Marco's office. Everything okay in here, sir?"

Cypress squirmed out of my stronghold and charged Curtis. "Dammit! Where is he?" she yelled. "Where'd you take my son?"

Curtis blocked her wrists and held her back. His eyes were solemn. He didn't say a word in response.

I looked at Marco, unsure of what might happen next. "Okay, how about everybody calms down. Cypress . . . " I extended my hand toward her. "Cypress. Sit down for a minute. We can figure this out."

She was furious. Her eyes were locked with Curtis's. She responded to my nudging, walking backward to the chair across from Marco's desk. I sat next to her. Marco and Curtis shared a brief conversation by eye contact. Marco took his seat, while Curtis returned to the bar through the flap door.

"If you've gained control of yourself, why don't you tell me what's gotten you so upset," Marco said smugly.

Cypress leaned forward in her seat. "You know exactly why I'm here, you arrogant beast," she growled. "And I'm not leaving until you give me my son."

———

I SENSED MARCO BEGINNING TO lose control. Cypress hadn't shut up for way too long and she wasn't showing any sign of slowing down.

Marco kicked his feet onto the desk, crossing his legs at the ankles. His arms folded at his chest, eyes fixed on Cypress.

"You're sick and twisted!" she shouted. Her limbs were bound to the chair after considerable effort on Curtis's part to get her secured, with all the flailing she was doing and the kicks and punches she jabbed in the process.

Marco's smug expression was a bit pompous and conveyed pleasure. Cypress yelled and swore, throwing out threats for as long as she had the energy, but her pleas only fueled Marco's ego. In his position of power, along with Cypress's desire for his product, he was fully aware of the financial burden that would keep her in his debt indefinitely.

"Put this over her mouth," he ordered, passing me a piece of ripped duct tape.

I affixed it to her mouth, standing behind to avoid eye contact. In exchange for not being bound to a chair, I emptied my pockets, including my wallet, keys, and cell phone. I did as Marco instructed, keeping quiet when a liquor distributor showed up at the back door with a shipment that needed to be unloaded into the back room refrigerator. Curtis monitored every move while managing the purchase order and engaging in small talk with the delivery driver.

"No problems?" Marco asked Curtis.

I looked at Cypress, disgruntled and furious. A look of helpless fear showed in her face.

"Marco," I interrupted. "There's got to be a way to resolve whatever's going on here. I mean, c'mon, is all this really necessary?"

Marco adjusted himself in his seat, bringing his legs to the floor and gesturing toward Cypress. "All this is because of your lady friend barging in here, to my place of business, yelling unspeakable accusations and demanding something I cannot give her."

Cypress thrashed her head from side to side, pulling her arms and shoulders to free herself to no avail. The sounds that came from her mouth were disturbing and she began to gasp deeply through her nose for more air.

"At least let her breathe!" I pleaded. "Can't the tape come off?"

Marco tipped his chin toward Curtis, suggesting that he could provide Cypress some relief. "Would you like the tape removed?" he patronized.

She nodded, anger shown in her eyes.

Curtis pulled the tape from her face. She shrieked in pain.

"Cypress!" I yelled. "Just keep quiet. Let me talk to Marco."

He looked at me with delight. "You think you have something to offer that might be of interest to me?"

"I'm just thinking that there's got to be something we can agree on. None of this seems necessary. She's upset, obviously. Let's figure out what's really going on."

Marco walked over to Cypress, just close enough that he could look into her eyes. He paced a couple of slow circles around her chair, engaging her eyes again upon his final return. "You believe that I have your son stashed away somewhere, yet I know nothing of what you're saying. Don't you think you're being presumptuous with me? The man who has done nothing but supply your habit, as often as you desire, as a friend to someone in need, asking nothing in return but adequate payment for my services?"

"I've paid for your services and I'm almost free and clear! Then you go and have my kid ripped from my house to prove some sort of sick point? That you get what you want when you want it?" Cypress yelled, a couple of tears trickling from the corner of her eyes. "Is that why you did it?"

Marco paced again, slowly. He leaned on the front of his metal desk, holding his chin. "It seems we've come to a standstill," he paused. "You want something from me that I don't have, and I want you out of my sight."

"That's great," I interjected. "Let me take her out of here, Marco. I'll handle it—you'll never see her again."

"Hey!" Cypress stammered. "You don't speak for me!"

"I'm trying to help you, here," I said with wide eyes.

Marco looked at Curtis. He picked up the phone. "Here's what I'm willing to do," he said, pausing to take a sip of something from the glass on his desk. "If we all agree, I will have Curtis remove the ties, and the two of you can leave quietly, returning to your lives as they were prior to ever meeting me—or, I will call my friends at the police department, report you for bringing illegal drugs into my establishment, and have you detained on as many counts of disorderly conduct and assault as possible."

"You're accusing me of bringing drugs here? That's a load of crap. You're the one pushing the drugs!"

Marco smiled, his lips pursed. "You shouldn't be surprised at what the police will find if I direct them to you."

"What?" Cypress squirmed violently in her chair, ripping the skin around her wrists.

"Let's go back to the first thing you said. We can do that! We'll leave and never come back," I redirected. I looked at Cypress, hoping for an immediate agreement.

"I will leave here to find my son," she said slowly. "And if I can't find him or if he's been harmed, you will see me again. That, I can promise you."

"I have no concerns in regard to your son, but let me repeat myself clearly. You and I will never be in contact again. If you choose to attempt a renegotiation of this agreement," he opened his desk drawer and pulled a handgun from the drawer, "I will be forced to take matters into my own hands, as I have done today. You will be the one facing the consequences of your actions. And on that day, your son will not be off limits."

Cypress stared fiercely, her chest raised and fell rapidly. "Let me go. Now! Before I change my mind."

Curtis snipped the ties. I grabbed my wallet, keys, and phone from the corner of Marco's desk and took Cypress by the hand. I pulled her out the back door, tossed her into the car and sped out of *The Lounge* parking lot.

"Where do we go now?" I asked.

"To the police!"

"We can't go to the police!" I argued.

"Why not? He has my son. I have to find him!"

I pulled into the next driveway on the right, stopped quickly and shifted into PARK. I turned off the car, faced Cypress, and handed her my phone. "Call him first."

"Call who first?"

"Call Toby. See if he answers."

———

CYPRESS'S GASP TOLD ME THAT Toby answered her call.

"Where is he?" I barked.

She swatted at me.

"Oh thank God!" she cried. "Where are you? Are you okay?"

"You're at Alex's? What the hell?" She sounded confused.

"Go! Go to Alex's house," she commanded. "We're on our way now," she told him.

In less than ten minutes, we ran through the open garage door and through the laundry room. We came to an abrupt stop, catching sight of Toby sitting in the family room with Alex, Marley and Dax.

Toby met Cypress in a relieved embrace.

I made my way around the sectional sofa and collapsed on the floor in front of Alex. "I'm so confused. Fill me in. Please." I put my hands around her knees.

She reached down to my arms and reassured me that she was okay. Marley crouched in the corner of the couch, her legs and knees hugged her chest. Exhaustion darkened her face while one hand propped up her forehead.

Dax stood to answer the doorbell, returning with two plain clothes police detectives. Both displayed a badge on their belts opposite a holstered handgun.

Cypress backed up hesitantly, the look on her face fearful.

Dax took control of the moment, inviting the detectives to sit at the nearby table and chairs. "We haven't had a chance to bring everyone up to speed yet, so maybe you can take it from the beginning."

Cypress leaned in toward Toby, speaking softly. "What in the hell is this? Do you know what's going on here?"

I tipped my head toward Marley, looking for answers in her stoic eyes. I looked to Alex for an explanation, but no one seemed ready to say anything.

One officer took a seat at the table, the other moved closer to the group. "Actually," he began, "it's better for us to speak to you individually before you speak to one another; allow the complete report to do the work, rather than all of you collaborating stories."

I threw my hands into the air, "I don't even know what that means." I looked at Marley again. "Are you going to help me out?"

The seated officer stood, gesturing to me, "That's good, really. I'll start with you."

"Start with me for what? I came here to talk to her son," I pointed to Toby. "I don't even know what has happened since he left their house this morning, and you want me to give a statement?"

"Yes, sir."

"I don't have any answers about anything. I can't give a statement when I'm completely in the dark," I insisted.

"That's exactly the statement I need from you, sir."

I shook my head, looking at Marley and Alex. Both nodded

gentle affirmations to do as the detective asked.

"Ma'am," the other officer spoke to Cypress. "I'd like to speak to you and your son at the same time. As a minor, he's entitled to give a statement in the presence of his parent or guardian."

Cypress took Toby's hand. They were directed into the kitchen, both sat on barstools. The officer stood next to them asking pointed questions and recording their accounts of the day. Cypress refrained from mentioning the altercation at *The Lounge*, and the officer asked nothing beyond their recollections from Curtis's presence at their home or the events that took place later.

From my position with the detective, I could hear Alex talking to Marley.

She spoke quietly at her mother's feet, contemplating the very real possibilities that other kids at her school might have issues with drugs in their homes. Money seemed to be an overwhelming subject of worry for people and if drugs are being used and purchased, it was likely that money would become an issue affecting the well-being of a family, the relationships within, and the question of safety as a response of what was going on between the user and the dealer. How could she weave these types of questions into her school column without completely revealing her identity, she wondered?

She'd been dating Toby for months before she even knew about Cypress using prescription drugs, she admitted. How many other kids at their school were living in a house where drugs were being obtained illegally or used for reasons they weren't intended? She wondered if Cypress felt that she didn't seem impaired enough, or break the law enough to consider her drug use a problem? Especially, in light of the T.A.D.A. campaign expressing the dangers—did people believe that drug abuse would only include illegal drugs—like cocaine and heroine, and not pills distributed in prescription bottles? Alex wanted to know how most people defined drug abuse, or drug use, for that matter.

The officer released Cypress and Toby, both ready to return home.

I finished my statement first and agreed to give them a ride. I promised to return to Marley's immediately afterward, so that when she and Alex were done giving their statements, the three of us would have a chance to talk. Dax walked us to the door, showing no signs of leaving Marley's side.

———

THREE ATTEMPTS AT THE GARAGE key pad all with the same result. "She finally did it. Dammit!" I grumbled. I hopped over the trimmed hedges, landing on the front pathway. I tried the front door and it, too, was locked. I rang the doorbell and waited, ringing impatiently until Dax opened the door with a somber smile.

"Where's Marley?"

Dax opened the door further, inviting me in with an open palm. I shook my head, passing him quickly.

Marley sat on the couch, Alex across from her in a recliner chair, covered completely with a blanket revealing only her sleeping face.

I took a seat next to Marley, eager with questions.

"I don't know," she blared. "Everything happened so quickly."

Dax entered the room, taking a seat in the second recliner chair.

"Can we talk about this privately?" I beckoned, cocking my head in Dax's direction.

Marley pulled her knees to her chest. "He's staying,

Andrew. He's as much a part of this as you are."

I sighed. "How can you even say that?"

"Because he is. There's no getting around it."

"Marley," Dax began, pausing.

"No, please. I want you to stay," squinting her eyes, she rubbed her forehead in her palm.

"Dad?" Alex whispered, waking from the chatter.

I went to her, squatting at the side of her chair. "How did you get in the middle of all this? Toby knew better than to pull you in with Marco."

She sat up, the chair back moving with her. "He didn't. Really. It just happened."

I stood, facing Marley. "Do you even realize what kind of crazy your mom has gotten herself into with that guy?"

"I do now," she nodded.

"That's it? That's all you have to say? You're the master of word play, Marley, and that's all you've got?"

Marley closed her eyes, leaning on the armrest, her head still in her hand.

"Dad," Alex appealed.

"What? Doesn't anyone have anything to say about anything that happened today? The detectives, the statements we were forced to make?"

Blank stares punched me in the face.

"Okay, if none of you want to talk, I have plenty to say. Earlier today, I was with Cypress in Marco's office at *The Lounge*, where he had her tied to a chair."

"What?" Marley gasped.

Dax leaned forward in his chair.

"You heard me. That bastard had his bartender zip-tie her wrists behind her back, bound to a chair in the back office."

"Why?" Alex sounded frightened.

"Didn't Toby tell you what his mom got mixed up in?"

Alex cringed, admitting nothing.

"Oh, that's right, you don't want to talk. Here's the bottom line: Cypress turned herself into a junkie. She picked Marco out of all the thugs in the world to be her supplier. What she didn't know or at least didn't have the clear head to realize, is that when you buy drugs and you can't pay—but your dealer still provides the goods, you run a tab that determines the length of your life."

The only eyes looking at mine were Dax's.

"You want to take a crack at this? Be the one person in the room who can tell me something of value?" I asked him.

"I can," he paused. "If that's what Marley wants."

All eyes were on Marley, she put her feet on the ground and opened her hands to begin some kind of explanation.

"The whole thing was put into motion by my mother."

"It wasn't the only thing she put into motion," I blurted under my breath.

"What does that mean?"

"She thought it'd be better if I told you," I paused. "Since you're all here, it makes sense to tell you now."

"Dad, what did she do?" Alex pressed.

"She feels awful about it."

"Come on, Andrew!" Marley was losing patience.

I looked at Alex. "She's pretty sure that you tested positive for marijuana because of the desserts she brought home from *The Lounge*."

"What?" Marley exclaimed.

"Finally, something that makes sense," Alex said, showing no concern for the reality of the situation.

"I want to talk more about that later. But right now, tell me what your mother put into motion." I reclaimed my seat on the couch, looking at Marley. "She's in the hospital," I said. "How was she involved?"

"She asked us to help her carry out a plan that she set up with Curtis."

"Shit!" I stood. "Why didn't you tell me? You've been in on this—no, you provoked the entire scheme?"

Marley's eyebrows furrowed, a familiar response I've witnessed over the years. I took a seat again, waiting for something—anything to come out of her mouth.

"Iris recently discovered the depth of Marco's business. She tried to keep everything under wraps because of my position with the drug abuse awareness campaign."

"And she didn't know about Toby's mom until just a few days ago," Alex added. "I didn't even know."

"I've been watching Toby, Alex . . . ."

"Watching him for what?" she asked defensively.

"I knew something was up and I just didn't notice the drug thing with Cypress."

"You still think he's up to something?" she pushed.

I looked at Marley but her shrug left me on my own.

"Alex, he's fine. His mother isn't fine, in fact, she's in a very deep hole that she may not be able to crawl out of. And what concerns me most is that he could pull you in to that mess."

Marley repositioned herself in the corner of the couch. "We're getting off topic. You and Alex can discuss your approval or disapproval of Toby some other time."

"So you don't have any concerns about Alex being with Toby?" I questioned.

"They're kids, Andrew. I don't want her around his mother, but I'm undecided about Toby."

"Mom!" Alex blurted. "You still don't like Toby?"

"I didn't say that."

"What's your position?" I asked Dax. "Since you're in the mix now, too."

He smiled. "My position on Toby?"

"Yeah. What do you think about Alex hanging out with Toby now that we know what his mother's into?"

"The only thing I know for sure," he started, "is that my son only asked for my opinion when he really wanted it. Otherwise, he picked his own friends."

"Thank you," Alex agreed.

I shook my head, never should have asked him, I thought. "Back to Iris. How in the hell did she get the police involved?"

"In a nutshell, it took a village. She'd already started mapping a plan with Curtis, who knew one of the detectives. Turns out, she and Curtis met many years ago. But their mutual friend, Mack, was a known drug user back then who started using at a young age because of someone like Marco. Apparently, he was very significant to her."

"How significant?" I asked.

"I'm not exactly sure. You know Iris, guarded about certain details, overly gratuitous with others. Curtis tipped her off to Marco's business practices and they used Rachel and Flick to carry out some of the preliminary work."

"What? Those two were in on this, and you still kept it from me? Iris told me about Marco when I sat with her at the hospital and she didn't say a damn thing about this grand plan."

"Andrew, this isn't about you. She wanted you to continue your charade with Cypress, act like your normal self, and have nothing to say—or be in a position where you'd have to stop yourself from saying something to the detectives when it came time for you to make a statement."

I paced the room. "What did Rachel and Flick do?"

"They planted a couple of cameras and recording devices at *The Lounge*, documenting Marco's meetings and conversations over the last couple of weeks or so."

"So they have proof of Cypress tied up in Marco's office?"

"I'm sure they do."

"What about Curtis? He's the one who did the dirty work."

Marley nodded. "And Rachel did the editing."

RACHEL

TIMING WAS IMPORTANT, SO I left Curtis's house when Marley and Dax arrived. They took the kids home and I headed to the station for final editing with Flick, eager to copy the tape and deliver it into police evidence.

"Well, that's a wrap! I'll give you a ride," Flick offered, smiling with a wink.

"Thanks for your help. Everything leading up to this crazy day has been strange," I said, patting him on the back of the shoulder. "But worth it—we're sticking to the plan," I reminded him.

"Then, I'll hold down the fort here," he said. "You go out there and save the world from bad guys."

I dropped the copy into my purse, scooting out the back door in time to meet the detectives at Curtis's house. I rounded the corner and noticed an empty navy blue sedan parked next to a motorcycle on the sloped driveway.

Curtis opened the front door and I could see the men inside. "Gentleman," I announced.

The sun had just set behind the mountains; streetlights began to illuminate.

"They got what they needed from Marco's storage site," Curtis explained. "We should be good to go as long as you have the video footage."

"Yeah, I've got it," I said, handing it over to the detective who made eye contact with me as I entered the room.

"Ross Stone," he introduced himself, shaking my hand. We exchanged a noteworthy glance.

"What now?" I asked eagerly. "How long until you take down Marco?"

"Rachel, c'mon," Curtis piped in. "You know they can't discuss it with you."

"Where's the fun in that? You guys just use me for my evidence and then kick me to the curb?"

Ross Stone gave her a look. "I'll walk you out."

I raised an eyebrow.

"When all this is done, would you be—"

"Yes," I blurted. "Sorry, that came out wrong. I mean, it came out right, but a little presumptuous." I blended a cringe with a smile. "Go ahead—finish your question."

A smile hinted from the corner of his mouth. "Would you be interested in meeting somewhere when this is done?"

I dug in my purse for a small zipper pouch of business cards. "That's what I hoped you were asking."

"Good," he took the card from my hand. "I'll call you."

I laughed out loud in the car, feeling ridiculous for jumping at the possibility of seeing Detective Stone again.

"It was so crazy!" I told Marley, after driving straight to her house from Curtis's place. "You know which one I'm talking about, right?" I asked. "The tall one with the dark hair?"

"I know exactly which one," Marley smirked. She held a cup of tea to her mouth, warming her lips on the edge while it cooled. "As soon as I saw that guy, I knew you'd be all over him."

CHAPTER 10

DAX

I DROVE MARLEY AND ALEX to the hospital around seven that evening. They'd both napped after Andrew left, waking to the ringing sound of Marley's phone. Iris wanted to see them in person to hear the details of the day's events.

"Thank you for doing this with us," Marley murmured.

I took her hand in mine and we walked through the doors together, Alex beside Marley.

The second floor of the hospital was dimly lit, Iris's door slightly ajar.

"Mother?" Marley announced, entering the room.

"Yes, I thought you'd never get here," she replied. "Dax, be a dear and turn on that second light, please."

I pulled in a third chair from a vacant room two doors from hers, closing the door behind me. We positioned ourselves on Iris's right side.

"I've been a nervous wreck all day," she admitted,

unusually. She used the remote to raise the head of her bed.

"We brought you some tea, Grandma." Alex poured from the thermos into a smaller cup.

"Come here, my darling," she reached out for Alex, embracing her tenderly. "I'm so sorry. I wish I could've done better by you."

Alex scooted closer on the bed. "You didn't know—and look at me, I'm fine."

Marley sat up and inched to the front of her chair, still fuming. "I'm so upset about you exposing Alex to drugs, but that's a conversation for another time. We did exactly as you asked and Curtis agreed to handle anything that might arise from this point forward."

"Yes, I spoke to him a bit ago, just briefly," she added. "And Marley, I feel terrible. I love Alex and you know I wouldn't hurt her intentionally."

Marley looked at me, then back to her mother.

"As soon as everything becomes public record, I'm going to step down from the campaign," she said.

Iris leaned toward Marley. "You will do nothing of the sort!"

"Mother, how can I possibly represent a drug abuse awareness movement and be in the middle of an investigation involving a drug dealer? It's scandalous!"

"Do you not see the opportunity? One that I know you can use to further your mission?"

Marley looked to me again.

"What do you have in mind?" I asked.

"From the time that Marley made the decision to be seen publicly through the lens of a camera, she made her requirements very clear. She would only report real life, real news, and honest stories."

"Mother!" she balked. "These circumstances are partially

fabricated. We were part of the sting before we even went to the police!"

Alex watched diligently, with table tennis precision.

"That's not entirely true," she retorted. "Curtis took care of everything. He's the insider. It was legitimate."

"How do you think it's going to look if it comes out that my daughter witnessed a drug-deal payoff in a public park?" Marley asked, her volume a very loud whisper. "Or that she tested positive—twice—because of foods in *our* home, laced with illegal drugs?"

I put my hand on Marley's back, she scooted back into her chair.

"Mom, she might be right," Alex said, siding with her grandmother.

"Thank you, my darling," Iris agreed.

"You could use a story like this to educate at your appearances for the campaign. I mean, none of us suspected Cypress of using drugs, but she's also a perfectly good example. I'd probably get a ton of feedback on the school site if I put out a few inquiries that point to illegal drug use. And it's not just illegal drugs, it's also the legal ones being used without prescriptions, right?"

"As long as Alex is already in this," I said, "I could probably convince my son to partner with her at a few of the campaign events. He's had quite a few run-ins with friends or friends-of-friends where this type of thing has come into play."

"More real life," Iris jumped in. "Before you make any definitive decisions, give this some serious thought. You've worked too hard to throw your career away on a guy like Marco. Use him to your advantage and continue promoting the cause. As much as I believe in free choice, that doesn't apply to children."

"You're the one who's been smitten with him, and now he's

threatened our whole family," Marley said.

"I don't think you'll have anything to worry about. Curtis said they'll have everything together and be ready to make the arrest tomorrow."

"Tomorrow? Why not today?" Alex wondered. "Should I warn Toby that Marco is still free?"

"Don't worry about Toby, dear. I've got Curtis taking care of that," her grandmother assured her.

"Now you've got him being watched?"

"What do you mean by that?" she asked.

"Dad's been watching him for months, thinking he was up to no good."

"Oh, god," Marley uttered, "Andrew. He doesn't know that the arrest won't take place until tomorrow. He better not run his mouth somewhere tonight and blow this whole thing."

"Give me a phone," Iris demanded. "Call his number and let me talk to him."

Taking the lead, Alex handed over her phone.

After a few moments, we heard Iris leave a poignant message.

"He's already gotten into it once with Marco today," Marley shared.

"What happened?" Iris questioned.

Marley looked to me to explain. She looked exhausted after the long day. I did my best to satisfy her probes.

"He's a grown man. He'll be fine," she said. "Marley, you can't back out of the campaign. It's too important."

"There's a lot that I need to consider, Mother. I don't want to jeopardize the integrity of the whole movement."

Iris took in a long deep breath, exhaling slowly before changing the subject. "Alex, darling, did you feel safe with Rachel today?"

"Yeah, I think she and Curtis went over every possible

outcome before he left for Cypress's house. I was really hoping that Toby wouldn't get involved, but when he showed up at the door, it was obvious that he'd gotten right in the middle of everything. I was just glad that we could explain the plan as soon as he got there."

"And does he have enough sense to keep his mother from going to *The Lounge* tonight?" Iris asked.

"He can try, Grandma, but Cypress does what Cypress wants to do. He learned that a long time ago."

We walked out of the hospital lethargically, Marley's head on my shoulder, and Alex's head under Marley's arm. I was in this with them and I have to admit, it didn't feel wrong.

IRIS

"YOU HAVE NO IDEA HOW relieved I am to see those discharge papers," I confessed to Marley. Sitting in that hospital room being probed and checked, questioned and bored out of my mind for all those days had really been wearing on me. Finally, Dr. O came to me earlier, stoic and honest.

"You're making it very difficult for me to approve your release, Iris," he stared. "The resistance you're presenting against my recommendation for assisted care goes against my better judgement."

I tried my best to respect his professional recommendations, but my response didn't reflect those intentions. "Why in the hell would I want to go from this godforsaken place to another cold and sterile facility, only to give up every shred of privacy and personal independence indefinitely?" I yipped.

Dr. O took a seat next to my bed. He crossed his right leg over the left and folded his hands over my chart on the top of his legs. We sat together in silence, gazing into one another's eyes for dozens of seconds.

"Have you changed your mind?"

I held our gaze, lifting one eyebrow.

"Are you going to speak with your daughter regarding the seriousness of your declining health?" he asked, repositioning his head to one side.

Silence continued to fill the space between us. He was handsome, well groomed and very academic in appearance, probably single, but I could't know for sure. His hands and wrists were void of anything gold, silver, or otherwise, though not all married types wore a ring to signify their life sentence. Probably a few years older than Marley, he presented a scientific air, one that I felt led to believe in when he talked to me about cancer and treatment options and the late-stage discovery. I hadn't been feeling great for awhile, but going to the doctor just wasn't my thing. By the time I gave in and scheduled my first appointment with Dr. O'Malley, my body was running its own show under the curtain of my skin. The test results determined a scope of treatments that didn't appeal to me, in the least.

"I haven't reconsidered my decision and I have no interest in assisted healthcare outside my home," I spoke solemnly. I knew that a time would come when Marley or Alex would recognize an observable change in me, but until then, I wasn't going to wait out any quality time I had left at a home for old people. Anything could happen and no one knew exactly what it would look like. For now, I wanted to get out from under the fluorescent lights, bask in the sunshine, and watch my granddaughter finish her last months of high school.

"You understand that I'll have to document your refusal?" he asked, tipping his chin down and raising his eyes.

"I do," I paused. "So now that we've cleared that up, how long until I can pack up and get out of here?"

Three hours later, Marley zipped my bag and positioned it by her feet when an unfamiliar volunteer appeared in the doorway.

"Hello," she scarcely smiled. "I'm here to wheel you downstairs."

I dangled my legs and feet on the side of my bed, eager for her to bring the chair into the room.

"Dax will bring the car around and meet us in front," Marley said.

Hearing that Dax came with Marley brought me unexpected delight. He seemed to soften her in the same way that Andrew brought out angst. I never really noticed how her uneasy nature and roller-coaster depression may have been rooted in Andrew's haste and inconsistencies. Dax's calm temperament might actually be rubbing off on my dear Marley girl.

MARLEY

I STOOD ACROSS THE INTERSECTION from *The Lounge* in a convenience store parking lot. I'd been there for two hours with Flick and Curtis, behind the barricaded perimeter set up by the police.

"Reporting live from a typically quiet neighborhood, Phoenix Police have arrested Marco Reyes, identified as a leader in illegal prescription drug distribution in the valley. Reyes took ownership of *The Lounge* nearly two years ago and some patrons say, it was a 'hidden gem'. We've been told that Reyes is in custody and should be escorted from the building shortly."

Flick panned the camera to my left, capturing Marco in handcuffs, as the officers directed him to a transport vehicle.

"According to Phoenix Police, Reyes has been under surveillance for quite some time and has been using his restaurant to solicit drug sales."

Curtis worked with Detective Stone to secure Marco's presence at the time of the planned arrest. The live coverage was short but Chris Dalton continued reporting from the station with edited video collected by Flick and Rachel, barring portions that would be used in court, already logged into police evidence.

After pulling the wires from my microphone and earpiece, I leaned on the side of the van. I looked at *The Lounge*. It was no longer a place that brought me comfort. It represented half-truths and deception, personal gain at the expense of others.

"You did a good job, Marley," Flick said. "That couldn't have been easy for you."

I nodded. "It wasn't easy, but I really felt like I had to be here, to see him taken away."

"It's out of our hands now," Curtis said, surrendering his in front of his body. He got into his car and drove away without another word.

EPILOGUE

"If you wait for fear to subside, you're going to be on the sidelines for a very long time."

—Robin Roberts
Good Morning America anchor

ANDREW

MAYBE I'M THE MOST FOOLISH man on earth. She didn't ask me to be there, I offered. She might even tell you that I insisted on escorting her to the courthouse. How could I let her stand in front of a judge without anyone there to support her? She'd made it very clear that Toby wouldn't attend. Maybe that was his father's doing. By evening on the day that Cypress was arrested, he'd moved Toby into his home with his new wife and their young children. He worked quickly to secure legal documentation, though technically both parents shared custody. Toby was days from turning eighteen and according to Alex, he didn't protest the move.

I took a seat in the first of six rows behind the short wooden partition, taking note of the few others in the room. Both detectives who took statements at Marley's home were seated in plain clothes in the last row. Two small groups of unfamiliar faces were seated in separate rows on the opposite side of the aisle. I hadn't expected to see Curtis, but it made sense when I saw him three seats down from Detective Stone.

As the judge leaned toward the microphone, reviewing the file, Cypress looked back at me, observably agitated. She stood when asked, and pleaded guilty to the possession charge. The judge gave her an opportunity to speak to the court and she fished a crumpled paper from her pocket.

"Your honor," she began. "I'm humiliated by the mess I've gotten myself into. What started as a way to control my physical pain became an out-of-control habit that I never planned on. My prescription medication worked fine for awhile, but I found myself experiencing deeper pain that wasn't fully controlled by those pills. I was offered another solution by a person I thought was helping me. In desperation, I gave his pills a try and felt an incredible improvement."

Cypress looked at the judge who offered no visible empathy. After pausing and attempting to control her shaking voice, she continued. "In the last four weeks since posting bail, I've met with my doctor. He's working with me on other means of pain relief and I've been clean for thirty days. I have a teenage son who no longer lives with me. He's seen me at my worst and I don't want him to think of me that way forever. Your Honor, please consider a lesser sentence for my actions. I fully commit to recovery and getting my life in order again. Thank you." She drooped dejectedly into her seat.

The judge sifted through papers affixed in a two-hole file prong. "You may remain seated," he lowered his chin toward Cypress and her attorney. "In accordance with your cooperation regarding a pending case, and dependent upon your agreement to complete the requirements, you are a candidate for deferred prosecution in the state of Arizona." He removed his glasses and looked sternly at Cypress. She straightened her posture. He explained, "Deferred prosecution means that the state will hold off on prosecuting you while you participate in a probationary term. During probation you are required to undergo treatment, comply with random drug tests, and attend classes to educate you further on the dangers of drug abuse. If you are successful, the criminal charges are dropped. If you violate the terms of your probation, however, you will be prose-cuted on the original charges and face the penalties prescribed by law. Do you understand these terms as they have been explained to you?"

"Yes, sir," she spoke confidently. "I do."

When I stood to wait for Cypress in the courtroom, both detectives and Curtis were already gone. I bit the inside of my cheek. Was this the beginning of a friendship? I've known lots of women intimately, and with the exception of Marley, none of them have been friends. Cypress wasn't like the others, she certainly wasn't like Marley, and I wasn't sure I knew how to be a friend, but surprisingly, I wanted to try.

ALEX

MOM AGREED TO LET TOBY ride with us to the station. Things were cool between us since he'd moved in with his dad, but we saw less of each other than before. Rachel scheduled recog-nition for my development of *DogEar* on a *Student Impact* segment at the network, a weekly highlight on school-aged kids who positively influence the community. I was very relieved when she said I could pre-tape the segment rather than run it as a live interview.

She sat me down behind the news desk with a green screen behind us. A guy named Flick worked the camera and had a good sense of humor, making it a little easier for me to settle in with Chris Dalton, one of the station's reporters that I only knew by name. He went over the questions he planned on asking me and we talked about the best way to answer them for the spot. The lighting changed to prepare for recording and my skin felt warm. Mom only stepped in when I asked her to check my hair and make-up, while Rachel stood on Flick's opposite side, smiling and nodding with encouragement. I wasn't sure where Toby stood in the shadows, but I knew he was there.

Chris Dalton introduced me as Alex Christopher, making no mention of my mom, the community's beloved news anchor, and I was pleased. I love her, without a doubt, but I appreciated being introduced as an individual standing on my own merit.

"And what inspired you to take the initiative to develop an interactive link to your school newspaper?" he asked.

"It was something I'd been thinking about for awhile," I said. "I knew it wouldn't be easy because it would require ongoing maintenance and technology support, but my grandmother said something one day that helped me make the final decision."

Out of the corner of my eye, I noticed my mom stepping slowly into the shadow behind the cameraman. I continued.

"She said, 'Don't expect everyone to agree with you all the time. Do what makes you happy.' So, I went to my newspaper advisor, she agreed and we took it from there."

The whole thing took about forty-five minutes. In the car, Toby asked about Grandma.

"She hasn't really been acting like herself," I said.

"She's been sleeping a lot," Mom added. "But the doctor

said she might be slow to recover after being in the hospital."

"The only thing she really wants to know is what's going on with Marco's case," I said.

"Marco," Toby sighed. "He's a guy I'd like to forget we ever knew."

At home, Mom spent time with Grandma in the recliner chair next to her bed. Toby and I channel-surfed until we both fell asleep on the couch. We woke to Grandma's whistling tea pot.

MARLEY

IT WAS THE FIRST DAY we didn't argue because as I drew breath, she was simply still. The blinds were drawn just as she preferred and I knelt next to her bed with my fingers embracing hers. The clocks were still ticking in every space around the world except for the room we occupied together where time had stopped for my mother, forever.

This was it, the end. Not just for her, Iris Christopher, but for me, for Alex, our routines and traditions, for the things I took for granted, and for her way of life that seemed the antithesis of mine. How long could I hold her hand before making a phone call for assistance or calling my daughter home to see her grandmother for the last time in this place?

"I still have so much to say to you, Mother. And God knows you have an arsenal of retorts for me." Without completely letting go of her soft hand, I pushed up from the ground and stood next to her bed. She was laying in her typical side position, covers tucked under her arm to just under her shoulder. I walked to the other side of her bed and kneeled next to her. My arm reached around her body and I cupped my hand around hers. Her skin felt cool.

I closed my eyes and nudged in closer. Feeling both

awkward and appropriate, I cradled her. The room was silent as the outdoor sounds crept in through the window. A lawn mower trimmed a nearby yard, a garbage truck scooped up a can, dumped it, and returned it to it's place on the curb. Birds spoke and sang in their own language, sirens blared from an emergency vehicle in the distance. My heartbeat suddenly increased. Instinctively I breathed in deeply, trying to catch my breath. In through my nose, slowly out through my mouth. I couldn't calm down. My eyes released tears down my cheeks until my shirt sleeves could no longer absorb them. I stared at my mother; both of us silent.

I couldn't leave her alone, but I needed my daughter. I wanted to drive to her school, see her in person, hold her in my arms, tell her what happened, and bring her home. I looked at Iris, knowing she couldn't tell me what to do. "Dammit, Mother!" I ranted. I knew I needed help to stay with Iris *and* retrieve Alex from school, but I wanted to be alone. I didn't want to explain anything to anyone in order to get help. I didn't want to see anyone besides Iris and Alex, and I didn't want my mother to be quiet.

I clutched my face in my hands, rubbing my eyes and my cheeks. I paced her bedroom with fleeting thoughts that seemed rational to me. I knelt at her bedside again, paying close attention to her face. I felt irritation of a different kind, one that put responsibility in my hands. Or was it guilt? Always guilt.

Had I placed such strict boundaries between us that I never really looked at you, Mother? I've been so intent on protecting myself from your potential wounds, no wonder I missed all the signs. Portions of past conversations drifted in and out of my memories. Then Marco appeared in my mind. For the first time that day, I gave him intentional thought. Sometime in the near future, I would pay him a visit.

A car door closed nearby and caught my attention. Turning my head toward Mother's bedroom door, I listened intently. Yes, the garage door was opening. I jumped up, touched my mother's cheek, and met Alex in the hallway.

"Hi, is it already after three?" I asked.

"Yeah," she slid past me and into the kitchen. Relieved that I'd closed Iris's door, I followed Alex clumsily. "It's Wednesday, right?" she mused aloud. "You're never home on Wednesdays. What's the deal?"

"Honey," I felt my facial expression change. My head tipped slightly. My mother spent her last days waiting to see Alex's *Student Impact* feature on the news last night.

"Oh my God," Alex bellowed, dropping her bag on the floor. She leaped toward her grandmother's bedroom.

Somehow, I managed to slide in front of her and we both reached the door at the same time. I touched her hand as I'd cupped my mother's earlier, taking another pause and breath. "Please. Wait." I hugged Alex tightly in the hallway. For the second time that day, I felt time stand still. "I'm so sorry."

"I want to go in," she urged me. "Right now, Mom."

We turned the knob together, opening the door to the remarkably quiet room. In the moments I'd been absent, Iris's jaw had dropped, slightly exposing her front teeth and the hue of her skin had paled. I caught Alex as she crumbled into my arms, holding her face and the tears that poured from her eyes. Together we melted to the floor and I rocked my baby girl in the wake of my mother's death.

In the time that followed, I watched Alex make her way into the bed with her grandmother, under the covers forging a gentle embrace. As I sat on the floor, I shed tears again, for the final loss of the mother I never really knew, and for my daughter who knew her better than anyone.

I WON, BUT IT FEELS like I lost. When I feared public scrutiny, the T.A.D.A. campaign embraced my family's association with Marco and his drug ring, spinning it to fit the movement's plea for drug abuse education. My network endorsement wasn't jeopardized, only backing the campaign more diligently, and Dax has walked with me through every uncertain step along the way. Simple statements were issued by both the network and the campaign in sympathy after Iris's death.

I suspect a different story, one that I will guard, but accept as a possibility. While her cause of death was recorded as cancer, the autopsy report also revealed high levels of Secobarbitol in her system, high enough to induce a final, peaceful sleep into death. It's legal, yes, and was likely prescribed by her doctor but I never found a prescription bottle, nor would her doctor's office confirm or deny a prescription. I know now, that she refused cancer treatments, but why would she need a drug for insomnia? If I'd known more, would I have watched more closely? Or was it another reminder that Iris lived her way, on her terms, until she was done?

My core team is broken in so many pieces. It's shattered in a way that will never heal to the way it was before. My players are missing and can't be replaced, though the thought of replacing them hurts just as much. My mother's position certainly has changed, but I know she'll remain on my bench, in my mind, and with me to the very end. Alex will move away for college soon; another player abandoning me. And if I'm being honest, Andrew left the team a long time ago. Dax has stepped up, a player I scouted for a very long time. I hope his experience as a seasoned athlete will provide guidance when I'm not performing at my best.

I thought I understood grief and loss. I've been out in the field, witnessing devastation and emptiness, filming people and places that were changed in an instant—never able to return to the original normal. And now that I know what profound loss feels like, I never should've been granted permission to step into those tragedies, the devastations, thinking I could soothe anyone's pain. I thought I understood, empathized, but it was impossible.

She was my mother. I should've known. Maybe I didn't want to know.

———

I STEPPED ONTO ALEX'S HIGH school campus for the first time since her graduation, met by her former journalism advisor, Eve Kingston. Flick introduced himself as we walked to the auditorium, preparing to introduce the campaign to high school students across the state.

Hidden in the wings, I watched the faces of the future file into the building, a host of personalities, emotions, and struggles, all disguised to mask the hard stuff. The house lights dimmed, leaving a spotlight on stage, and the first slide in the presentation appeared on the screen. Eve introduced the T.A.D.A. campaign and welcomed me to the podium.

"On behalf of the campaign and network news, I'm here to talk about the dangers of drug abuse. You might hear the words drug abuse and think only about illegal drugs like cocaine, heroine, or crystal meth—maybe even alcohol, since you're all underage." I paused, hearing a few giggles in the audience.

In a room full of kids who were nearly grown up, they showed occasional signs of lingering adolescence. I wanted to make sure that *what* I said was exactly what they needed to *hear*—a story that needed to be understood.

"Or maybe you think about people who are uneducated, unlike yourselves, or homeless, maybe people who just mixed with the wrong crowd. The truth is, drug abuse is very real and anyone can be a victim. Statistics regarding drugs used for unprescribed purposes are astonishing and increasing every day. And the numbers rise dramatically when specific factors that lead to abuse are multiplied."

We proceeded through a few slides. The pictures told stories, captioned with words under a canopy of music; a message that could make the difference in at least one life. Designed for this particular age group, the presentation highlighted high school students. Young men and women, successful in many ways, who suffered from drug abuse followed by rehab, and those who took their own lives; unclear which acted intentionally or accidentally.

I took my place again at the podium and for the first time, publicly shared my own story. A portion of it would be featured on the evening broadcast. I talked about my mother and the profound impact that her choices made in my life. "Every single one of you can think of someone who doesn't understand you, who doesn't get you, and who you don't relate to. It's okay, we're not meant to be the same. We all do life differently."

I talked about Alex and her contribution to *DogEar*. "My daughter understood how it felt to need a safe, anonymous place to talk and share advice without being judged. Since her graduation, your campus has continued to use *DogEar* as a powerful, meaningful discussion board."

I took a moment to find Dax in the wings. He smiled just enough to show his support, he believed in me and what we were doing for people who needed to hear our words.

"When I joined the campaign to speak on behalf of victims and families, I was an outsider, I thought, just a spokesperson. I didn't know all the details, although I presumed I was prepared. In just a matter of months, I learned that every single person in my circle of friends and family have either used drugs irresponsibly or they are linked to a victim of drug abuse. Every single person in my circle. I had no idea that drugs could be concealed so easily."

Typically, I followed the script. I was nearly done with the presentation but I decided to engage with the students more personally. Flick's camera rested on his shoulder, he stood in the side aisle and caught my eye with a glimmer in his. He knew what I was doing.

"The T.A.D.A. campaign is sweeping the country, reaching out to everyone, because this message is important. I have a partner in this movement, right here in the state of Arizona." The whispers in the auditorium grew in excited anticipation. "He travels with me on behalf of the campaign and he's also very well known in football . . . please welcome, Mr. Dax Townsend!"

The kids went crazy. Dax commanded their attention with a sincere smile, a gentle wave, and a single word. He was another real face with real experience, who could speak and be heard. His presence was engaging.

Finally, it had all come together. I learned to embrace the power in my position and speak words that could maybe, possibly, begin to heal.

THE END

About The Author

K.H. FINDER earned a Bachelor's degree in Social Work and a Master's degree in Education from Arizona State University, including alumni membership in the Sun Devil Marching Band. She works as an educator, volunteer, and loves to travel. She contributes to www.cranky-writer.com as *The Optimistic Crank* and works as a copywriter for various online forums. She lives with her husband and three children in Chandler, Arizona.

Acknowledgements

I AM INFINITELY GRATEFUL TO my husband for his patience and poised confidence. His generosity makes it possible for me to dream and create, to volunteer in a multitude of roles, and to live our grown-up lives more splendidly than I ever imagined.

From very young ages, I tricked my children into believing in me as a writer. At times, I tricked myself into believing the same, in order to push through intermittent thoughts of shelving another manuscript. But over the years, their genuine acceptance for my efforts in writing have motivated my work, and I'm so lucky to have their unconditional support.

This work would not have been completed without the weekly nudging, collaborating, tech-support, and accountability from my writing partner, *The Big Crank*, author Scott A. Combs. Since the inception of Cranky Writer (www.cranky-writer.com) in 2007, I believed that publishing would become a reality, always *The Optimistic Crank*. Never though, did I anticipate the length of time it would take to get here.

I am humbled by my parents for recognizing my strengths, nurturing my interests, teaching me to be independent, to set personal goals, and to make choices wisely.

With sincere thanks to Michelle—who reminds me that a good laugh goes a long way; Brooke—whose kind gesture in the earliest days became a significant daily reminder; and Julie—who demonstrates the unlimited value of living out loud. To Sandy, Laurie, Susan and Brandi—thank you for digging deep with me, the most important work is never easy. To my family, friends, and the community of supporters who've shown genuine interest in my writing—you continue to propel me forward, especially in the slowest currents, reminding me that if the journey was easy, I'd miss out on so many adventures along the way.

Join

THE CONVERSATION

Please leave a REVIEW on:
Amazon
Goodreads
Twitter
Facebook
Any of your favorite websites

Connect

WITH THE AUTHOR

On Facebook: https://www.facebook.com/KHFinder
On Twitter: https://twitter.com/AuthorKHFinder
Send an Email: kim@cranky-writer.com

Launching a book is a daunting task. Writing is only the first step. Making it available beyond the author's immediate circle is dependent upon reader support. Tell your friends, share with your book clubs, review it online.

Your time is valuable, thanks for reading.

You are appreciated!

35668987R00200

Made in the USA
San Bernardino, CA
01 July 2016